Praise for Jan Watson

"This is a settle-in-and-savor type of a read. . . . With rich texture and detail and unforgettable characters that lodge themselves in your heart, Jan transports us to a world without modern convenience, where we live with the people of the land. Danger, tragedy, faith, romance— it's all here in spades."

JERRY B. JENKINS, coauthor of the Left Behind series

"Watson's success lies in her ability to create characters that are enjoyable, endearing, and timeless . . ."

ROMANTIC TIMES* MAGAZINE ON *WILLOW SPRINGS

"Colorfully descriptive language, engaging characters, and words that flow like honey make this a rich, satisfying historical novel. As charming as its predecessor and easily as good; highly recommended."

LIBRARY JOURNAL* ON *WILLOW SPRINGS

"[*Troublesome Creek* is] one of the best books I've read all year. I couldn't put it down."

EVA MARIE EVERSON, author of the Cedar Key series

"This first-time novelist captures the reader's heart as pages quickly turn to reveal plot twists and a story of real-life family love."

CHRISTIAN BOOK PREVIEWS ON *TROUBLESOME CREEK*

"Jan Watson has a true gift for weaving in details that make the mountains of Kentucky almost like another character in the story."

"*Torrent Falls* is a great story demonstrating the reward of remaining faithful to God and His laws."

"Watson brings forth intimate characters with a strong sense of family, obligation, and faith and evokes sensitive and realistic issues. Readers will enjoy the latest journey set in the mountains of Kentucky."

"Packed with characters full of feminine strength, *Still House Pond* paints a picture of nineteenth-century rural life, while offering a hint of romance and a dash of suspense."

"[In *Still House Pond*] Watson brings together lovable and unforgettable characters, a small-town feel, and suspense that gently grips the heart."

"*Still House Pond* spins a charming tale. There were moments where I could not wait to turn the page and discover where the story went next."

Skip Rock Shallows

Skip
Rock
Shallows

JAN WATSON

TYNDALE HOUSE PUBLISHERS, INC., CAROL STREAM, ILLINOIS

Watson, Jan.
Skip Rock shallows

Visit Tyndale online at www.tyndale.com.

Visit Jan Watson's website at www.janwatson.net.

TYNDALE and Tyndale's quill logo are registered trademarks of Tyndale House Publishers, Inc.

Skip Rock Shallows

Designed by Julie Chen

Edited by Sarah Mason

Published in association with the literary agency of Benrey Literary LLC, P.O. Box 12721, New Bern, NC 28561.

Scripture quotations are taken from the *Holy Bible*, King James Version.

This novel is a work of fiction. Names, characters, places, and incidents either are the product of the author's imagination or are used fictitiously. Any resemblance to actual events, locales, organizations, or persons living or dead is entirely coincidental and beyond the intent of either the author or the publisher.

Library of Congress Cataloging-in-Publication Data

Watson, Jan.
  Skip Rock shallows / Jan Watson.
    p. cm.
  ISBN 978-1-4143-3914-6 (sc)
  1. Women physicians—Fiction. 2. Coal miners—Kentucky—Fiction. I. Title.
  PS3623.A8724S55 2012
  813'.6—dc23   2011052921

Printed in the United States of America

18   17   16   15   14   13   12
 7   6   5   4   3   2   1

To the memory of my coal-mining papaw, Alec Pelfrey,
and to the memory of my sweet granny, Julia Brown
Pelfrey. How I wish I could share this book with you.

Acknowledgments

The writing of a book is never a stand-alone project. I've been more than blessed to have the support of all the folks at Tyndale House Publishers during my writing career. Special thanks go to Jan Stob, Babette Rea, and Sarah Mason at Tyndale, and to my literary agent, Janet Benrey.

During my research for *Skip Rock Shallows*, a good friend arranged for me to tour the Kentucky Coal Museum in Benham, Kentucky, and the Portal 31 Demonstration Coal Mine in Lynch. Thank you, Carlton Hughes.

I have the greatest respect for the men and women who mine the coal that provides comfort and ease for millions of others. Please forgive any mistakes I may have made in my attempt to realistically portray the mysterious, awe-inspiring world of the coal miner.

And as always, thank you to my family and to my friends, who are as close as family. I love and appreciate each one of you.

I went down to the bottoms of the mountains; the earth with her bars was about me for ever: yet hast thou brought up my life from corruption, O Lord my God.

JONAH 2:6

CHAPTER I

1908

Stanley James knew there'd been an accident before the blast of the whistle shattered the stillness of the morning. He felt the slightest tremor against the soles of his feet when he bent to lace his high-top work boots. His arm jerked and the rawhide string snapped. Coffee sloshed from his cup and ran across the table like a tiny river overflowing its bank. It dripped onto the knee of his just-ironed coveralls. Stanley swore.

"There's no call for that purple language in my kitchen," Myrtie said in that disapproving way she had. She mopped the spill with a bleach rag before he had a chance to move out of the way.

"Wake the gal," Stanley said.

"It's early yet, Stanley, and she was up late last night."

It would be right pleasant, Stanley thought, if just once Myrtie would do what he asked instead of throwing a wall of words up against him.

Myrtie's eyes grew round as the first warning shrieked. She covered her ears as if it came from right next door and not a mile up the road.

"I'll go get her," she said, folding the rag on the tabletop. Pausing at the door, she looked back. "Will you have time to eat your breakfast?"

Stanley was at the cupboard getting down a box of carbide. "Wrap up some biscuits and fix a thermos. We'll carry it with us."

Myrtie hesitated.

"Wake the gal first, Myrtie. Tell her to shake a leg."

"Stanley, you've got no call to remark on her limbs."

"It's a saying!" Stanley shouted over the alert. "It means hurry up."

"Don't be telling me what to do, Stanley James. I'll go as fast as I want to."

It didn't much matter, Stanley thought. What good would a slip of a gal be against an explosion or a cave-in?

❧

Lilly Gray Corbett was awake. She liked to get up early and climb partway up the mountain to attend to her devotionals

2

under a stand of regal pines. The trees looked down over the valley, where wood-sided shotgun houses jostled each other for elbow room. She leaned against the rough bark of one of the trees, enjoying the fresh green scent of its needles, searching in her Bible for a verse in Isaiah, the one about being called.

When she heard the far-off whistle, her mouth went dry. It was one thing to study about accidents and mangled bodies, quite another to actually attend to one. Carefully, she retraced her steps toward home.

Last night had gone well, though. The baby girl she'd delivered slid into the world without as much as a thank-you. The young mother would have done just as well without Lilly's assistance. If you didn't count the number of births she'd attended with her mentor, Dr. Coldiron, this had been her first delivery—or baby catching, as her mother would say.

Maybe folks were beginning to trust her a little. She'd been here at Skip Rock for two weeks, opening the doctor's office daily, but last night was the first time she'd been called out.

When she reached the end of the one-cow path, Mrs. James met her. "Better hurry, Dr. Corbett. Stanley's in a dither."

Lilly would like to see that—Mr. James in a dither. She'd never seen him break a sweat. He was as deliberate as a plow mule, and he worked just as hard.

Mrs. James ushered her around the side of the house like she was a birthday present. "Lookee here, Stanley. I found her."

Mr. James looked Lilly up and down. "Them skirts ain't going to work."

"Stanley James!"

"Get the gal some overhauls," he said, while fitting pebbles of carbide into a small, round lamp. "We might be going down in the hole."

Dressed and ready, Lilly hurried to catch up to Mr. James. She nearly had to run to match his long stride. He didn't want her there, she knew. In his world, women weren't doctors and they didn't belong in the mines.

Lilly wasn't so sure she didn't agree about the mine part. If her stepfather could see her now, he'd have a heart attack.

The overalls were too long and she kept tripping over the hems. Mrs. James had cinched the waist with a piece of twine, but still they ballooned around her. "I'll fix them proper when you get back," she'd said. "Next time we'll be ready."

Next time? Lilly swallowed hard. What had she gotten herself into?

It seemed to Lilly that she was predestined to be a doctor. Her mother was a natural healer. Her father and his father had been medical doctors. It was in her blood, if not yet in her bones.

She had earned her degree at the end of May and before you could say *whippersnapper* was on her way to the mountains to gain some experience. Sadly, the elderly doctor she was to shadow had died just days before she arrived.

It was no wonder Mr. James's face had fallen when he met her at the train station. He'd stared at the paper in his hand and looked again at her. "Says here you're a man."

She set her hatboxes on the platform and stuck out her hand. "I guess you can see I'm not."

Instead of shaking her hand, he waved the piece of paper under her nose. "Larry Corbett? Larry's not a gal's name, and a gal ain't a doctor."

"I'm Lilly, not Larry," she said. "Dr. Lilly Corbett." *Doctor?* Would she ever get used to using that title?

Mr. James held the paper at arm's length, as older folks do. "Humph," he said.

She picked up the two round, beribboned boxes and lifted her chin. "Shall we proceed?"

What could the poor man do? He stuffed the paper in his pocket and reached for the traveling trunk the porter wheeled out. He said not a word on the buggy ride to her lodgings and kept his face straight ahead. But every so often his eyes would slide sideways as if he was taking her in. It was obvious he found her wanting.

Mrs. James, on the other hand, seemed delighted to see her. She fussed over Lilly as if she were a prodigal daughter as she showed her to the one-room tar-paper shack out behind their house. She even helped Lilly unpack, exclaiming over each garment she hung from pegs beside the door.

"If this ain't the prettiest," she said when she unfolded

Lilly's long silk gown and her matching robe. She laid them across the bed. "I ain't never seen the like."

"Thank you," Lilly said. "It was a gift from my aunt Alice. I guess she thought I was going to Boston or New York."

"I never heard of them places," Mrs. James said. "Are they over round Lexington? My sister's been to Lexington."

"They're just cities. Just big places." Lilly moved to one of the two windows on either side of the door. "Does this raise? Do you have a screen?"

Mrs. James's face colored. "No, I don't have such, but I could tack a piece of greased paper over it, if you want it open. It's clean. I washed it myself."

Lilly felt bad that she had embarrassed her benefactor. The Jameses were kind to provide room and board for her in exchange for a smallish stipend. It was all arranged through the medical school and the mining company. Lilly would be here for the summer practicing her trade.

"Goodness, no, this is fine," Lilly said. "I was thinking I might like some fresh air, that's all."

"Best leave the winders down and the door closed. The air here ain't as unsullied as it once was—it gathers in your lungs and sets up like wallpaper paste. But you know, beggars can't be choosers. We're that glad for the work. As Stanley says, it's a clean breath or a day's pay."

Mrs. James took a snow-white rag from her apron pocket and wiped the windowsill. "You can push it up after dark if you want. Seems like the night dew settles the dust. I'll have Stanley see if the company store carries ary winder screens."

Opening the door, she shook the rag out over the stone stoop. "We're saving up, though. I got a money jar hid behind the grease can." A wistful note crept into her voice. "Soon's as we get a bit together, we're fixing to buy a place over to Stoney. They ain't any mines besmirching the mountains there."

Coming out of the memory, Lilly stopped for a second and rolled up her pant legs. She would take scissors to them herself when she got back.

CHAPTER 2

WOMEN, CHILDREN, and a few elderly men gathered on their porches and watched as Lilly and Mr. James hurried down Skip Rock's main street on their way to the accident.

"Stanley!" one old fellow called out. "Is it a bad un?"

Mr. James never slowed down. "Don't know yet, Otis. I heard the whistle same time you did."

"If 'tis, you'll be needing a real doc," Otis hollered at their backs. "That poser ain't gonna do no good."

"Don't I know it," Mr. James said under his breath.

Lilly hoped he hadn't meant for her to hear him. If she wasn't so scared, she might have taken offense. She'd heard those same sentiments expressed in many different words all the while she was at university. She'd even caused an orga-nized protest among the male students early on. Some had marched on campus with signs proclaiming, *A woman's place is in the home* and *Fair sex. Weak mind.* She thanked the good Lord for Dr. Coldiron, who had put a stop to the shenani-gans with warnings of expulsion. Theirs.

She didn't have time to rehash that, though, for they were passing the giant wooden coal tipple and fast approaching the portal of the number 4 mine.

A man covered in coal dust met them at the entrance, carrying a lantern in each hand. His eyes shone brightly from his darkened face. He hardly gave Lilly a glance, directing his few words at Mr. James. "It's Darrell," he said. "Roof fell."

"Bad?"

"Reckon he'll lose a leg if he don't bleed out first."

Mr. James turned his back on Lilly. "Hold on," he said.

Lilly stayed behind while Mr. James followed the fellow a few steps into the mine. She heard him give an exasperated snort.

"Are you coming or what?"

"I thought you said to wait."

"What I said was 'Hold on.'" He ran one finger under the wide leather tool belt buckled at his waist. "Grab ahold of this and don't let go. Myrtie will pitch a fit if I lose you."

Lilly did as she was told, clutching his belt with one hand and her doctor's bag with the other.

"Women!" Mr. James went on. "This morning I said 'shake a leg' to Myrtie and she went off like a busted cocklebur."

"I got you," the other man said. "My old lady's ornery as Job's off ox."

"Tell you the honest truth, Bob, it's like they speak a different tongue," Mr. James said derisively, as if Lilly were deaf and not clinging to him by his belt.

The air inside closed around them like a thick, damp curtain. Men who looked like stoop-shouldered gray ghosts walked past single file.

"I ordered everybody out that don't need to be in," Bob said. "I figured that's what you'd want, Stanley."

"Yeah."

The floor slanted downward as they walked through a twisting man-made tunnel. Lilly could feel the strain on her knees. She had to pace herself to keep from bumping into Mr. James. The ceiling seemed to be getting lower and lower, the cave darker and darker. The lamps cast feeble yellow light at their feet. Mr. James and Bob walked with their heads below their shoulders, like turtles. Soon Lilly was stooping also. Her chest tightened with fear; she had a dread of closed-in places.

A memory of her grandfather in his coffin overtook her. She had screamed when the lid was closed and refused to go to the cemetery for the burial. How could anyone stand and watch as dirt thudded down on their loved one? Now she wanted to scream again. Scream and flee. But how would she ever find her way out alone?

"Mr. James," she gasped, "I can't breathe."

He didn't even stop. "Sure you can. You just go in and out. In and out."

In and out, she chanted in her mind. *In and out.*

Bob flashed his light on a small wire cage that sat on a shelf rock. A yellow canary stared back. Lilly was appalled. Poor little bird.

Without thinking, she let go of the belt and approached the cage. "Why would this bird be here?"

"Bird's dead, we're dead," Mr. James said.

How did they know the bird wouldn't die of loneliness or fright? Lilly wondered, hooking herself back up to Mr. James.

"Unh. Unh. Unh." Low grunts accosted them from somewhere up ahead.

"Darrell's still drawing air," Bob said.

"Yeah."

They arrived at a wide vestibule-like area, where a rock had indeed fallen on the miner. Darrell was lying in a narrow passageway that shot off the backside of the vestibule. The rock effectively plugged the passageway. All Lilly could see of Darrell was one bare foot. His boot lay on its side as if he'd just popped it off. But his low moans added urgency to the scene.

Several men worked on shoring up the roof on their side of the site with timbers, but as far as Lilly could ascertain, nobody was doing anything to help the fallen man.

"Did you bring a doc?" one man asked.

Mr. James stepped aside. As lamps were raised, all eyes seemed to be on Lilly.

"You're joshing," a man said.

"Nah," Mr. James said. "The company sent her."

One man spat on the floor. "They sent a skirt? Shows what *the company* thinks we're worth."

"That's right," another said. "Mules. We ain't got no more rights than mules. No telling what will happen now."

The men's anger swirled, mingling with the coal dust, settling on Lilly like poison. She knew the superstition about a woman in the mine bringing bad luck, but didn't they realize their bad luck had already come about? How could her being among them make it any worse?

"Bring a light," she said, kneeling at the fallen man's foot. Her hands probed his ankle for a pulse. It was faint, but it was there. "Is anybody over there with him?"

"We can't get around," Bob said, holding his lamp down for Lilly. "Even Billy here couldn't pass through."

Thin to the point of gaunt, Billy didn't look old enough to grow whiskers. He had no business in this place.

"Has anybody tried to move it?"

"We was waiting on Stanley," Bob said. "He's the face boss." He squatted next to Lilly and lowered his voice. "We don't know what will happen when we move that thing. If it goes the wrong way . . ."

Lilly caught his drift. It could fall backward over the trapped man, crushing him.

She watched Mr. James study the predicament. His stubbly beard rasped when he ran his hand over his chin. He motioned for Bob and Lilly to move aside before he crouched down. "There's a few inches' space either side of Darrell's foot. We could jack the rock up, I expect."

"Could someone climb over?" Lilly asked.

"Too dangerous," Mr. James said.

"I wouldn't mind to try."

"Danger's not to you."

Lilly's face flamed. She was glad for the dimmed light. How silly of her. If she climbed atop the rock, the pressure would increase on Darrell. Maybe she should just keep still.

Noises louder than Darrell's filled the cavern. It sounded like the mountain itself was groaning. Dust streamed down, dancing in the lamplight. Men ducked and ran for cover while Lilly stood stunned. What was happening?

Mr. James grabbed her hand, but she tripped over her britches and fell. He dropped beside her and covered her head with his arm as pieces of shale rained around them. Then all was ominously quiet—until Darrell screamed, "Don't leave me here to die alone!"

Mr. James stood and hauled Lilly up. "I understand if you want to leave," he said. "The rest of the ceiling could give way any second."

"I'm staying," she said. Shaken into action, she slithered into a narrow space between one side of the rough slab of rock and the wall. She went in sideways. There wasn't even room to bend her arms. "Hand me a lantern," she said.

"Careful you don't set yourself ablaze," Mr. James said while passing the lantern to her.

With a sidestep shuffle she maneuvered along the cramped space. Halfway there, a piece of the rock stuck out like an arm, blocking her. Alarm prickled like pinpricks up and down her arms. What if she got stuck? There was nothing for it but to slide back out.

Mr. James shone his light into the space. "Are you all right?"

"A piece of the rock impedes me," she said. "I don't think I can get through."

"Don't leave," Darrell whimpered. "Don't leave me."

"Lord, be with us," Lilly prayed. "Please help me."

Pressing her back against the wall, she slid down. With her knees up under her chin, she inched herself, her bag, and the lantern underneath the outcropping. Her scalp scraped against the jagged stone. A lock of her hair caught tight. She couldn't reach up to untangle it, so she jerked her head sideways and nearly cried out from the tearing pain. Her outstretched arms felt like lead weights, but she made it. She could see the passage dead-ended a few yards from where Darrell was trapped. Bent nearly double, she shuffled over to the fallen miner.

"I'm in," she shouted as she shone the light on Darrell's face.

"Who are you?" he asked.

"I'm a doctor," Lilly said. "I'm here to help you."

"Am I going to die?"

Lilly took a good look at the rock. It effectively pinned his shin to the ground. He might lose his lower leg, but otherwise he seemed unscathed. "No, Darrell, you're not."

"What's it look like over there?" Mr. James called.

"The rock is thinner on the downward side. It's caught his left leg below the knee."

"Set your lantern down by his leg so's I can see its shine."

Lilly brushed pebbles from the floor and put the lamp down.

"Yep, there it is," Mr. James said. "I'm passing a stout pole through. Holler when it clears."

In less than a minute a piece of timber inched past Darrell's knee.

"We're going to lift the rock a fraction. You see if you can pull Darrell free."

"Wait until I say. I'm going to apply a tourniquet first."

Lilly snapped open her kit and removed a length of India-rubber tubing. Darrell turned his head to the side and watched.

"I'm just going to pass this under your leg, Darrell. It won't hurt."

Darrell gritted his teeth. "It ain't like I'd notice. It's already as full of pain as a rain barrel's full of wiggle tails."

If the situation had not been so dire, Lilly would have laughed. Darrell had a way with words.

Carefully, she slipped the tubing under his thigh, wound it round tightly above the knee, and secured it.

"What's that for?" Darrell asked.

"Right now the pressure from the rock is cutting off your circulation. When it's lifted, the blood will flow again. This tourniquet will keep you from bleeding too much."

The fearsome overhead groaning started up again. Dirt sifted down.

"Get a move on," Mr. James hollered.

Lilly took a kneeling position at Darrell's head and put her hands under his armpits, ready to haul him loose. "All set!"

The rock inched upward. Lilly pulled. Darrell didn't budge. She bemoaned her slightness. She didn't have the strength for the task. "You're going to have to help me, Darrell. Bend your good leg and push yourself backward while I pull."

Working together, they managed to free his foot. "It worked, Mr. James! He's loose!"

"Listen close, little gal," Mr. James said from the other side of the rock. "We're going to hoist this thing again, and when we do, you need to put your hands in the middle of the rock and shove it this way."

The ceiling creaked like rusty hinges and loose pebbles pinged against the floor behind her. "I'll try," she said.

"It don't need muscle. Just set your mind to it," Mr. James said. "Trust me."

Cold sweat broke out across Lilly's forehead. Gingerly she touched the rough surface of the obstacle. How could Mr. James and the other men get out of the way in time? What if the boulder fell on them? What if it came her way? "Move back as far as you can, Darrell," she said and squared her shoulders.

"Ready?" Mr. James said.

"Ready!"

The rock teetered on the pole. "Push, gal, push!"

All her strength centered on the solid rock, Lilly took a deep breath and pushed. With a loud thunk the barrier smashed into the vestibule, breaking into ragged chunks. Lilly could see Mr. James and Bob and another man standing free. The others had left.

"Come out of there, Doc," Mr. James said.

"I can't leave my patient," she said.

"We're coming for him soon as you're out. Hurry up now."

Grabbing her doctor's kit and the lamp, Lilly scrambled overtop the rubble. Mr. James and Bob hurried to Darrell and lifted him into a two-man sling they made with crossed arms. The third man held his lantern up and guided them as they went. It was a difficult thing to do—carrying a grown man over a pile of rubble while stooped.

"Get on now!" Mr. James said. "Don't tarry."

Lilly started running.

"Watch your feet!" Mr. James wheezed the words. "They's holes you could fall in."

Lilly watched her feet. She was so scared, she thought they'd not even touch the ground. But there was the bird. She couldn't just leave it to die. She could hear the men coming as she shoved her kit under the arm that held the lantern and snatched the cage on the fly. Timber crashed and the sound of falling rock rolled up the mine like thunder. Dust filled her nose as dense as cotton batting. She strained to breathe until finally she was out. The men followed shortly.

Someone handed her a cup of water. It was cold and tasted of rock and coal and smoke. It was delicious.

She drank it down, then turned to Darrell. The tourniquet needed attention. Loosening it, she watched for blood flow. Satisfied, she tightened the tubing again. Some men hurried up with a stretcher and laid Darrell on it. They covered his body with a woolen blanket. Lilly removed it, rolled it, and used it to prop up Darrell's foot so that it was higher than his heart.

"I need to tend to this," she said. "Take him to the surgery."

Lilly followed the stretcher. A tall man with broad shoulders and coal-black hair walked alongside her. He carried her kit and cupped her elbow. She thought to shake his hand off, not wanting to appear weak, but truthfully, she was glad for the support.

Once inside the office, the men put Darrell on a waist-height operating table.

"I need hot water," she said, "and lots of it."

People gathered outside the door, murmuring among themselves. A man came in with a big black Bible. He laid his hand on Darrell's forehead and began to pray.

Outside, a near-grown boy added a thick cord of wood to a hastily assembled campfire. A woman poured clean water into a kettle hanging from a tripod over the fire. Wisps of smoke drifted by the open door.

Lilly could tell these people had been through times like this before. Everyone seemed to want to be of service.

As soon as the water was steaming, Lilly scrubbed her filthy hands and arms up to the elbow with strong lye soap and frequent changes of water; then she dipped them in a solution of 1:2000 per chloride of mercury. Mrs. James stepped in and tied a white, long-skirted, bibbed apron around Lilly's neck and waist. It flowed nearly to the floor and was starched stiff as an ironing board.

As Lilly had ascertained before, the previous doctor had kept the office surprisingly well stocked. There was nothing Lilly needed that she didn't find, from silk sutures to rolls of gauze. She would be all set as soon as she got an assistant.

"Who would be best to help me?" she asked of Mr. James. "I need a stalwart soul. We'll be here a long time."

When Mr. James brought a young man in and introduced him as Ned Tippen, Lilly shooed him out. "Scrub up first," she said. She stood, elbows bent and hands held upward, careful not to touch a thing as she waited to begin the repair of her patient's mangled shin.

Mrs. James picked up the antiseptic solution. "Should I take this out for Ned?"

"Just mix a tablespoon of it into a full pan of rinse water," Lilly said. "We don't want him to burn his hide off."

Whip-poor-wills began their eventide croon before Lilly finished putting Darrell back together. Her back seemed to have a permanent crook and her neck was stiff. She balled her fists and pressed them into her lower back.

Lilly thanked Ned, whom she had learned was a first cousin to Darrell. Once their patient began to come out of the anesthesia Lilly had administered, they transferred him to a bed in the alcove of the surgery suite. Ned volunteered to spend the night so Lilly could get some sleep.

"I don't know," Lilly said. "It's a half-mile walk to the

Jameses'. What if you needed me? I wouldn't want Darrell to be left alone for a minute."

Ned opened the door that had been closed during the procedure. The yard was crowded with folks all waiting. "The rest of his family's here," he said. "I'll send one of them if he takes a turn."

Lilly shook her head. "Surely they won't spend the night."

"Surely they will," Ned said. "You couldn't drive them off with a pointed stick."

CHAPTER 3

LILLY LEANED BACK in the galvanized tub and sighed. Even Aunt Alice's modern claw-foot bath had not felt this good.

"I put some rose hips in there," Mrs. James said from the other side of a privacy screen. "Don't they smell pretty?"

"I think I've died and gone to heaven. You are so thoughtful."

"Do ye want a vinegar rinse for your hair? I've got it ready."

"Um, just a minute," Lilly said. She sank back in the water, then scrubbed her scalp with the castile soap she'd brought from the city. Her fingers sought and found a nickel-size sore from where she'd caught her hair on the rock. Gingerly, she probed it. She hoped it didn't cause a bald spot. She'd always been vain about her hair.

"Okay," she called.

Mrs. James waddled around the screen holding a full bucket of water with both hands. Her eyes were closed tightly. "Do ye care if I look?"

Lilly laughed. "I expect we've both got the same equipment."

"Yours might be a little better placed," Mrs. James said and then tee-heed.

Cool water streamed from the bucket over Lilly's head and into the tub. She gasped.

"I should have warned you, but nothing brings out the shine like cold water and vinegar."

"It feels wonderful to be clean. Thank you."

Mrs. James averted her eyes as she held a towel for Lilly to step into.

Lilly wrapped herself up and then tied a towel around her head turban fashion. The coal-oil lamp sputtered on a table.

Mrs. James pulled a straight-backed chair up close to the wall. "Sit here on yon side of the door, where cain't nobody see you, so I can empty the tub."

Lilly sat and dried her hair while Mrs. James carried buckets of dirty water outside. Lilly could hear her slosh the bathwater over the side of the stone stoop. "Too dirty to save," she said as if Lilly would think she was wasteful. Mrs. James reminded her of her mother and her use-it-up-or-do-without attitude.

While Lilly combed her hair, Mrs. James carried the near-empty tub outside, rinsed it, and hung it from a nail beside the door.

"I just wanted to say you done a good job today," she said when she came back in. "I heard Stanley saying you saved that fellow's life."

"Mr. James and the other men were the ones who knew what to do. Me, I was scared silly."

"Well, don't think what you did was unnoticed." Mrs. James straightened a lace runner under the lamp. "I almost forgot." She took an envelope from her pocket and handed it to Lilly. "From a beau, I suspect."

Lilly Gray Corbett MD, Rt. 1, Skip Rock, Kentucky flowed in Paul's precise script across the front of the dove-gray envelope. "Could be," Lilly said.

"I'll be leaving, then," Mrs. James said. "You just holler if you need anything."

"Thank you. I'll be going back to the office later to check on . . . goodness, I don't even know Darrell's last name."

"It's Tippen, Darrell Tippen. He's Turnip Tippen's youngest. Darrell's a fine young man. By the way, I've been meaning to ask you to call me Myrtie."

"All right, if you'll call me Lilly."

"Oh, I couldn't do that. It wouldn't be respectful, you being a medical doctor and all."

"But, Mrs. James—Myrtie—I don't want to be treated any differently than anyone else."

"Yes, you do. You'll never get on with these people if

25

you carry water on both shoulders. They need to see you're set apart, else they won't have any respect for you. It's hard enough you being a woman working alongside of men without giving up your station, so to say."

Lilly had braided her hair into one long tail while they talked. She wound it into a thick bun, which she fastened with pins at the nape of her neck. "You sound as if you speak from experience."

"You wouldn't know it now, but I trained as a teacher before I married Stanley. But you cain't be married and a teacher both, so it's said. Folks would rather the schoolhouse stand empty than to have a married woman in it."

Lilly turned up the wick on the lamp. "Why is that, do you suppose?"

"It's menfolk having their way," Mrs. James said as she headed for the door. "They're all afraid won't be anybody to home when they come in for supper. They don't ever get over needing a mommy."

As soon as the door closed, Lilly dressed in a white button-front shirtwaist and an ankle-length navy-blue serge skirt. She held the envelope to her heart before she opened it. There was much truth to what Myrtie said. Lilly would heed her warning, but for now there was news from Paul— her dear Paul.

She slid the pages out. She was sure to get encouragement and laughter from his words. He was the funniest fellow. Scooting her chair closer to the light, she read:

Dearest Lilly,

I trust this missive finds you hale and hearty there in the land of family feuds and moonshine. As for myself, I have just returned from a stroll through the invigorating streets of Boston and will shortly go to meet friends at a local pub for a bit of food and conversation. I fear for your mind, darling Lilly, in that backward place and wish you had accepted the internship in Lexington. Your intelligence and exceptional charm will be wasted there. Skip Rock? Really, what were you thinking?

I can see from miles away that I have stepped, though ever so lightly, on your pretty toes, and if I were there, you would give me a fine argument concerning privilege and heritage and all that folderol. Truly, dearest, forgive me. My longing for you overrides my common sense. The sense that tells me you are right and I am wrong. Far from being the weaker sex, you put me and our other colleagues to shame with your bent to save the world one downtrodden person at a time.

Ouch. I ducked that shoe you threw my way.

Tomorrow I report for duty at Hamilton Hospital. It is certain to bring me down a peg, and I will be begging you to let me come to Skip Rock, where all is simple and serene.

Lovingly yours,
Paul

Lilly tucked the letter under her feather pillow, then plopped down on the brightly embroidered counterpane. Paul's letter stirred the homesickness that she hid in her heart like a faded photograph.

It was late. Her family would no doubt be in bed. The lamps would be turned out and the screened windows all flung open to catch the soft night breezes. Her sisters, Molly and Mazy, might be awake, whispering secrets back and forth. Her brother Jack would be dead to the world—he slept as hard as he worked and played. Did her youngest brother, Aaron, still sleep in the hammock outdoors when the weather was hot? She didn't know. It had been two years since she'd been back to Troublesome Creek, two long years since she'd felt the touch of her mother's hand or seen the twinkle of pride in her Daddy John's eye. And that had been a quick trip between semesters, not the long visit she pined for.

She never would have thought her studies would separate her from her home place for such a length of time. Even though she'd lived with her aunt Alice and her cousin Dodie while attending the university, it wasn't the same as home. It was better than being alone, though. She didn't know if she would have survived the first semester at college without Aunt Alice.

Oh, my goodness, that first year had been hard. Lilly knew she was in trouble when she walked into the lecture hall and beheld a long and complicated chemical formula marching in chalk across three blackboards. Three blackboards! It was daunting to say the least. But with prayer and determination she had learned and thrived.

Absentmindedly, she smoothed the counterpane with one hand. Dr. Coldiron had been surprised when Lilly chose to intern for the summer in a coal camp. She was surprised herself, for she'd expected to stay at St. Joseph Hospital in Lexington to continue her training. But then the letter had come to the university from the old doctor who worked for the coal company in Skip Rock, pleading for assistance. That letter was an arrow straight to Lilly's heart. She wondered if he knew he was ill when he wrote it—if he knew his time was short.

After finding her extra pair of shoes tucked under the bed, she went to the chest of drawers for a pair of hose. The drawer was stuck and squeaked like a mouse when she wrenched it open. She'd have to ask Mrs. James for a candle stub to run along the sliders.

Myrtie. I must remember to call her Myrtie. Mrs. James might be offended if Lilly was too formal. Now Mr. James— that was a different story, but she had heard him call her *Doc* instead of *gal.* Maybe he was lightening up a tad.

She pulled the laces tight on her sturdy brogans, ever so thankful for modern times. No more buttons on shoes and no more buttonhooks. Progress was a wonderful thing.

Sticking her feet out before her, she made a face. These shoes might be proper for the place, but they were also ugly— lumpy, black ugly. She much preferred the pretty pumps still wrapped in tissue paper and tucked away in the bottom of her traveling case.

Ah, well, once she and Paul were wed and she doctored in Boston, she'd wear only pretty shoes and pretty dresses covered by a lab coat instead of aprons—and her pearls. Aunt Alice had given her the strand of lustrous pearls as a graduation gift, and Lilly wore them always, even with overalls. She must have looked a sight today, operating in those too-big britches cinched in by twine, her face still black with dust, her apron two sizes too large.

A flush of pride warmed her. She knew she'd done a good job on Darrell's shin. Putting bones back together was like a complicated jigsaw puzzle, requiring patience and dexterity. She had plenty of each, she wasn't too modest to say.

Lilly closed the door to her cabin gently. The high yellow moon gave plenty of light to guide her way. In a treetop somewhere close by, an owl hooted, plaintively calling, *"Whoo-whoo"* to a distant sweetheart. Or so Lilly fancied. She'd always been one to give notions to animals as if she could discern their feelings.

The dark gloom of homesickness stole across her heart again. Once you gave in to that old high-lonesome feeling, it craved attention like a drunk craves whiskey. She wished she had a dog to walk alongside her as she made her way to the clinic. She missed her old beagle, Steady, and the way she'd push her long nose into Lilly's hand when they went for walks along Troublesome Creek. She couldn't help but smile remembering their good times together. Steady had been dead for years now, but still Lilly yearned for her sweet companionship. Maybe when she got to Boston . . .

Shivering, she tightened the shawl she'd thrown around her shoulders against the night air. It was spooky walking after dark in an unfamiliar place. The trees cast long, wavering shadows in the moonlight, and something fast and low to the ground scurried across her path. She should have kept to the street that ran smack down the middle of town instead of this path alongside the railroad track. She'd thought this way would be less distracting, as she was sure the townsfolk weren't used to a woman walking out alone so late.

Something caught her eye. Was that a man darting between the trees?

"Who's there?" she asked. She slowed without stopping and looked into the deep shadows. Nothing stirred. It was just her mind playing tricks, conjuring up specters, she was sure as she hurried up a side street to Main. She wasn't fearful as much as cautious. Past experience had taught her to be wary.

When she got to the clinic, folks who were obviously camped out for the night stepped aside as she made her way to the door. *There must be a lot of Tippens hereabouts.* She hated to close the door in their expectant faces, but her patient came first.

Ned Tippen sat in a straight-backed chair beside his cousin. He stood and moved the chair aside.

"How is he?" Lilly asked, checking Darrell's bandages and the circulation in his toes.

"Stirred enough to ask for water, then conked right back out."

Lilly held the water to the light. "He didn't take much," she said. The glass invalid straw clinked against the side of the glass when she set it back on the table.

"I didn't know whether to force it or not," Ned said.

"Sips are enough for now. We'll try some barley water tomorrow and progress to clear broth as he tolerates." Lilly shook down a thermometer and drew Darrell's elbow forward across his chest. She slid the thermometer between the folds of his armpit. Holding it in place, she timed five minutes by her watch. "His temperature's 101. Not unexpected. Have you ever given an alcohol bath, Ned?"

"No, ma'am, but that don't mean I can't."

"All right then," Lilly said as she assembled a basin of water, a jar of rubbing alcohol, and clean linen. Once Ned had the technique down pat, she stepped outside.

Darrell's family gathered round. "How's he doing?" a man who was an older version of Darrell asked.

"Are you Darrell's father?"

"Turnip Tippen," the man said, doffing a worn cap.

A portly woman pushed her way in front of Turnip Tippen. "Why are you banning his family from in there? What gives you the right? Are you doing some kind of experiments on my boy?"

A murmur with an undercurrent of anger arose from the crowd.

Lilly was taken aback. Nothing she'd learned in medical school prepared her for the outright hostility she felt emanating from the woman's body like heat off a potbellied stove.

Mr. Tippen stuck out one strong arm and swept the woman behind him. "Shut up, Tillie. This here's a doctor."

"Don't look like no doctor to me!" someone in the crowd shot back.

"Mrs. Tippen, Mr. Tippen, wait just a second," Lilly said. She cracked the door and slipped inside. Ned was sponging Darrell's uninjured foot. Otherwise the patient's body was covered. The assuring scent of diluted alcohol drifted from the bath. Everything was in order. She opened the door. "Come in," she said to the parents.

"Ned," Mr. Tippen said.

"Uncle Turnip. Aunt Tillie," Ned replied while patting Darrell dry with a clean cloth.

Mrs. Tippen gasped and covered her face with her apron. "He looks bad," she said, her voice muffled. "How's he going to make it with one leg?"

Mr. Tippen shook his head and looked askance at Ned.

Lilly touched her shoulder. "Come and look, Mother."

She guided the woman to the foot of the bed and turned back the cotton sheet to show Darrell's swathed lower extremity. "See, he still has his foot. You can touch his toes."

Mrs. Tippen put out her hand as if to touch her son but pulled it back. "It's purple as an eggplant. Why's it swole up like that?"

"We expect the swelling, and the color is the result of—"

Mrs. Tippen's wailing cry cut Lilly off midsentence. The woman sank to her knees on the floor at the foot of the bed and folded her hands. "Oh, Lord," she prayed, "spare my baby. Take me instead."

"Here we go," Mr. Tippen said. "The storm's a-coming in."

Lilly took the measure of Tillie Tippen. She'd seen her sort before—no matter what the circumstance or how dire the situation, women like Tillie could somehow steer all the attention straight to themselves like they were the only ship on a rolling sea. She swabbed the thermometer with alcohol and stuck it under Darrell's arm again. After several minutes, during which Darrell's mother heaved and sighed, she read the line of mercury.

"Much better—99.8. Good job, Ned," she said, her fingers seeking Darrell's pulse.

"Is that normal?" Mrs. Tippen asked as she got up from the floor.

"It's very close and really quite good, considering," Lilly said.

"But it's not normal?" Mrs. Tippen's voice rose like the crest of a wave. "So he's probably going to die. Is that what you're saying?"

Darrell's pulse quickened under Lilly's fingertips. "Mrs. Tippen, your son is doing very well, but he needs his rest. You need to step out now."

"But . . . but I should be here. I'm his mother."

Mr. Tippen took his wife's elbow and led her to the door. "We sure thank you, Doc," he said. "Our boy's in good hands; I can tell."

"I don't much like her attitude, Turnip," Mrs. Tippen said before the door closed behind them.

Ned shrugged. "Sorry about that. Aunt Tillie is a hand-wringer."

"She's just worried. I would be wringing my hands too if this were my son. He's in real trouble if gangrene sets in, but I didn't want to alarm them unnecessarily. We'll cross that bridge if we come to it." Lilly placed a clean top sheet over Darrell and then expertly removed the soiled one from underneath so that he was never exposed.

"If she'd of seen his ankle afore you put it back together, she'd not be vilifying you." Ned fanfolded the top of the sheet across Darrell's chest.

"You're good at this," Lilly said.

Ned's face colored under the compliment. "You think so?"

"Yes, I do. Someone taught you well."

Ned turned in his chair. He pulled back one britches leg and thumped his wooden leg. "Same thing as happened to Darrell happened to me."

"Goodness," Lilly said. "I never even noticed. How long ago . . . ?"

"Three year now."

"Do you still work in the mines?"

"I cain't make myself go back, but I'm going to have to. Since Daddy died, I'm my family's main support."

Lilly liked Ned's quiet manner. He had a good turn about him. "What have you been doing since you left the mine, if you don't mind my asking?"

"This and that, mostly tending to folks who don't have family to take them in." When Darrell stirred, Ned offered him a sip of water. "I took care of Cholly Bright for going on two years. Folks said Cholly was tetched, but he was only old."

Darrell moaned, "Hurts." The sheet fell away when he lifted his injured foot.

Lilly went to the pharmacy cupboard and turned the key in the lock. She'd give Darrell some morphine to ease the pain.

"Why don't you stretch your legs?" Lilly asked, then clamped her hand over her mouth. "Gracious, Ned, I'm sorry."

Ned just laughed and got up. "I'll go have a smoke and stretch the one I've got. Be right back."

Shortly after the morphine injection, Darrell quieted. His eyes fluttered open.

"Are you comfortable?" Lilly asked.

"Will you marry me?" he said, clutching her hand.

"Well, not tonight, Darrell." Lilly smiled when he drifted off and the grip on her hand relaxed.

Narcotic medication made folks say the strangest things. Once she'd assisted at a difficult posterior delivery. Dr. Coldiron had been expert with the forceps and liberal with the drugs. When the young mother had swum up out of a laudanum fog, she grabbed Lilly's hand just as Darrell had done. "I have to tell you something," she'd whispered in an exhausted voice. "This baby is not my husband's."

Lilly had hoped it was the pain medication talking.

Once Ned had stretched his leg, Lilly walked home. The air felt cool and good. She breathed it deep into her lungs, chasing the dregs of coal dust away. She wasn't as tired as she should have been. The events of the day and the continued concern for her patient had her wound as tight as an eight-day clock.

Fumbling with the knob, she almost missed the cage sitting by her door.

"Goodness, where did you come from?"

The canary huddled forlornly on the floor of its pen. Lilly carried it inside and lit the lamp. She poured a little water into a saucer and put it on the floor of the cage with a crumble of dry corn bread left over from her supper. The bird shook his feathers and hopped onto his perch. A tiny cloud of grit lifted up, then sifted back down over the teeny creature like a pall.

Stepping outside, Lilly dipped a clean cloth into the rain barrel sitting under the eave. The wooden barrel held the heat of the sun, so the water was still lukewarm. She thought of Darrell's earlier remark about the wiggle tails, but it was too dark to check for worms. Myrtie was so particular, Lilly figured she'd never let her rainwater go bad. She wrung the cloth nearly dry before going back to the canary.

The bird didn't resist when she cupped it, but she could feel the nervous trill of its heart against her palm. "Poor little biddy," she murmured. "Let's get you cleaned up."

The wall clock chimed three before she climbed into bed and pulled the soft quilt under her chin. The bird chirped thrice as if he were mocking the clock. Lilly didn't hear if he did the same at four.

CHAPTER 4

Tern Still couldn't believe his luck. And it was all because of a roof fall. His granny always said, "Even a thorn tree casts a shade," but he wasn't sure he'd believed her until today.

Long about midnight, he gave up on sleep. He went to the window that overlooked the street and tried his best to raise it. He started to pound the stuck sash with the heel of his hand but thought better of it. He didn't want to wake the other souls in the boardinghouse, especially Mrs. DeWitt. She'd have his head on a platter. That woman ran a tight ship.

He should have taken his bedroll and slept out under the trees. It would have been more comfortable than this stifling little room with its garish cabbage-rose wallpaper, threadbare rug, and lumpy mattress. Boardinghouse life. Tern was tiring of his vagabond ways, and he'd never thought that would happen. The food was good, though.

Quickly he dressed, sitting on the side of the iron bedstead to pull on his scuffed boots. His blue work shirt and jean trousers were cheap stuff and he disliked the feel of them, but if he was going to pass for a miner, he had to look like one. It wasn't as if he'd never done the work. Much like that boy Billy, who hung around the tipple each morning hoping for work off the books, he'd started working down the mines when he was seventeen. Boy, he knew the work, all right.

He plucked his billed cap off the bedpost where he'd hung it, eased the door open, and stepped out into a narrow hallway that led to a set of stairs. In seconds he was outside. If it weren't so late, he'd go by the livery station and get his horse—take a long ride out to where the air was still clean and the mountain streams still pure. He settled for a mindless walk around town. Somebody's hound tracked his trail, but it didn't bark. Dogs never took him for a stranger.

Of course, he wound up right where he didn't mean to go, a little ways up the mountain on a path that put him directly above the tar-paper cabin in back of the James place, where Lilly Gray Corbett was staying. Just the thought of her and his heart was beating like a trip-hammer.

He should be sleeping instead of spying. It had been a rough day, and tomorrow promised more of the same. Sometimes he didn't recognize his own intent.

When the roof caved this morning, he'd stayed put while

everyone else ran for their lives. He couldn't make himself leave Darrell Tippen—not even to save his own worthless hide. The others were right to run, trying to stay ahead of the dreaded black damp that dropped you in your tracks or the methane from firedamp and the explosion that could blow you right out the mouth of the mine—if you were lucky. At least that way your family had a body to bury. But noxious gases hadn't formed. The bird didn't die. Men were soon trooping back in and shoring up the roof with timbers until Bob made most of them leave again.

Tern got some odd looks from the other miners for hanging back. That had been a dumb move. It wasn't like he really knew the Tippen guy. He needed to be careful, really careful. He had to blend in with the others or else he might stir suspicion. Right now, all anybody knew was what he wanted them to know. He was just a fellow down on his luck, just passing through Skip Rock, just trying to make a few bucks until the next town. He wasn't any different on any given day from Billy or Charley or Buck.

The mating calls of insects waxed and waned with the fall of his feet, but when he hunkered down on the path, the noise became incessant. It was music to his ears. If you paid attention, you could hear that each bug played a different winged instrument. The black field cricket's chirp faltered in and out like a pulse, but a tree cricket's tune was long and steady. If he had to pick a favorite night song, though, it would be the katydid's.

Kay-tee-did, kay-tee-did. He heard the familiar sound

made when the insect rubbed the ridge of one thinly veiled green forewing against a scraper on the other. Tern quieted his mind and listened hard to hear the sound most folks never did. *Kay-tee-did-not,* the leaf on legs trilled. *Kay-tee-did-not.*

The buzzes, clicks, and rasps of the night serenade lulled him. The town and the mine seemed far away and of little significance from where he sat on his heels—until a door opened onto a stone stoop far below, and a young woman stepped out into the night.

Lilly. He'd known it was her the moment he first saw her in the yellow light of the lantern that morning. He had dared to cradle her elbow in his cupped palm, supporting her as others carried Darrell Tippen to the surgery suite in the doctor's office. Of course he'd heard the gossip that there was a new doctor staying with the Jameses and that it was a woman, but he'd never imagined it was Lilly.

Obviously, she hadn't recognized him. That was good. His momentary lapse could have given it all away. The feel of that small elbow in his rough hand made him out of heart, ill with the lovesick longing of the boy he thought was long since buried in the deepest recesses of his mind.

As he watched now, she walked briskly, stepping with purpose into the puddles of light cast by the lantern she carried. He supposed she was going back to the office. But why was she taking the long way around instead of walking down Main? A woman like her wasn't safe alone at this time of night. There were some rough characters working in the mines and living in shanties or pitched tents on the outskirts of town, men imported for their backs and their brawn and their closed mouths. Like him, they'd be here today and gone tomorrow. They would go wherever a new mine opened or an old one paid better wages. He would go whenever the government sent him.

Tern felt compelled to follow along, making his way among the trees in the dark of the moon until the long, waving frond of a blackberry bramble reached out to impale him. It was so unexpected that he almost cried aloud as thorns raked his side through the fabric of his shirt. He pulled the bramble loose and flung it away. It snapped back, bringing more with it, circling his forearm like a witch's bony talons. Taking a deep breath, he stopped to extricate himself. If he was right-natured, this never would have happened. Usually he was sure-footed as an Indian scout, more at home in the forest than in a house, but he'd walked right into the prickly, unforgiving shrubs. He shook his head. *Man, get a grip on yourself.*

She went where he figured she would. A small group of folks stood back as she opened the door to the doctor's office and closed it behind herself. He could hear rumblings of discontent. People didn't like that she had replaced Doc Jones. They acted like she was a spider in their dumplings. Stupid. They had held the old doc's wake days before she arrived. But of course, their minds were set against any woman being in the belly of the mountain. People had a right to their superstitions, but Tern wished they could have seen Lilly at work this morning. It might have made some inroads into their false notions. Way he saw it, any doctor was better than no doctor.

Stanley James was coming up the street and heading toward the set of people. Hands in pockets, Tern stepped backward, fading into the shadows while keeping his eyes on Stanley. If anybody figured him out, it would be Mr. James. The heel of Tern's boot caught on something, throwing him off-balance. A bird squawked as its cage tipped over and rolled like a tin can toward the mouth of the mine. Tern scrambled to stop the blasted thing, sure everyone would be staring at the commotion.

As luck would have it, a woman in the crowd set to bawling at the same time the bird set to squawking. Tern breathed a sigh of relief as he righted the wire pen. He remembered seeing Lilly carry it out. She must have forgotten about the bird in all the chaos that ensued.

He'd better get out of here before somebody noticed and wondered why he was hanging around. Mr. James would look after Lilly.

Tern picked up the cage and slipped away. Halfway to the boardinghouse, he stopped under a gas lamp and looked inside the cage. What would he do with a bird? He could take it back to the mine in the morning, but that might give him away. Folks might wonder why he had it in the first place. Besides, Lilly Corbett saved it for a reason.

Images of a girl flickered in his mind. Plain as if it were yesterday, he saw her climbing the low rock wall that divided her family's land from his. She was maybe twelve then—not much younger than he had been. Clearly, he'd caught her infringing on Still property. But when he'd told her of her insult, she'd sassed him with a surety of self he had never witnessed in a female.

When he was a boy, he thought she was the most beautiful creature he'd ever seen. Heaven help him, she still was.

The first time he'd seen Lilly, she was trespassing. The last time he saw her, she had kissed his cheek. A lot of terrible things took place between that trespass and that kiss, and they were all his fault.

His heart dropped with the realization that he could never act on his feelings for her. It was just as well he was a man living a secret life—just as well Lilly Gray Corbett would never have to know who he was or who he had been. He was the last person on earth she would ever want to see again. If he was sure of anything, he was sure of that.

He put the birdcage on the stone stoop outside her lodgings and walked away, wishing he could discard his secret longings as easily as he'd discarded the caged bird.

CHAPTER 5

LILLY WOKE WITH A START. For a moment she didn't know where she was. The room was deep in shadow. What time was it?

The bird gave a rusty chirp like he was tuning up for something. Time to get up—that's what time it was. She hurried to the washstand to begin her morning toilet by dipping her damp toothbrush into a tin of Colgate's dental powder.

Once she was dressed and her hair neatly combed, she cracked the door to let in some air. A chill morning mist swirled like smoke around her ankles.

A tap at the door signaled that Myrtie James stood on the other side with her breakfast.

"Oatmeal," Myrtie said. "I should have asked if you take it with brown sugar or sorghum. I didn't know, so I brung ye both."

Lilly tipped a small white pitcher and poured a copious amount of thick yellow cream into her mug of coffee. She didn't have the heart to tell Myrtie she would prefer tea. "Mmm, this is bracing, just what I needed this morning. Thank you, Myrtie."

A sheer film of dawn's first light fought the shadows and, dominating, set the bird to singing. His tiny chest puffed out and his head thrown back, he saluted the morning. He sang with such vigor Lilly was surprised he didn't fall off his perch.

Myrtie nearly dropped the pint jar of sorghum she was twisting the lid from. "Well, I never," she said. When Lilly declined the sorghum, she put it back on the tray and bent over the cage. "A bird in the house brings bad luck. Where'd it come from anyway?"

"He's the bird from the mine. I carried him out yesterday, and then someone left him on the stoop last night."

"You don't say. You mean this here's the forewarning bird."

The bird hopped to the floor of the cage and pecked at the corn bread scattered there. "Forewarning? I guess so," Lilly said.

Myrtie's hand closed around the cage's thin wire handle. "Well, I'll just take him to the house. Stanley ain't left out yet. He'll want to take him back."

"Take him back? Surely not. The little thing almost died yesterday."

"Well, honey, lots of folks almost died yesterday," Myrtie said with a frown. "This bird's job is to caution—give the men a chance to get out before the black damp overcomes them."

The cereal she'd just swallowed formed a painful lump in Lilly's throat when she watched the canary's cage swing to and fro as Myrtie carried it across the yard to the main house. Myrtie's words made her feel like a scolded child, and she fancied the little budgie was looking back at her, waiting to be saved once again.

Oatmeal congealed in the bowl while she skimmed some Scripture and hurried through her prayers. She hoped God wasn't offended when she prayed for the bird after she prayed for Darrell. Animals had always been her weakness.

As she headed toward the small hospital, she wondered who had left the bird at her door. She hoped she soon found out, for obviously they were like-minded, and she could sure use a friend.

Skip Rock was a hard place, so unlike Troublesome Creek you wouldn't think they were both situated in the mountains of Kentucky. Even church here was hard. She'd gone with Myrtie Sunday last, and even in Myrtie's company, folks barely acknowledged her. But she had smiled and soldiered through. Maybe next Sunday would be different.

A woman swept her wooden porch. She leaned on her broom, her face lost in the shadow of a shapeless bonnet, watching as Lilly passed by.

"Good morning," Lilly said.

Her reply was a barely audible "Morning." She turned her back, brushing vigorously at something under the porch swing with the stub of a straw broom.

A white-and-tan dog sauntered up, sniffing at Lilly's heels. She stopped and offered her hand. He looked up at her with soulful brown eyes before taking a tentative sniff. When she walked on, he followed. All along Main Street, dogs popped out from underneath porches and behind houses, happily joining their parade. She might as well have been the mayor. All they needed was a brass band.

One of the dogs was sleek and muscular with a blue-black coat. She figured him for a coonhound. He edged out her first companion, asserting his authority, strutting next in line behind her. A hapless cat saw the procession coming and quick as a wink darted up an ash tree. The coonhound peeled away and treed the cat, baying like it was the full of the moon and the cat was a masked raccoon.

Poor kitty, Lilly thought. She'd check on it when she came back this way. The dog would surely get bored by then. She'd have to remember to keep a biscuit in her pocket for her morning companions.

"Get!" Stanley James yelled as he joined her, swinging his booted foot at the dogs, carefully not making contact. One by one they slunk away back to their outposts, back to their private territories.

"I didn't mind their company, Mr. James," Lilly said.

"Always liked dogs myself," he said.

"I didn't think you and Mrs. James had any pets."

"Lost Sam round about a year ago now. He was a smart one."

"I'm sorry."

"That's the way, ain't it?"

Lilly took three steps to his every one. He might have joined her, but much like the coon dog, he was dominating. "What happened to Sam?"

"Took on the wrong varmint. Dog's no match for a bear."

Lilly's hand went to her throat. "Oh, dear." She had to suppress the urge to touch Mr. James in sympathy. "Will you get another?"

"Maybe. Maybe not. Ain't ready to take on that sorrow yet."

"But don't you think the joy of having one outweighs the grief of losing one?" Lilly asked.

"Yeah . . . well, I ain't certain sure of that. Sounds like you been there yourself."

"I once had a beagle. I named her Steady and she was just that. She never let me out of her sight. She was the truest friend I've ever had."

"So what happened to steady Steady?"

"Old age sneaked up on her, but she was happy right to the end—chasing rabbits in her dreams." Lilly sniffed. Steady always brought tears.

"Humph." Mr. James cleared his throat and walked ahead. Lilly wondered if he was discomfited to be seen having a conversation with her. It might put him at a disadvantage with the other men. Women in their place and all that. She was swimming upstream here for sure. She wondered if she would ever find her place among these people.

Darrell's face was lathered for a shave when Lilly got to the clinic. Ned Tippen was sharpening a straight razor on a leather strop. He ran his thumb over the razor's bright edge. "I wrote down what the thermometer told me this morning," he said, glancing at a scrap of paper on the invalid tray. "It was 99.8."

"That's the same as last night," Lilly said. "Very good." After taking the pearl-headed pin from her hat, she took it off, stuck the hatpin into the crown of the castor-brown felt, and hung it on the coatrack just inside the door. She slipped a fresh apron over her head, tied it at the neck and waist, and then peered into a hanging mirror to smooth her hair. She liked everything tidy.

"Reckon it's all right if I open the curtains?" Ned asked. "I might slit Darrell's throat shaving him in this gloom."

Lilly opened the curtains. The room brightened.

The lather on Darrell's face cracked around his crooked grin. "I feel like a new man this morning, Doc."

"Stop talking, Darrell, else I'll have to soap you up again," Ned said, hanging the strop on a tack in the wall.

Lilly busied herself counting supplies and wiping down the counters with bleach water.

"I'll do that, Doc," Ned said, "soon's as I get done beautifying Darrell here." He nudged Darrell with his elbow. "Might take a right smart while to pretty this mug."

"Don't you have any toilet water?" Darrell said. "Good barbers always finish with a slap of good-smelling toilet water."

"Well, Cuz, I reckon you'll have to make do this morning," Ned said.

Lilly enjoyed their banter. It reminded her of her brothers and sisters. Darrell had to be doing much better if he could participate in Ned's teasing. It seemed her worry had been for naught. She recalled the words of her mentor, Dr. Coldiron. "Don't get emotionally involved," he counseled his students. "Fret and worry only get in the way of sound medical practice. Do what you can, do it well, and then let it go."

Now all she had to do was put the wise professor's saying into practice—easier said than done.

CHAPTER 6

CHAPTER 6

IT HAD BEEN A LONG DAY, and it was nearing dusk before Lilly made her way up the winding mountain path. Her devotional time had gotten short shrift this morning, and she hoped to make up for it now. When she reached her favorite spot, she spread a shawl on which to sit. A profusion of common purple violets carpeted the ground around her, and just under the trees, a few trilliums still bloomed brightly red. Her daddy called trilliums wake-robins because their blossoms heralded the return of the orange-breasted birds in the spring.

From her seat, she picked a bunch of violets, winding one long stem round the others to make a posy. With the tiny bouquet in her lap, she opened her Bible to Psalms and began to read.

Sing aloud unto God our strength: make a joyful
noise unto the God of Jacob. Take a psalm, and
bring hither the timbrel, the pleasant harp with
the psaltery. Blow up the trumpet—

"Hey! Hey, you," someone blatted loud as the psalmist's
trumpet.

Sighing, Lilly turned to see who was disturbing her peace.

A flash of color caught her eye from the far side of a
beech tree before a girl stepped out onto the trail several feet
distant. Lilly guessed her to be fourteen years old. Tall and
narrow as a boy, she had not yet developed a feminine figure.
Her light-brown hair was plaited in two braids unadorned
by ribbon. She wore a red-print feed-sack dress and over that
an apron that tied at the neck but hung loose at the waist.

Lilly laid her Bible aside and stood. The posy tumbled to
the ground. "Might you be looking for me?"

"Depends," the girl said. "Are you that doctor lady?"

"Depends," Lilly shot back. "Who's asking?"

"Armina Eldridge's asking, if ye need to know," the girl
said as she stepped closer.

"Pleased to meet you. I'm Dr. Corbett," Lilly said. "What
do you need of me, Armina?"

"I don't need nothing," the girl replied.

"Then why were you looking for me?"

Armina's forehead knit into a frown. "'Cause you're that
doctor woman. Right?"

Lilly nodded. "Um, yes. That would be me."

"Well then, listen here. I want to know how come you ain't stopped by to see my aunt Orie. Old Doc never missed a Wednesday."

"I'm sorry, Armina, but I don't know anything about your aunt Orie."

Armina's light-colored eyes looked out from her freckled face with the sharpness of daggers. "That's plain dumb. How can you not know of Orie Eldridge? Ever'body knows of her."

"Is your aunt Orie ill?"

"Huh! You reckon Old Doc come every Wednesday for the tea and crumpets?"

Lilly forced a slow breath. If the doctor was making weekly calls, this case didn't sound emergent. "It's nearly dark. If you give me directions, I'll come and see your aunt tomorrow."

Confusion clouded Armina's thin face. "But tomorrow's Thursday."

"Yes . . . so?"

"Aunt Orie expects her doctoring on Wednesday."

"I'm sorry, but tomorrow's the best I can do."

A sudden wind stirred their skirts and sent Armina's apron flapping. Holding it down with one hand, she looked Lilly over. "I'll come by and fetch you directly after breakfast," she said. "It ain't a place easily found."

Turning her back, Armina hiked up the steep trail, sure-footed as a mountain goat. Before she angled away around a bend, she stopped to fetch something from the tall grasses beside the path. "Come on, Bubby," Lilly heard the girl say as she plopped a roly-poly baby on her nearly nonexistent hip. "It's a-fixing to come a frog strangler."

Dozens of grasshoppers whirred down the trail from where Armina had disturbed them. Lilly watched their progress from one clump of brush and weeds to another. One of the long-legged insects landed on her wrist, cocking his wee brown head, studying the bit of flesh beneath him before, with a short burst of speed, he jumped to test the yellow fruit of a horse nettle.

Lilly laughed. "Hurry up," she said as the marble-size globe bobbed under his weight. "Your friends are leaving you behind."

The coming rain gave warning with its clean yet earthy scent. Lilly wrapped her Bible in the shawl and hurried down the mountain. With a laugh she ran across the yard and into her house, beating the rain by seconds. Her still-warm supper sat waiting on one of Myrtie's prized tea-leaf plates: a ham steak, corn pudding, baking soda biscuits, and green onions fresh from the garden. A cold glass of milk and a slice of apple pie finished her repast. If she wasn't careful, she'd soon be as fat as the baby Armina had hefted to her hip.

It was still dark and misting rain the next morning when she rapped lightly on the Jameses' front door. She wanted to let Myrtie know not to bring her breakfast round. The apple in her pocket would suffice.

The tantalizing smell of bacon teased her resolve when Myrtie opened the door. "Goodness gracious," she said after Lilly told her she was on her way to work. "Why so early?"

"I've got to make a house call this morning," Lilly said, "but I have to see about Darrell first."

"If you'd of told me last evening, I'd of brought your breakfast before I fed Stanley."

"I'm sorry. I didn't think of it until just now."

Lilly could see Mr. James sitting at the table. His fisted hands, a fork in one, a knife in the other, rested beside his empty plate. "Step in," he said. "It don't take but a minute to eat an egg." He put his fork down and, without moving from his seat, pulled out a chair for Lilly.

Feeling like a child, Lilly took the chair. She really shouldn't let Mr. James direct her time, but Myrtie was already stacking silver-dollar pancakes and two over-easy eggs on her plate. Her stomach rumbled at the sight. Mr. James slid a pitcher of syrup across the table with one hand and cut into his stack with the other.

Myrtie watched from the stove. Lilly wished she'd sit down and eat with them. As soon as Mr. James emptied his coffee cup, Myrtie was there with the pot. She refilled the cup, then stirred in a splash of cream and two teaspoons of sugar, although the sugar bowl and cream pitcher sat right in front of Mr. James. He never had to ask for a thing. Myrtie anticipated his every need. Lilly was appalled. Myrtie was being treated like a servant. In Lilly's home on Troublesome Creek, her daddy was as likely to fix her mother's cup of tea as her mother was to pour his coffee.

Lilly couldn't help but notice a folded one-dollar bill tucked under the rim of a saucer. It must be for Myrtie's money jar. She wondered if her landlady was getting close to her goal. Probably not if Mr. James gave her only one dollar at a time. Of course, he might not want to move; maybe that was just Myrtie's dream.

"How's Darrell holding up?" Mr. James asked.

"He's doing very well. I'll send him home to finish his recuperation soon, barring complications."

"I heard his mother pitched a fit on you," Myrtie said as she packed bacon and leftover pancakes into Mr. James's lunch bucket.

"You wouldn't be fishing for gossip, now would you, Myrtie?"

"I'm just asking, Stanley, not telling. Gossip's like jam; it don't bear fruit if you don't spread it."

Lilly sipped her coffee. She felt caught in the middle by the couple's teasing. "Darrell's family has been quite helpful. They bring meals for both him and Ned, and his mother keeps a kettle boiling doing up the wash."

"Good cook is she?" Myrtie asked.

"Give it up, Myrtie," Mr. James said as he pushed back his chair and bent to tie his shoes. "Where are you off to?" he asked.

Lilly wiped a drip of sticky syrup from her chin. "I'm going to call on Orie Eldridge. Her niece is coming to show me the way."

"Orie Eldridge, you say?"

"Yes, I met Armina yesterday when she came by to say I'd missed a visit. She was quite insistent." Lilly placed her knife and fork across the top of her plate and tucked her folded napkin under its edge. "I'll visit in her home this time, but next week her family will need to bring her by the clinic."

Mr. James exchanged a look with Myrtie. "That ain't likely to happen."

Standing, Lilly bit back the question that sprang to the tip of her tongue. Mr. James would have to learn that she was in charge of her patients and she would decide how to deal with them.

As she left, she heard Myrtie scold from behind the screen door, "You should have told her, Stanley."

"Gal seems bent on doing ever little thing by her lonesome," he said. "She'll find out soon enough."

CHAPTER 7

THE HOUND DOG was waiting for her at the edge of his yard. Lilly tossed the half pancake she had saved from breakfast to the ground. He slurped it up, stood still for her to scratch behind his ears, and then trotted up the street toward the clinic, as fine an escort as she had ever had.

Though it was not yet full light, Ned was outside, slapping something on the door with a wide brush.

Lilly's eyes watered from the sting of gypsum. "What in the world are you doing, Ned?"

Startled, he jumped, nearly dropping the bucket, before he opened the door as wide as it would go. "Just sprucing things up."

"At six in the morning?"

"Darrell's sleeping. I had a little time on my hands."

"You're acting guilty as a fox in the chicken coop, Ned. Please close the door."

Ned's chin dropped to his chest. "I'm sorry. I just didn't think you needed to see this."

The door swung shut. A leering skull shone faintly through the wash, and black crossbones still marred the door.

"It'll need several coats of whitewash," Ned said. "I mixed some plaster of Paris from the back storeroom—hope you don't mind. I didn't have any paint."

"Why would someone do this? Is it supposed to be a warning?"

"It's my fault. I reckon I fell asleep. I didn't hear a thing."

"I think covering this up is a good idea, Ned. Let's keep this to ourselves, shall we?"

Lilly reached for the knob, but Ned beat her to it. "I'll let you get back to work," she said. "And, Ned, thank you for caring."

"You're more than welcome," he said, dipping the brush into the bucket. "I'd best hurry before this sets up on me."

Lilly had barely finished Darrell's a.m. routine before Armina rapped on the doorframe.

"You ready?" she said when Lilly stepped around the privacy screen Ned had pulled in front of the door left propped open. Bubby bounced on Armina's slight hip.

"I'll be back this afternoon," Lilly called to Ned, who was in the back. "I'm making a house call."

"Watch careful for snakes," he replied. "They'll likely be sunning today."

"I've got my walking stick," Lilly said. "I'll make a ruckus."

The path was steep and twisted into hairpin turns, but they made their way easily enough until they came to a wide and stagnant creek.

Armina gathered her skirts to one side, secured them under Bubby's bottom, and waded in up to her knees.

Lilly paused on the bank. The water was murky and smelled of rotten leaves and dead fish. Something sinister slithered by.

"I reckon you'll want to take your shoes off," Armina said.

"Isn't there a bridge somewhere about?"

"You afeered of snakes?"

"Well, I don't want to step on one," Lilly said, "and this water is not very clean."

Armina swirled the water with one foot. "This here's Swampy. It's always brackish." She bent down to pick up a good-size rock and lobbed it underhanded, up the bed. Oily water splashed. "There now. The snakes will all go up under the riffles. They won't hurt you none." The tail of her skirt broke loose and trailed behind her as she made her way to the far bank.

With her shoes and stockings in one hand and her skirts over her arm, Lilly followed.

Once they crossed the creek, it was not far to the Eldridges' cabin nestled deep in the hollow of the woods. The cabin sat four feet off the ground, balanced on rocks stacked underneath each corner. A trace of smoke wafted upward from a massive stone chimney. They climbed six wide wooden steps up to the porch. Armina crossed silently on bare feet, but Lilly's footsteps rang out hollowly.

The door opened inward. Armina stood back and allowed Lilly to step into the cool shadows of the one-room house. As her eyes adjusted to the dim light, she saw that everything was clean and orderly. A kitchen table was laid with tin cups and plates as if for dinner. A shelf against one wall held a gray granite bucket and round granite pan. On the wall beside the bucket, a long-handled gourd dipper hung from a leather string looped over a nail. Warmth emanated from the cookstove in one corner.

The biggest woman Lilly had ever seen sat in a huge chair placed in front of the empty fireplace. Her dimpled elbows were planted on the arms of the chair, and she rested her double chin in one palm. Aunt Orie, Lilly surmised.

"Mrs. Eldridge? I'm Dr. Corbett. What can I do for you today?"

"Honey, I cain't hardly draw any air."

Each word was punctuated with a singing gasp. She sounded like the full gospel preacher Lilly had once heard at a brush arbor meeting.

"Doc said she's got the dropsy," Armina said.

"May I?" Lilly asked, pulling her black stethoscope from her bag and placing the bell over Mrs. Eldridge's heart. The heart galloped—straining. Her short, labored breath crackled through the bell when Lilly put it on her chest. "Could I listen to you from the back?"

Mrs. Eldridge leaned forward heavily. The chair popped and creaked. Tiny hands lifted the tent of Mrs. Eldridge's skirts and a little girl crawled out from under the seat. She didn't go far, however, for the tail of her dress was caught tight under one of the legs.

"Sissy, sit still now," Armina said, plopping Bubby down on the floor beside her. She'd carried the boy nearly a mile up the side of the mountain.

The toddler poked Bubby's button nose. "Node?"

"Shh, Sissy," Armina said.

"Twins?" Lilly asked.

"Same as," Armina said. "Ten months apart—he's eight months but already outweighs her. She'd be easier to pack when I have to leave the house, but I cain't wag both and she don't fuss." She wet one fingertip and wiped a smudge from the boy's cheek. "Bubby and Sissy, double trouble."

"They sure are cute."

"Yeah."

After listening to the patient's lungs, Lilly knelt and used the bell for auscultation of the four quadrants of the ponderous abdomen. Obvious to her, heart disease was causing copious amounts of fluid to collect, which pressed against the diaphragm, thus the labored breathing. "May I?" she asked again before hanging her stethoscope around her neck and lifting the hem of Mrs. Eldridge's long skirt. Lilly had to stop herself from shaking her head in dismay, for as she had expected, the lady's feet and ankles were hugely swollen. The flesh dented when she pressed with her fingertip. She'd learned to rate the pitting with numbers: one plus, two plus, three plus, or four. This had to be four plus plus plus, if there was such a score.

"Do your feet and ankles hurt?" she asked, sure of the answer. She couldn't imagine how the poor woman walked about.

"Pains me some." Long wheeze. "Mostly wearies me."

"Do you want me to get the bucket?" Armina asked.

"Bucket?"

"For the water. Old Doc drains her belly ever couple of visits. He ain't been here for a long time. That's why she's got so bad."

"Hmm," Lilly said, giving thought to the problem. Surely there was a chapter in one of her medical texts titled "Drawing Water Other Than from the Well."

"Pity," Mrs. Eldridge gasped.

"Pardon?" Lilly asked.

"Old Doc," she said.

"Tragedy," Lilly said, truly. She could have learned a lot from Old Doc.

A white enamelware bucket clanked against the rough wooden floor. "Here you go," Armina said.

Bubby grasped the black-trimmed rim and pulled himself up. His grin spread ear to ear before Sissy jerked him back down.

"Good girl," Armina said. "Last thing I need's for him to start walking."

From where she knelt on the floor, Lilly could see inside the bucket. It held a long, skinny packet of gauze and a brown rubber suction bulb.

"It's Aunt Orie's silver tube," Armina said. "I boiled it clean just like Old Doc showed me."

Of course, Lilly thought, a trocar. Old Doc drained the fluid from Mrs. Eldridge's abdomen by way of the sharply pointed surgical instrument contained in a metal cannula. Her mind scrambled backward through many lectures and demonstrations to a day in clinical when she'd observed the treatment of a patient with the same symptoms as these. The difference was the woman that day had been skin and bones. The only thing big about her had been her belly, whereas Mrs. Eldridge was markedly obese and not just from retained fluid. It would be a challenge, but fat or skinny the treatment would be the same.

"I'll need to wash up," she said, standing.

A teakettle whistled. "Water's hot," Armina said. "I'll fix you a pan."

"Let's get our patient settled first," Lilly said. "Mrs. Eldridge, will you be able to walk to the bed?"

"Don't stand on ceremony," she labored to say. "I'm plain Aunt Orie."

"Of course," Lilly said. "Thank you."

Armina positioned her body in front the chair. "Grab hold."

It was then Lilly noticed the knotted rope suspended from the ceiling. Aunt Orie reached overhead, grabbed the rope above the double knot with both hands, and heaved herself upright. The chair tipped forward and Sissy scooted free. Bubby laughed and clapped his chubby hands.

With support on both sides, Aunt Orie shuffled lock-kneed to the bed, which Lilly saw was made up with linen sheeting folded over a rubber mackintosh sheet. Managing to turn herself around, Aunt Orie dropped down. The mattress sighed under her weight.

"Lie on your side as close to the edge as possible," Lilly said.

Armina positioned a stack of pillows. "We know what to do."

Lilly waited for Armina to pour the hot water before she scrubbed up. It was always best to remember whose kitchen you were in so you wouldn't overstep your bounds.

Armina washed and oiled her aunt's belly before Lilly removed the gauze from the trocar. In one sure and steady move, Lilly plunged the instrument into Aunt Orie's flesh. With the encouragement of suction, a stream of fluid flowed freely as water through the cannula and into the bucket on the floor. After the first gush, the flow settled into a steady drip.

"Good," Lilly said. "You don't want to shock the body by removing the fluid too quickly."

"It's just like tapping a maple tree for sugar water," Armina said.

Aunt Orie relaxed and closed her eyes.

"She'll nap now."

"That's good," Lilly said as she applied a pad of lint and

strapping around the puncture site. "How much did Old Doc usually get?"

"Oh, it'll drain a couple gallons." Armina smoothed stray wisps of hair from her aunt's forehead. "She'll feel better for a while."

Lilly recognized the look of resignation in Armina's eyes. She'd seen it many times in people who nursed loved ones for whom they had no real hope.

As she cleansed her hands, Lilly wondered about the circumstances of the Eldridge family. Young as she was, Armina seemed perfectly at home with her aunt's care, but surely she didn't also have the care of the two babies.

Armina poured tea into two cups. "I thank ye for coming," she said. "I feared for Aunt Orie once Old Doc passed on."

Lilly took a seat at the kitchen table and sipped the hot tea. "Who helps you with Aunt Orie?"

"Right now there's just the three of us—me, myself, and I," Armina said as she tossed her braids over her shoulders. "Aunt Orie's sisters drop by ever other Sunday on their way home from church. They don't stay long enough to take their hats off, but Uncle Bud helps out. He comes over from his place of a morning. He weeds the garden, keeps the wood box filled, and milks the goat."

"Goat?"

"For the kids," Armina said. "The nanny goat's and these."

Sissy toddled to Lilly's side and held her arms up. Lilly bent to lift her.

"Sorry," Armina said. "She's always begging for something."

Bubby skirted Lilly's chair and crawled to Armina's. She picked him up and kissed the top of his fuzzy head.

Lilly broke a piece of the cinnamon biscuit on her plate and fed it to Sissy. The little girl was so slight she barely made a dent in Lilly's lap.

"Are Sissy and Bubby brother and sister?"

"Yeah, they're my sister's kids. She's gone, but she'll be back sooner or later." Armina tied a dishrag loosely under Bubby's chin. "She followed their daddy off somewheres. He's supposedly working."

"Hmm," Lilly said, disengaging Sissy's hand from her pearl necklace. "How old are you, Armina?"

"I'm seventeen next week. How old are you?"

Lilly smiled. Fair enough. "I was twenty-three last November."

"How'd you come to be a doctor? I thought only men were doctors."

"I was not much younger than you when I decided I wanted to go to medical school." Lilly added a cube of sugar to the tea in her cup. An aroma akin to that of root beer tickled her nose. Her mother had made her this special drink whenever she was ill. Lilly hadn't had sassafras tea in a long time.

"Wasn't you afraid you'd be an old maid?" Armina gave Lilly a calculating look. "I guess you wasn't."

Lilly laughed. "I suppose not," she said. "My daddy always said I had a one-track mind. Once I decided what I wanted to do, there really wasn't much time for romance."

"Maybe it ain't too late. Do you have a boyfriend?"

Bubby kicked his legs out and started fussing. Armina lifted him to a standing position. He bent his knees and jounced up and down.

"My sister always kept a beau," Armina went on. "I hope to get me one someday."

Lilly felt like a young girl sharing secrets, but there was something compelling about Armina's questions. "I do have a fiancé. He's a doctor also."

"So where's he at?"

"He's in Boston. That's a big city in Massachusetts."

"That's where they had the Tea Party." Armina gave a sly grin. "Reckon it was sassafras?"

Lilly laughed again. This girl was smart—smart and funny. Sissy drooped against her arm. "She's gone to sleep. Should I put her down?"

"The crib's on the other side of the bed. With any luck Bubby will go down too; then I can get some work done."

Lilly laid the little girl in the crib and covered her with a knit baby blanket. She checked Aunt Orie's drain, then picked up her doctor's kit.

"Are you comfortable with your aunt's care?" she asked. "Do you have any questions?"

"No. I take good care of her."

"Yes, you do," Lilly said as she left. "You'll let me know if you need anything . . ."

"I expect we'll do fine. Always do," Armina said.

Lilly paused at the bottom of the steps. "See you next Thursday."

"Wednesday," Armina said with a steely look. "Aunt Orie likes her doctoring done on Wednesday."

CHAPTER 8

CAREFUL TO KEEP to the footpath, Lilly tramped down the mountain. Halfway home she stopped and took the canteen from her linen satchel; her mouth was dry as talcum powder.

"Bother," she said, shaking the empty vessel. She'd neglected to refill it at the Eldridges'. Surely there was a spring nearby. She knew the animals and birds didn't drink their fill at the sour water of Swampy. She hung the canteen around her neck by the strap of its canvas holder and looked around. It would be a nice break from the hustle of the day to spend a few minutes searching for cool, clear water.

Shortly after she stepped off the path, she entered an isolated cove lush with an unspoiled hardwood forest. She wandered farther in, noting oak, buckeye, walnut, sour-wood, ash, and beech, as well as the expected underlying scrub cedar and stunted fir. The leafy tops of the soaring hardwoods intermeshed, enclosing her under a protective canopy. As if poured through a heavenly sieve, sprinkles of sunlight glittered through the shadows, pooling like melted butter on the forest floor and highlighting the tips of beech fern with gold.

In awe, she continued into the depths, arms outstretched, trailing her fingers over the sometimes-sleek, sometimes-rough bark of the trees. *Tap. Tap. Tap.* She heard the staccato drum of a woodpecker's sharp beak probing a hollow limb for insects. She inhaled the ancient, undisturbed, verdant scent of the forest like a history lesson, imagining the passage of time trapped by rings inside the trunks of the trees. More than likely, on this very spot, an Indian scout had crept silently through the trees, his moccasin-covered feet leaving nary a trace. Perhaps the redskin had tracked the wily Daniel Boone or the elusive Simon Kenton; perhaps he had his eye on a sleek deer or a fatted buffalo and stopped where she now stood to insert an arrow into his bow.

Under her feet, a maidenhair fern tickled her ankles with long, drooping leaflets. She stooped to pick one. As a girl, she'd often gathered these fronds to make flowing green wigs for her dolls and once for her dog. Poor Steady had been so embarrassed.

She stopped to remove a worm that inched up her sleeve, measuring her for a new suit of clothes, and deposited him gently on a moss-covered rock. Many times she'd lined her dolls' beds with just such velvety moss.

The hush of the forest was so deep that the bright notes of a wren amplified accordingly, and a cardinal's song ricocheted joyously from branch to branch overhead. She strained to hear the slightest splash of water against rock—sure sign of a spring. It was there, she thought, somewhere on the other side of the massive tulip poplar barring her path. A tree fit to hide Goliath himself.

A tiny prickle of fear buzzed her consciousness like a bumblebee searching for a honeysuckle vine. She swallowed hard, disappointed that she had let an unpleasant sentiment enter this hallowed space. It was no use. No matter how hard she tried, she couldn't bury her past. Like the stench of rotten fruit, it wouldn't be ignored.

Feeling abandoned in an unfamiliar place, as unseen walls closed in on her, she panicked and fled. The canteen bounced against her hip, pulling her back to the present. Her anger flared. She'd be tarred and feathered before she would run this time. Instead she pulled up some Corbett grit and shouted, "Get thee behind me, Satan!" Shaking her fist in the face of all fear, she marched right back to the tulip tree.

"'Yea, though I walk through the valley of the shadow of death, I will fear no evil,'" she recited as she skirted the trunk of the tree. "Thank You, Jesus," she prayed as her emotions calmed.

Her reward was indeed on the far side of the tulip poplar. A steady stream of water gushed from the base of a rock- and grass-covered hillock. Gray-green lichens and tiny, fossilized shells dotted the surface of the centuries-old stones covering the knoll. Enchanted, Lilly knelt and wet her face in the spring before filling her canteen. The icy water felt and tasted delicious, a rare treat on a summer's day.

A child popped his head above the knoll. At least Lilly thought it was a boy. Maybe it was the bowl-shaped haircut. As soon as she spied him, he disappeared. Before she could react, he popped up again and did the same maneuver at least half a dozen times before she darted around the hill and caught him in his game. She caught him, but he stunned her.

There was something dreadfully wrong with the lad. His bare chest and arms were splotched with large reddish-purple dots—like hemorrhagic spots of petechiae magnified a dozen times. Her mind searched for answers. The usually pinprick dots of petechiae were indicative of blood-clotting disorders, severe fevers, and—oh, surely not—typhus.

As soon as the boy realized Lilly was on his side of the hill, he laughed and dashed away. Lilly gave chase, discarding each hypothesis as she went. He was too vibrant to be very ill. Winded, she slowed her pace and, instead of chasing the boy, followed the runnels in the grass left by his flying feet.

Soon she came to a meadow rimmed by the forest. Wildflowers of every sort grew there in wild abandon. Smack in the middle of the meadow was a tumble-down cabin with a wide plank porch that listed to one side like a boat in a storm. And smack in the middle of the porch was a bearded man holding a shotgun with the barrel pointed her way.

"Stop where ye are!" he said in a voice as deadly as the gun.

Lilly didn't have to be told twice. She stood stock-still at the edge of the yard.

"State your business," he said with a slight wave of the gun as if she needed encouragement. "If'n you're with the gov'ment, I'll finish you off where you stand."

"I was following the boy," Lilly said. "I'm a doctor."

"Ain't no such thing as a woman doctor," the man said with a guffaw. "'Sides, we ain't got no call for any doctoring."

The man weaved or the gun weaved; Lilly wasn't sure which. She held her doctor's bag at chest level. "Is your boy sick, mister?"

The man yelled over his shoulder, "Cleve! Get out here!"

The boy popped out of the open door. "Yeah, Daddy?"

"Air ye sick?"

"No, sir."

Lilly noticed odd circles under the lad's eyes. They were the same alarming color as the rash on his chest and arms.

"He ain't sick. Be on your way."

A woman appeared in the doorway. A fretful toddler straddled her hip, and she was obviously close to term with another child. "Hiram, you loggerdy head," she barked. "Put that gun away and ask our guest in. Honestly, you got the manners of a porcupine." She pinched the boy's earlobe. "You been aggravating the lady, Cleve?"

"No, ma'am." He hopped around the porch while rubbing his ear. "Ouch! Ouch! Ouch!"

The man staggered a little as he broke the shotgun and removed some shells. Lilly wondered if he was drunk.

With a generous wave, the lady motioned Lilly inside. There were two straight-backed chairs at the kitchen table, which was laid for dinner with the scrubbed-clean lids of lard buckets, rims up, and a few assorted utensils. *Brilliant,* Lilly thought of the lard can plates. *I never would have thought of that.* A dough board packed full of reddish grape-size fruit decorated the center of the table. A packing crate pushed up against the wall held the water bucket and a wash pan. The only other furnishings in the room were a mirrored wardrobe, a coal cookstove, and a corn-shuck mattress on the packed dirt floor. The flue pipe that accessed the chimney to the cookstove lay in pieces atop the stove. A can of blacking, a long-handled brush, and a soiled rag made Lilly think she'd interrupted the lady cleaning the segmented pipe. She remembered how her mother would chase all the kids outside when she took on the same chore every spring. The black suet made a terrible mess. It had to be done yearly, however, or the pipe could catch on fire.

Hiram ceremoniously pulled out a chair for Lilly before he plopped down in the other. "Air ye a doctor for real?" he asked.

"For real," she said.

"Then mayhap ye can doctor me," he said.

"What seems to be the problem?"

Lilly observed the boy while his father prattled on about bouts of dizziness and ringing in his ears. "Tobacco juice ain't helping," he said.

"Pardon me?" she asked.

"Lynn biled some tobacco and a big sweet onion for a poultice, but it don't cut the pain no more." He covered his right ear, which was stained dark brown, with his hand. "Used to work good," he said with a puzzled look.

The baby cried and rubbed her tiny red nose against her mother's shoulder. The whole family needed doctoring from what Lilly could tell.

"This quare woman was a-drinking from the spring," Cleve chimed in.

"Well, we all forgot our manners," Lynn said. "Hiram, take this girl child while I fix the doctor a drink."

Lilly reached for the baby instead. "May I take a look at the little one?" she asked.

The boy leaned against her arm while she searched in her kit for the otoscope. The baby shrieked in terror as Lilly attempted to look inside her ear with the tip of the pointed instrument.

"Do mine first." Hiram scooted his chair closer to Lilly's. "She won't be so scared if she sees me have it done."

The mother set an assortment of cracked cups and mugs on the table, stuck her finger in one, and popped it in the little girl's mouth. "Don't study everything so hard, Hiram."

Distracted, the toddler let Lilly probe her ears. "She has an ear infection. I suspect you do too," she said to Hiram before she examined him. His ears looked worse than the baby's. No wonder he was dizzy. "How about you, Cleve? Do your ears ache?"

"Nah," he said, "but I'd like to look through that there thing."

Hiram held his head to one side while Cleve took a look-see. Lilly was struck by the father's tenderness in the midst of such poverty—even if he didn't offer his wife a chair. Lynn slid a cup of pinkish liquid in front of Lilly.

"Umm," Lilly said, stalling for time, "this looks tasty."

"Sumac-ade." The boy swallowed a large draught. "It's good."

"My word, I thought sumac was poison."

The man picked a bunch of fruit from the dough board. "Red is safe; see how the fruit grows on the twig tips? Unless you strive to be as big a fool as Adam in the Garden, don't dare to taste the white sumac. You'll know it even if it's not ripe, for it'll dangle loosely and not from the tips." He pulled a tiny winged projection from the stem and held it up for all to see. "The poison sumac don't have wings either."

If she hadn't been holding the toddler, Lilly would have smacked her own forehead. The boy had decorated his body with sumac juice in the same manner that she and her child-hood friends once dipped feather quills into the purple ink of the pokeberry plant. She'd spent many a hot summer after-noon with her friend Kate decorating rocks and writing notes on the underside of sycamore leaves to send to make-believe pen pals in foreign lands.

"Drink up," the man said. "Lynn here mellows the juice with honey."

Lilly took a small bottle of wine of opium mixed with

anise and sweet oil and set it on the table. "Let me write instructions for treating your earache first." She never liked to leave medicine of any type without specific written directions. When she was a student, she'd left a glycerin suppository bedside only to have her patient swallow it whole. No harm done; everything came out all right in the end, as the saying goes, but it scared her silly nonetheless.

Shake well, she printed on a pad, *and drop three to five drops into the affected ear. If no relief in five or ten minutes, repeat, and follow along as needed.*

Lynn studied the script as seriously as if she were memorizing a Bible verse. Carefully she unscrewed the dropper from the glass bottle and drew up a minute amount. Watching her mother intently from Lilly's lap, the little girl opened her mouth wide as a baby bird's.

"Do I put it on her tongue?" Lynn asked.

"Goodness," Lilly said, "I forgot the most important part." She uncapped her fountain pen again and drew a picture of the dropper and three drops dripping into an exaggerated ear canal. "This should be clearer."

Lynn treated her husband first, letting the little girl watch. The toddler turned up first one ear and then the other in perfect imitation of her daddy.

"Good job," Lilly said, picking up the white stoneware mug full of pink sumac-ade. Surprisingly, it tasted refreshing, but too sweet for her taste.

After half an hour of nonstop dialog, Hiram pushed back

his chair and retrieved the shotgun from behind the door. "Come on, Cleve; supper ain't catching itself."

"I saw a squirrel big as a fattening hen on that pin oak by the spring, Daddy," Cleve said, pulling a shirt on over his head.

"Let's go get him, Son. Time's a-wasting."

"You'll have to make a spit to cook him on outside," Lynn said. "I ain't going to have the stove put back together before suppertime."

"Be on the lookout for apple trees, Son. Meat roasted over dried apple wood will flat out melt in your mouth." He slid shells into the breech, allowing Cleve to pocket extras. "You might not think it, but an apple tree drops a lot of wood— branches fall off in the slightest wind."

The screen door slapped closed behind Hiram and Cleve. Lilly was glad to have a moment alone with Lynn, and she was glad for a break from Hiram. The man surely loved the sound of his own voice.

"Ye can go if you need to," Lynn said. "Hiram's careful where he shoots."

"I'd love to visit a moment. I could help you black the stovepipe."

"That's real nice, but you'd ruin your clothes. It can wait. Want some more ade? There's plenty."

Lilly held her palm over her mug. "No, I'm good."

"So where are you from?" Lynn asked. "I heard tell there was a new doctor in Skip Rock, but I never figured on a lady."

"I grew up on Troublesome Creek, in Breathitt County. Do you know of it?"

"I can't say as I do. We come from Virginia. We ain't been here a year yet."

"Do you have someone to help with your confinement?"

"Hiram's a pretty good help." Lynn dropped her eyes, busying herself by making circles around the rim of her cup with her thumb. "I don't want to put anybody else out."

"I would be more than happy to help you." Lilly laid her hand over Lynn's. "It's my job, you know."

When Lynn raised her eyes, Lilly saw the sparkle of tears.

"Ain't God good?" Lynn said. "I was praying for an angel just this morning and now here you are, sitting at my kitchen table, bold as brass."

"I don't know about the angel part," Lilly said with a laugh, "but I do know God meets our needs if we but ask. 'The effectual fervent prayer of a righteous man availeth much.' That's from James, I think."

Lynn clapped her hands. "That's my favorite Scripture. I can't believe you just said that! See, you are an angel."

"Tell me about your deliveries, Lynn. Do you have difficulty?"

Lynn tipped the pitcher and poured more sumac-ade into the cup over Lilly's protestations. Now she would have to drink it. The pink tea was all Lynn had to share.

Lynn reached across the table and rubbed the crown of her daughter's head. The little girl thumped her head backward into Lilly's chest. *There will be a bruise under my collarbone tomorrow,* Lilly thought.

"You can see this one's got a big head," Lynn said. "Where Cleve was easy as pie, Dolly nearly kilt me."

"How close to delivery are you?" Lilly asked although she could tell it wouldn't be long.

"Three weeks, tops. She's already dropped."

"You know it's a girl?"

"Yeah, Hiram did the yarn and needle test. You know, the one where you hang a darning needle from a length of yarn over a woman? If it swings it's a boy, but if it spins it's a girl? Well, mine spun like a top. I've never known that test to fail."

"Hmm," Lilly said. Another superstitious old wives' tale. "Would you like me to check the baby's presentation?"

"Please," Lynn said. She went to the door and closed it. She cleared the table and spread a tattered sheet before she laid herself flat upon its surface, using another sheet for a drape.

The toddler played at Lilly's feet as she palpated the huge mound of Lynn's uterus. Unrolling her fabric tape measure, she noted the size from top to bottom and from side to side. Indeed the baby had already dropped. "I'm guessing you're making frequent trips to the outhouse," Lilly said.

"Funny how you forget about all them aggravations once the baby's born," Lynn said.

"As they say, if you remembered all of that, you wouldn't have but one."

"Ain't it the truth?"

Lilly helped Lynn up and off the table. "I think you're doing well. I don't anticipate any problems with your delivery, but you know there are no guarantees. Things can change from one minute to the next." Lilly folded the drape into neat squares. "This is your third, so you'll likely go fast."

"I'd be glad for that," Lynn said, resetting her table.

"That is understandable, but a fast birth can be dangerous for both mother and baby. Do you have anyone who could come to help you for a while?"

"I could maybe send for my sister."

"That would be good. In the meantime, what can I do to help?"

"You already answered my prayer. I can't ask for more than that."

When Lilly left the family, she had a quart jar of sumac-ade in her linen bag and a promise from Hiram to come fetch her when Lynn was in early labor. She also took away important lessons: Look for the easiest diagnosis first—it might be as simple as sumac juice!—and don't assume a person can read. Actually, don't assume anything.

CHAPTER 9

Tern Still leaned in close to the wavy mirror in his rented room and applied a styptic pencil to the scrape on his chin. It stung like fire, but the wound clotted. He ran his thumb over the blade of his straight razor. Even though he'd stropped it good, there was the nick. He'd have to add a whetstone to his shopping list. That was the problem with moving around all the time. You never had everything you needed in one place. Something was always left behind.

He opened the top dresser drawer and fitted a key into the lock of a smallish wooden traveling case. He removed his gun and leather holster to get at a book that rested on the bottom of the case. Sliding the slim volume into a pocket of the black frock coat he wore on weekends, he replaced the gun and holster and turned the key. Once, he was quite the dandy in the high-buttoned jacket, which he had worn with a yellow silk vest and tan woolen trousers. Now, he liked it for its deep pockets and its knee length and because it hung loosely over his rough denim jeans.

Downstairs in the dining room, Tern took a seat on one of the benches at the long, picnic-style table. There were chairs at the head and foot of the table, but Tern never took one of those.

Mrs. DeWitt's hired girl passed steaming bowls of grits and platters of eggs and ham and poured hot coffee into a dozen mugs. This room and board was the nicest Tern had ever stayed in. Mrs. DeWitt charged by the week, making it an easy come-and-go. Tern didn't really like sharing his space with so many men, though—too many questioning eyes.

He sliced his over-easy eggs with a knife, then forked up a bit of yellow. The guy sitting to his left poked him and pointed with a utensil to the hired girl. "Cute as a bug's ear. Wonder if she'd fancy stepping out with me." The fellow's name was Leroy, but all the men called him Elbows.

Tern smiled as if he cared. Instead of replying, he chewed his eggs and swallowed a gulp of coffee, burning his tongue in the process.

"A bunch of us are going into town later," Elbows said. "Want to go along?"

"I'll take a bye," Tern said. "I've got a lot to do." He nearly spilled his coffee when Elbows nudged between his ribs again.

"What's to do on a Saturday night but bury the week with some white lightning? It'll cure what ails you."

Yeah, Tern thought, *and make you spill your guts too.* Whiskey and secrets didn't go together. "Thanks; maybe next week."

Elbows flicked the collar of Tern's frock coat with his nicotine-stained index finger. "You ain't one of them Bible-thumpers, are you?"

Tern could feel the heat of anger creeping up his neck. It took all his thin patience not to knock the man's hand away.

Suddenly the room was still. All the other men were craning their necks looking his way. "Hardly," Tern said with a derisive snort. Planting his forearms on the table, he leaned in and dropped his voice conspiratorially. "Say, did you hear the one about the government inspector who visited the farmer's garden?"

Elbows's face relaxed as if ready for the joke. "Can't say as I have."

"Story goes the government fellow visits the farm, taking particular interest in the corn crop. 'Do you people have any trouble with insects getting in your corn?' government guy asks the farmer. 'We sure do,' says the farmer, 'but we jes fishes them out and drinks the squeezings anyhow.'"

"Doggies, that's a good one." Elbows laughed and slapped his knee.

"I've got a better one than that about the farmer's daughter," another guy said from his chair at the end of the table.

Now all ears were tuned his way.

Mrs. DeWitt appeared from the kitchen. "Take it outside, fellows," she said.

Saved by the bell, Tern thought as he headed outdoors, settling his cap on his head until it felt just right. There were rocking chairs on the broad plank veranda of the boarding-house, but Tern was not one for sitting. Once he'd gone by the commissary, he'd swing by the livery station, get his horse, and head out. Apache would be glad for the exercise—all the pinto got weekdays was a quick ride.

The company store was a tricky place on Saturday mornings. Too many ladies in one place at one time gossiping and shopping. But Tern needed that whetstone, and the place would likely be closed when he finished his ride.

He stuck his hat in his pocket and went in. Men's stuff was clear in the back. He wondered if that was on purpose. Holding his elbows close to his sides, he walked down the center aisle to a shelf chock-full of shaving mugs, rounds of soap, cheap cologne, brushes, and razors—and a lone whetstone. Fine with him; a whetstone was a whetstone. You didn't need a selection.

He tested a brush against the palm of his hand. His had left some bristles in his shaving mug this morning; might as well pick up one of those too. The soaps had different scents—that one too much menthol, that one too spicy. He preferred just soap. Who needed it to smell like something else? What was wrong with just smelling clean?

So a brush, a whetstone, two soaps—maybe a new shirt? He only had three and they were looking worn. He paid

Mrs. DeWitt extra for a clean and ironed shirt every day. He'd hate to give up that particular vice. He supposed it was a vanity—his penchant for neatness.

Cradling his supplies against his chest with one hand, he stopped at the display of men's shirts. One was in blue-and-white-striped cotton with the new fold-down collar. It would look good with his gray suit, the one that was hanging in the closet at his place in DC. He reached down to feel the sleeve and dropped one of the soaps. It rolled across the oiled-wood floor and came to a stop against a decidedly feminine shoe.

He gazed from the foot to the face and nearly choked. It was her. It was Lilly.

She bent with a graceful dip of her knees and retrieved the errant round. "Your soap has run away." Her smile dazzled him.

His mouth went dry and when he went to thank her, he couldn't speak. She held out the soap. His hand brushed hers. Sparks ran up his arm, around to the back of his neck, and down his spine. He felt like she had set him afire. He dropped the soap again.

"Goodness," she said. "It's rolled under the counter."

"I've got another," he managed to say. His voice cracked like a schoolboy's.

"So you do."

"Yes," he said. He couldn't tear his eyes away. Her dark hair was pulled back from her face and dressed in some sort of soft roll caught up with a white ribbon. He searched for and found the shiny streak that started at her widow's peak and shot through her hair like quicksilver. He'd been fascinated by that errant mark when he was a boy. Her heart-shaped face was like fine porcelain and her eyes were the same stormy gray of his dreams. She was taller than he imagined she would be but tiny—small-boned. Her waist could be circled by two hands. He'd give all the gold in Fort Knox to touch her again.

"I'm Dr. Corbett," she said, sticking out her hand like a man.

"Joe," he replied. "Joe Repp. Pleased to meet you." Her dainty hand disappeared in his large, rough one.

"I'm sure I'll see you around camp, Mr. Repp. Enjoy your shopping."

And then she was gone. He stood in the aisle hardly aware of where he was. The very air around him seemed charged, and her fragrance lingered sweet as summer roses.

"Excuse me—" a woman's voice interrupted his reverie—"do you want me to tally them things up for ye?"

His mind clicked into gear. A heavyset clerk had taken Lilly's place. "Um, yeah," he said, handing them over. "And one of these shirts if you don't mind. Size large."

At the counter, the clerk thumbed through a small pad and inserted a piece of carbon paper between two pages. "Do ye want to be on the books until payday?"

"No, I settle as I go."

With the stub of a pencil, the clerk added up the charges. "Them shirts is expensive," she said as if giving him a chance to back out.

"That's okay."

"You owe three dollars and twenty-seven cents." She ripped out his copy of the receipt, wiped the smudges from her fingertips on the front of her apron, and tucked the tab in the shirtfront before wrapping his purchases in brown paper. She spun a string ball, cut off a piece, and tied the parcel closed.

He handed over three bills and change. "One of these soaps is under the counter yonder."

"I'll get it," she said with an upside-down smile. "You come back now. Hear?"

It was a short walk to the livery station where Apache was boarded. Tern could hear the animal's welcoming nicker before he approached the holding pen. He stroked the horse's long nose, then offered him half an apple. Apache snorted thanks and crunched his treat as Tern shoved the brown-paper parcel into his saddlebag.

Once they were out of town, he let Apache set the pace. The horse's muscles bunched with energy beneath Tern's thighs as his hooves pounded on the macadam road. Tern leaned forward in the saddle and lightly slapped Apache's long neck. "Feels good, doesn't it, boy?"

It was early yet and the air was still cool and crisp. They veered off the turnpike and onto a lightly graveled side road that led eventually to the river. Tern kept Apache on the narrow shoulder and out of the deep ruts cut by the wheels of wagons. The forest on either side of the road was alive with colors. The pink and white of dogwood and serviceberry, the shadowy lavender of lilac, the varied shades of leafy green called singly for his attention like women dressed for a dance.

Tern's mind wandered to the last party he had attended in Washington, while he was still clerking in the office of a congressman from Kentucky. He slacked the reins and Apache ambled along, stopping now and then to munch a bit of grass. One young lady in particular had taken a shine to him that last spring he was Tern Still. Elizabeth's father was a diplomat, and her mother was a peevish, self-important woman who peppered Tern with sharply honed questions whenever he visited her daughter. She was singularly determined to get to the underbelly of his upbringing.

He was truthful but evasive in those days. Besides being a man who held his own counsel, he figured much of what Elizabeth's mother prodded for was none of anybody's business. He'd buried his past as deep as a seam of coal, and nobody was going to dig it out.

Truthfully, he'd never even missed Elizabeth. Though she shed pretty tears that night of the party, his heart had lightened the minute he walked through the French doors of her father's mansion, across the sparkling terrace, out into the night, and into his new life as a federal agent.

His opportunity had come about following a series of underground mining disasters; there was talk in Congress of forming a US Bureau of Mines. In preparation, the government had been looking for men with experience in the coalmining field: educated, trustworthy men who were willing to go incognito to study and report back on the true working conditions in the mines. The Monday after the party he applied, and with a good word from his congressman, he was accepted on the spot. Now he could be anybody he wanted to be. His family history didn't matter a whit. Except to Lilly, that was—it would matter more than a whit to her. He must see that she never discovered who he really was.

He leaned back in the saddle, the sun warm on his face, and let it all go. Who needed love anyway? For him, love was as ethereal and unattainable as a mirage. Ever since he'd met Lilly Corbett, he was like a man crawling across the desert on his belly, constantly denied a cool drink of water.

He gave a rough bark of a laugh at his own fanciful thinking. At the sound, Apache snorted, then trotted on up the lane, not stopping again until they reached the shallows.

Tern dismounted and picketed the horse up the riverbank in a more private spot. He loved this place for its quietude. There was something about the rushing water that cleansed his spirit and brought him back to plumb.

From the bank, he selected a small, flat stone and sent it skipping across the water. Ripples formed and broke, ever widening around the stone until it sank with a plunk. Not his best throw ever, but the rock had nearly made it to the far bank.

After ascertaining that he was truly alone, he retrieved his book from his jacket pocket. Later he'd find a fishing hole and catch a mess of trout to take back to Mrs. DeWitt, but for now he settled against the broad trunk of a sycamore and lost himself in the words of Henry David Thoreau.

CHAPTER 10

NED TIPPEN STUCK HIS HEAD round the open office door and called, "Hey," to Lilly.

"Hey, yourself," she said, marking her place in a book with one finger. "What are you up to today?"

"Nothing much. Thought I'd stop by and see if you needed any help."

Over the last couple of weeks, Lilly had come to rely on Ned. Once Darrell's mother insisted on taking him home against her advice, most of what she did was home visits. She had started with a list of shut-ins left by the old doc, and Ned had proved invaluable with his keen knowledge of the twists and turns of the unmarked and unpaved roads hereabout.

Just Sunday after church, he'd hitched up the clinic buggy and driven her five miles to the Jacobs place, where she'd delivered a nine-pound boy. He got her there in the nick of time.

She knew many folks would turn her away, so strange did they find a woman doctor, if not for Ned's intervention. He was heaven sent.

Lilly motioned him in. "Do you know the Eldridges? I've been going up every Wednesday to visit them."

"The ones that live on Swampy? Got that house that sits up on rocks like stilts?"

"Yes."

"That aggravating Swampy Creek runs wild as a turkey ever time it rains. Orie's old man's been dead awhile now, God rest his soul. But afore he died, he raised the house because Orie's deathly afraid of the snakes that wash up in the yard whenever Swampy overflows its banks. She was always bragging on him for that. Somebody said she'd taken off sick. Come to think of it, I ain't seen her in a long time."

Lilly inserted a thumb card between two pages and closed the book. "She's very ill. I'd like to bring her here to the clinic and try a new treatment."

"Sounds like a plan. When you aiming to go up there?"

"In just a bit," Lilly said. "I'm not sure if she'll agree to leave home. I just want to broach the subject today, get her to start thinking about it."

"Who's taking care of her now?"

"Her niece Armina is staying with her."

"Oh yeah, Bud Eldridge's her uncle. Seems like there was two of those gals. Didn't the older one move off somewhere?"

"Evidently she is with her husband. Armina is watching her sister's children plus taking care of her aunt. She's a remarkable young lady."

Ned stroked his chin. "Be hard to get a buggy up there. Might have to bring her down on a litter."

Lilly tapped the desk with her fingertips, deciding how much to tell Ned. The last thing she wanted to do was to denigrate her patient. "Mrs. Eldridge is hugely obese, Ned. I'm not sure half a dozen men could carry her down that mountain."

"Orie was always a big woman." His eyes took on a wistful look. "She makes the best mincemeat you ever put in your mouth. She used to bring her pie whenever the church had dinner on the grounds. Folks would queue up for a slice."

Lilly thought she had rarely known a man with as sunny a disposition as Ned Tippen. His easygoing way reminded her of her stepfather. In the three weeks they'd worked together, he hadn't uttered one unkind word, though he certainly had reason to. She'd helped him dress the red, raw stump of his amputation more than once and knew the pain he lived with. Truthfully, the doctor who'd treated him after his accident had not done a very clever job. She would consult with Paul when she visited him and his family in September. Paul would know the latest. He was already an excellent surgeon.

"So do you want me to go along today? Want me to saddle a couple of horses?"

"I'd love for you to. You can see the lay of the land and help me figure the best route to bring Mrs. Eldridge here."

"Give me two shakes," Ned said.

"All right," Lilly said, already collecting her things, "just charge my account at the livery station."

Truthfully, Lilly would rather walk. Though she liked horses, she wasn't an accomplished rider. The only experience she'd had was on a gentle mare of her mother's and that was not much beyond the barnyard. But Ned couldn't very well hike that far on his wooden leg, and like he said, they would be hard-pressed to get a buggy up there.

Soon Ned was back. He helped her into the saddle and handed her the reins. "I'll lead; you follow. I know an old drift road that'll get us there quick-like."

Lilly realized anew that quick-like in the country was different from quick-like in the city as Ned led her on a different route than the one she had walked with Armina. Her mount was a bit frisky, and she held the reins with a firm grip. It seemed a long way to the ground from where she sat sidesaddle.

She felt fairly comfortable until they came to the river. *Gracious,* she thought, *why would Ned want to cross a river on horseback?* Suddenly, being knee-deep in Swampy didn't seem so bad.

Ned waited for her horse to come alongside his. "This here's the shallows. Skip Rock's down, so it'll be even easier to cross than usual."

The river tumbled over moss-covered stones; it was so clear she could see the sandy bed. Relieved, she followed

Ned into the water. Sunlight danced on the surface like gemstones spilled from a jewelry casket. My, this was a beautiful place. She'd have to come here again and bring a book and maybe a picnic lunch. She bet there would be a perfect spot up the bank a ways. Daydreaming, she shifted her weight in the saddle. The reins slacked in her hands. Her mount took full advantage and pranced sideways before rearing up, seemingly determined to rid itself of her.

With a yelp she slid backward, over the hump of the saddle and onto the horse's wide backside. Stretching forward, she grabbed a bit of mane and wrapped it around her hand.

"Whoa!" she heard Ned yell and saw his horse turn back. "Whoa there!"

Just as she was losing her grip, he grabbed the harness and brought her horse up short. On her knees, skirts flying, she scrambled back into the saddle. Her heart thumped like a scared rabbit's. She pressed her knees tightly together to stop their shaking.

"Are you all right?" Ned said, keeping a grip on her horse and leading them to the far bank.

"I'm all of a piece," she said. "Nothing hurt but my dignity." She tucked a strand of hair under the rim of her hat. "I must look a sight."

"Looks don't matter none if you ain't hurt. Trade rides with me."

"You know, Ned, I think I'll keep this one. This was a lesson learned. I was woolgathering instead of paying attention. Give me a minute."

They reined in and she dismounted. The horse's nostrils flared and he jerked his head when she tried to stroke his long nose. She clicked her tongue, making soothing noises like she'd learned to do with all the wild things she'd doctored during her growing-up years: baby rabbits needing around-the-clock feedings, broken-winged crows, discarded kittens, and once a fox kit caught in a trap.

"Will you look at him, Ned? There must be something wrong."

Ned ran expert hands along the animal's flanks before lifting each foot and examining the shoes. The horse stood steady under Ned's attention.

"Can't find a thing wrong," he said.

"Maybe he slipped on a slick spot," Lilly said as Ned handed her back up. "Okay, we're ready."

She sat tall in the saddle and minded their way. The path narrowed, choked with raggedy cedar boughs and the low-hanging branches of trees. Wild honeysuckle scented the air with its sweetly delicate fragrance.

"I ain't been this way in a coon's age," Ned shot back over his shoulder as he dodged a branch. "Careful as you go."

Lilly ducked, changing her position and easily passing under the limb. Suddenly her mount snorted as if sounding a warning. Stretching his neck out long and low, he shot through the woods like Lucifer himself was on his tail. Trees streaked by, each threatening to dislodge her. One errant limb clipped her hat and tore it from her head. All she could think to do was lean forward over the horse's elongated neck.

She patted his sweaty hide firmly. "Easy, easy," she said, over and over again, determined to hold on until the horse was out of steam. How far could he run anyway?

"Rein in! Rein in!" Ned's startled shouts followed her dashing mount.

Ahead Lilly could see an old dry-stacked stone wall. It was time to learn to fly. She felt the horse's muscles bunch for a jump. "Lord, help us," she yelled before, smooth as sweet milk, they were over the wall and slowing.

Ned soon caught up, clutching her straw bonnet in one hand. "That's enough of that. You could have been killed! We're trading places, and I'm riding Mr. Ball of Fire here back to the stable."

Lilly was standing on legs that felt like limp dishrags. Her horse stood placidly, munching on a clump of grass. "He's mean as a striped snake, Ned. Whatever comes over him?"

Ned guided her to a seat on a fallen log, where she sank down and fanned her face with the tattered hat he gave her.

"Sorry about your hat. It sailed right into my hands. Maybe you can fix it."

Lilly poked her finger through the hat's crown. "Glad this wasn't my eye."

"Let me get you some water," he said, lifting the flap from the leather bag attached to her horse's saddle. The horse nickered and did his sideways dance again.

"It's this saddle," Ned said. "He flinched when I fiddled with it." Running a hand under the seat, Ned flinched himself before he pulled out a cocklebur the size of a banty egg.

His usually sunny expression turned stormy. "I'm gonna crack somebody's head for this."

Lilly took the canteen he offered, unscrewed the top, and drank. "What do you mean?" she asked when her thirst was slaked.

Ned shook his head when she offered the canteen to him. "I mean someone did this on purpose and I aim to cuff the dirty dog."

"Surely not. Why would you think so?"

"I hate to be the one to tell you this, Doc, but ain't everyone in your camp, so to speak."

Lilly stood and shook out her riding skirt. She thought of the forewarning bird someone had set on her porch and the crossbones painted on the clinic door. Not to mention church. She'd faithfully attended every service that she could and still she was met each Sunday with the frosty disdain of cold shoulders.

"I can't imagine why people don't see that I'm only here to help them."

Ned pulled a seeding blade from a clump of grass. He chewed on the stem for a few seconds before he answered. "Folks hereabouts are so proud, they'll go to their reward never having changed an opinion—like it's some sort of badge of honor to be backward. They don't like newcomers stirring things up, and pardon me for saying so, but they don't trust flatlanders."

"But I'm not a flatlander. I was raised in Breathitt County on Troublesome Creek. My mama was a Brown and my stepfather is a Pelfrey."

"A Pelfrey, you say?" A grin split Ned's face. "My mama was a Pelfrey from up Troublesome Creek. God rest her soul. She didn't talk much about her family, but I heard her mention she had a bunch of cousins. I remember her remarking on a John Pelfrey who married a midwife name of Brown."

"Goodness, Ned, that's my mother and my stepfather. We're—what—second cousins?"

Ned let out a whoop, grabbed her, and swung her around. "I can't believe it! Don't the Lord work in mysterious ways?"

Lilly steadied herself against Ned's arm to make the world stop twirling. "It's good to know I'm among kin." She gave him a light hug. "I'm sorry to hear about your mother. Has she been gone awhile?"

"She passed on five years ago this November, but I still miss her every day." Ned hung his head. "Too bad it's such a far piece to the Pelfrey family graveyard. I feel guilty for not keeping up her site."

"You don't have to worry about that. Daddy keeps it clean. I'll take you home with me next time I go, and you can see for yourself."

Ned's face lit up with a mischievous grin. "I can't wait to tell Uncle Turnip and Aunt Tillie. She's gonna swallow her chaw."

Lilly grabbed the saddle horn. "Help me up, Ned. If we don't get a move on, it will be dark before we finish at the Eldridges'."

"You sure you want to ride this devil again?"

Lilly patted the horse. "He's docile as a kitten without that bur under his saddle. Let's go."

CHAPTER 11

THE ELDRIDGE HOMESTEAD was just as Lilly had left it on her previous visits. Everything was tidy. Even the hard-packed dirt yard, which sported random tufts of browning grass, was swept clean.

Ned took the reins to Lilly's horse. "I'll wait out here."

Armina appeared in the doorway with the babies in her arms. Then, quick as a hummingbird, she darted out of sight.

Lilly found the young woman in the curtained-off pantry. Wedged on a shelf behind her, Bubby and Sissy anchored a ten-pound sack of pinto beans and a graduated set of yellow-ware mixing bowls. "Goodness, Armina, what are you hiding from?"

"I didn't expect company." Armina smoothed a strand of hair that had dared escape her tight braids. "You should have told me if you were bringing somebody."

"May I?" Lilly asked as she reached for Sissy. "I'm sorry if we startled you. I needed Ned to come along today."

Armina lifted Bubby down and followed as Lilly held the curtain aside. "I don't see why," she said, bouncing Bubby on her hip. "If you was afeered to come alone, I would have fetched you."

"I'll explain after I examine Orie," Lilly said. "How's she been?"

"About the same, I guess . . . maybe talking a little more."

Lilly untwined Sissy's fingers from her pearl necklace and set her on a bright rag rug at Orie's feet. She knelt and placed her hand on Orie's wide knee. The woman seemed to be asleep. Lilly shook her knee slightly and Orie opened her eyes.

"Aunt Orie, how are you feeling?"

Orie Eldridge smiled and put her hand on top of Lilly's. "La, girl, I reckon I've felt better," she said in her wheezy way.

"Your heart's laboring, but your lungs are not as wet as they were last week," Lilly said when she finished her examination.

"Perhaps I'm getting well," Aunt Orie said.

Lilly looked into the gravely ill woman's eyes and saw a spark of hope. "There is a new treatment I'd like for you to try. You'd have to take pills. . . ."

"Drastics? Old Doc never gave me such a thing. Dandelion tea, strong as I can stand—that's all Doc recommended."

Lilly chose her words carefully. "Dr. Jones took good care of you. I can see that. He wouldn't have known of the new treatment for congestive heart failure."

"Say what?" Armina broke in.

"Congestive heart failure," Lilly said. "It's akin to dropsy."

Aunt Orie took a coughing fit. Her whoops stole her breath, and her face turned the purplish-red of a pickled beet. Her king-size chair teetered back and forth dangerously. Lilly feared the thing would collapse and dump Orie on the floor.

Armina fanned her aunt's face with a church fan. Sissy whimpered and scooted under the bed. Bubby crawled after her.

Lilly retrieved a rubber suction bulb from her kit. It was the only relief she could offer while Orie fought for life-giving oxygen. The woman could die right before their eyes. This simply couldn't continue.

When the hoots turned to gasps and finally to ragged breaths, Armina sponged beads of sweat from Orie's forehead with a wet washrag. "There, there, Auntie. You'll feel better now."

"Them drastics," Aunt Orie said when at last she could speak. "What'll they do for a body?"

Lilly studied what to say. She could almost hear the words her mentor, Dr. Coldiron, would choose: *"Why, they'll fix you right up—you'll be your old self in no time."* He believed it was kindest to couch the truth in platitudes to keep up a good front. It was generally accepted by modern physicians that the shock of full knowledge could send a seriously ill person into a final decline. The dear doctor was the soul of kindness, but anything less than the total truth went against Lilly's grain. Besides, Aunt Orie was tough enough to take it.

"The medicine will give you a fighting chance, Aunt Orie. At the very least, you'll be more comfortable."

"All right then." Orie cupped her palm. "I'm ready to try. Armina, fetch me some of that water yonder."

Lilly knelt by the chair again. "I took a script to the pharmacy in town. They had to send out for the medicine. I should have it filled soon." She closed Orie's palm and gave her hand a gentle squeeze. "If you agree to take the medication, you'll have to come to the clinic so I can monitor you for a few days."

"Oh no. No. I cain't do that." Orie shook her head so hard, her jowls slapped. "I cain't be leaving these kids to fend for themselves."

"It's your choice, of course. I can't force you."

Orie dropped her head. Her chins flattened against her broad chest like pancake mix in a hot skillet. "Cain't Armina give me them drastics? She's good at doctoring."

"Yes, she is, but I wouldn't be comfortable putting her in that position. I'm sorry, Orie. I know this is hard for you."

A single tear tracked down Aunt Orie's face and disappeared in the folds of her neck. "I feel like death's a-standing on my porch with a warrant, just waiting to serve me." She took a minute to gather her strength. "I don't want to die and leave these young'uns. I'll do whatever you want if it can borrow me some time."

Two sets of eyes peered fearfully from underneath the bed. Sissy crawled out and toddled over to hang on Aunt Orie's skirt. Bubby tried to stand before he had cleared the bed frame. He bumped his head hard. His loud bawls mixed with Sissy's snuffling and Aunt Orie's whistling breaths.

Armina stuck an extra pillow behind Aunt Orie's back, stooped to swipe Sissy's nose with the skirt of her apron, and dragged Bubby out from under the bed. She brushed his silky hair back from his face. "You'll have a goose egg. Let's make you a cool compress."

With Bubby on her hip, she went to the washstand and took a sip of water from the long-handled gourd dipper. "This ain't cold." The granite bucket clanged against the side of the stand. "I'll be right back."

Lilly scooped up Sissy. "I'll come along."

Armina nudged the cowbell on the table by Orie's chair. "Ring if you need me."

The sun bore down, bright as the yolk of an egg, as Lilly followed Armina to the well house. Like the cabin itself, the structure was well built and several degrees cooler than outside. Armina lowered a wooden bucket attached to a rope down the well, hauled it back up, and poured fresh water into her granite bucket.

Sissy rocked against Lilly's hip. "Pash?" she crowed. "Pash!"

Armina dipped her fingers in the water and flicked them in Sissy's face. The tiny girl recoiled from the cold drops as she shrieked with laughter. "Do Bub. Do Bub."

Bubby turned up his face and Armina splashed him. It did Lilly's heart good to see the childish joy, but once again she wondered how Armina kept up with her burdens. It seemed decidedly unfair.

Back outside, heat waves shimmered on the surface of the yard. Lilly shaded her eyes against the brightness.

Ned approached and reached for the water bucket. "Let me help."

"I don't need no help!" Armina said, jerking it away. Half the water slopped over the side of the bucket, drenching her skirts and Lilly's too.

Armina inhaled sharply. The water might as well have been a snake. "Just look what you've done!"

"Aw, I'm sorry," Ned said.

"Pash!" Sissy shouted. "Whee!"

Lilly shook her skirts. "It's all right, Armina. It's only water. We'll dry."

"Well," Armina said, "a body shouldn't interfere unless a body's been asked."

Ned folded his arms and stood back.

Armina looked him over. She heaved Bubby higher on her hip and held the bucket toward Ned. "Since you asked."

Lilly clamped her lips against laughter when she saw the look of fear and awe on Ned's face. He looked like he'd just stumbled upon a mountain lion, a magnificent mountain lion.

"Yes, ma'am," Ned said.

Armina puffed up like a wet hen. "Ma'am? Do I look like an old-maid schoolteacher?"

Ned seemed at a loss for words, but he took the bucket and headed toward the well house.

Lilly watched Armina watching Ned's halting walk. Her eyes widened, then narrowed, but she didn't ask. That was good, for Ned's story was Ned's to tell, not Lilly's.

A clamor emanated from the fenced lot beside the barn. When they turned to look, a white goat with pointed horns gave up butting the fence and stuck its head over the rail to bleat hello. The bell around its neck tinkled merrily.

"See goes?" Sissy asked.

Armina sighed. "Dumb thing wants a carrot. Nanny's spoiled plain silly, like everything else around here." She gave Bubby to Lilly. "If you'll take them over to the lot, I'll run to the garden."

Ned passed them carrying the water bucket.

"Don't take it inside," Armina said. "Aunt Orie don't know you're here."

"Where do you want me to put it?"

"Set it on the porch," she said with a roll of her eyes. "Men—I don't know why the good Lord bothered."

Lilly seated both children on the top fence rail, keeping her arms firmly around them. The nanny explored Sissy's bare toes. Sissy giggled and pulled her knees up. Bubby thumped the goat's head in an awkward attempt to pat.

"Be easy, Bubby," Lilly said.

Finished with his chore, Ned swung the boy up to sit astraddle his neck. Bubby's eyes grew wide with amazement. He clutched fistfuls of Ned's hair.

The nanny pranced over to Armina, who held a bright-orange carrot fresh from the garden. With dainty precision, the goat nibbled the carrot until all that was left was the lacy foliage.

"She saves the top for dessert," Armina said.

Bite by bite, the greenery disappeared. "All gone," Sissy said with a shrug. "Goes be full."

Armina walked down the fence line. The nanny followed.

Ned lifted Bubby over his head, then reseated him. "Want to go for a ride?" Bubby drummed his heels against Ned's chest when Ned whinnied and jounced the little boy on his shoulders.

Sissy was having none of it. She pointed to the horses tethered in the shade of a tree in the side yard. "Dere's horsey."

Ned stopped in his tracks. "I think this one takes after that one," he said under his breath, tilting his head toward Armina.

Lilly nodded. "Smart as a tack."

"And just as sharp."

"Horsey," Sissy demanded.

"Is it all right if I take them for a short ride?" Ned asked when Armina came back.

Armina snorted. "You think you can handle the two of them at once?"

Ned shifted Bubby from his shoulders to one arm, walked over to his horse, and expertly swung himself and the baby up. The pointed end of his wooden leg rested like a foot in the leather stirrup.

Lilly waited for Armina's nod before she handed Sissy up.

"I'll hold on tight," Ned said.

"If you let anything happen to them kids, you'll think you got your head in a bear's mouth."

Ned gave Armina a slow smile. Deep dimples appeared in his cheeks. "Well, you know what they say about having your head in a bear's mouth."

Armina's eyes flashed. "I expect I don't need no enlightenment from you concerning bears."

My word, Lilly thought, *the sparks from these two could set a house afire.*

"All right then," Ned said. "We'll be back in two shakes."

"Ned's really a very nice fellow," Lilly said as he rode away.

"Could be," Armina agreed, "but he ain't my type. I don't need me no cripple."

"I'm not matchmaking, Armina."

Armina flipped her braids. "I still don't know why you brung him here."

"I need Ned to help me figure out a way to get Orie to the clinic. It will be difficult at best, what with her health and her . . ."

"She'll be there if I have to pack her down this mountain myself! I ain't never giving up on Aunt Orie."

It was way past suppertime before Ned and Lilly reached the shallows of Skip Rock River.

"Thank you for your help today," Lilly said as their horses drew up side by side. "I think the trail you showed me will work perfectly for getting Orie Eldridge to the clinic, once it is bushwhacked."

"No problem, Cuz." He sat up tall in the saddle. "It sure enough makes me proud to call you cousin. Imagine, me being kin to a doctor. Don't that beat all?"

"Imagine that we found each other. God truly does work in strange and miraculous ways. If my horse hadn't tried to throw me, we might never have taken the opportunity to talk as we did."

"Somebody's still going to pay for that bur under your saddle!"

"I'd rather you let it be, Ned. It might be best to not add fuel to the fire."

"I'll do what you ask, but it goes against the grain."

After they crossed the shallows, they dismounted to stretch their legs and water the horses.

"Talk about going against the grain—what was going on between you and Armina?" Lilly asked.

"Whew, she acted like I was a skunk in the chicken house. I feel like I been skinned alive. That gal's a spitfire."

Lilly grinned. "So what do you do when you get your head in a bear's mouth?" she couldn't help but ask.

Ned cupped his hands, making a step for Lilly. When she was safely in her saddle, he replied with a wink, "You work real easy until you get it out."

"Know a lot about bears, do you, Ned?" Lilly teased.

"I know enough to keep my distance."

We'll see, Lilly thought as she nudged her horse forward. *We'll see.*

CHAPTER 12

TERN STILL YAWNED MIGHTILY. Faint rays of light pierced the early morning gloom as he walked to work. He took off his cap and reseated it. Man, it was already hot for so early in the day. He couldn't remember the last time it had rained. He was so beat, he could barely figure what day it was. He flexed his right arm, testing the muscle. It was sore as a bad tooth. And even though he'd flushed his eyes with an eyecup last evening, he was still wiping grit from the corners.

Yesterday's assignment had made him ill at ease. Mr. James tapped him to bore shot holes in the face above the cut for inserting explosives to blow down the seam. He'd spent hours working in Number 5 with a breast auger. The bruise on his chest bore witness. He didn't mind the work, but being singled out for such an exacting duty set him apart. Leaning into the breastplate while turning the long drill took finesse as well as muscle and marked him as an expert . . . and he didn't need the attention.

He made his way to the lamp house, where the gear was stored and serviced. As he came alongside the building, he heard angry voices and paused by an open window. He didn't want to interrupt, but he didn't want to be late to work either. He needed to step inside and get his tally markers. Before every shift, each employee took several brass tags with identical numbers stamped on them, pinned a set to his clothing, and put a single one on a small hook on the name board. He'd hang his under Joe Repp. It came to him how foolish that was; it wasn't like anyone would come to claim his dead body if he got crushed or poisoned. Not a person would know his true identity outside of the government agency for which he worked, and they would never blow his cover.

Oh, well, it was strictly his decision to go underground—in more ways than one. His family, such as it was, wouldn't miss him anyway. He hadn't seen his brothers in years, and it was his fervent wish to never to think about his father again.

Beyond the window, the argument raged on, calling his attention. Tern rested the bottom of one foot against the outside wall and leaned back, waiting. He could make out Stanley James's voice. That didn't surprise him because Mr. James kept his desk in the lamp house instead of in the office building. He wanted to stay close to the men. Tern respected him for that.

Tern's ears pricked and he chanced a quick look through the grimy glass pane. Mr. James had his back to the window. A short, bald man thrust one finger toward Mr. James's chest, punctuating his bossy commands. He had to be a company man—a big shot from the Black Lump Coal Company—who made a living off the backs of others. Tern could tell by his shiny suit and the way a stub of a cigar bobbed in the corner of his mouth.

"They're not animals!" Mr. James said. "They've souls just like you—or maybe not. I ain't for certain sure the company hires men with souls to oversee the real workers." Tern could fairly see steam coming out of his ears. "That'd make your job a sight easier, wouldn't it, if you didn't have to answer to the Lord?"

"You'll do as you're told if you want to keep your job," the suit warned, his voice suddenly as cold as a blue moon in winter. The stub of his cigar arced through the window, barely missing Tern's right ear.

The office door banged open. Tern crept to the rain barrel at the corner of the building and crouched down where he could see but not be seen.

"At what price are you reopening Number 4?" Mr. James asked. "These men got wives and families depending upon them."

"There's plenty more where they came from. Now paddle or suck mud." The man struck a match against the porch railing and lit a fresh smoke. He inhaled a lungful, then drew another cigar from his inside jacket pocket and offered it to Mr. James.

Mr. James dropped the cigar to the floor of the porch and crushed it with the heel of his boot. Tern held his breath.

The company man's eyes turned hard and mean as a hungry coyote's. "It doesn't matter a whit to me or to Black Lump who supervises this setup, James. We've been pleased with you up to this point. Your outfit produces more clean bituminous coal than any other in the state, but don't think you're irreplaceable."

He stomped down the steps and snapped his stubby fingers just once. His flunky jumped to the hitching post and unhitched the two horses tethered there.

Tern rose slightly, holding on to the barrel for support. He thought the company man looked much bigger astride the powerful roan.

"Next man supervising this team won't be a local; I can tell you that." The fellow flung the words over his shoulder between sucks on the cigar, puffs of gray ringing his head like smoke signals.

As the company man rode off, Mr. James kicked the door. It banged shut against the frame, then bounced open, hitting him square in the chest. He didn't curse, though; Tern gave him credit for that.

"Whatcha hiding from?"

Startled by the voice at his back, Tern tipped the rain barrel. Water sloshed over the rim, pouring into his work boots before he righted it. "Just stopped to tie my shoe," he said, standing. His feet made squelching noises as he went around the corner and into the lamp house, but he wasn't about to give Elbows the satisfaction of seeing him empty his boots. Now he'd have to work all day in wet shoes. His feet would be as sore as his arm by suppertime.

Elbows clung like a shadow as Tern sorted through the tags. Tern liked to use the same one each time. It was why he tried to get to the lamp house early—before anyone else took number 10. If he didn't snag those particular ones, he'd be uneasy all day.

Elbows stuck his arm around Tern and plucked a random set from the bucket. Tern shoved his arm away.

"You're particular as a girl," Elbows said as he hung his tally ticket on the board. "Must be why you always smell so good." He slapped his knee and cackled at his joke on Tern.

As Tern's hand tensed around the number 10 tags, the ache in his arm increased. He wanted in the worst way to punch Elbows in the nose. "It's called soap," he said, nearly cutting his tongue on the edge in his voice. "You should try it sometime."

"Don't see why," Elbows said. "The more grease you got on you, the better you slide through them tight places. Besides, the girls like a manly man."

Elbows parodied straightening his collar and slicking back his dirty hair. "You got a girl, Joe? Or are you too pretty for our women? Maybe you should try the new doc. She might be more your style." Elbows threw back his head and crowed like a banty rooster. "You better hurry up if you do, for I'd like a taste of that myself."

Tern saw red, but before he could react, Mr. James's chair scraped the floor as he pushed back from his desk. In a flash, he grabbed Elbows by the arm and half dragged him to the door. "That gal's under my care, you little weasel," Mr. James said, flinging Elbows out onto the porch. "Now get out of here before I fire your sorry butt."

Elbows landed on his knees before scrambling to his feet. "Sorry, boss," he said, mewling like a sick cat. "A man's gotta have some fun now and then. I meant no harm."

Mr. James stalked back into the room, pushed his chair in place, and sat down heavily. "I'm pulling you out of the new operation, Repp. Company wants Number 4 reopened and I need a man to lead a team. Think you're up for the job?"

"Sure, Mr. James, anything you want."

"Pick you a crew. I don't care who, but pick careful." Mr. James flicked a pencil with his index finger. The pencil skittered across the desk and landed on the floor.

Tern picked it up and put it back. "Do you think the men will answer to me—me being new and all?"

"They will if they want to keep their jobs. I'm naming you because there's something true about the way you handle yourself. And you're cautious—you'll need to be in Number 4. I don't trust that mine a'tall."

So why work it? Tern wondered. *Why not tell the company men to go hang themselves?* He heard a clot of miners talking as they passed the open window. That was why, of course.

Times were hard and men needed work, work that kept food on the table. Miners had always taken their chances. They always would.

Mr. James stroked his stubbly chin and looked square into Tern's eyes. Tern matched his stare.

"That's settled, then," Mr. James said. "Your pay will take another boost. I suspect you'll be happy about that."

"Yeah, of course." He tipped his cap. "Thanks, Mr. James. I won't let you down."

"Stanley. Call me Stanley."

"Sure thing—Stanley."

Left shoulder leading, Tern shoved through the men who were coming in. He saw Elbows dusting dirt from the knees of his pants before looking up to give Tern a knowing smirk.

Tern choked on anger hot and thick as coal smoke. Acting nonchalant, he walked until he was hidden from sight behind a massive oak tree. He should have throttled Elbows for daring to mention Lilly! Instead he stood by impotently as Mr. James stepped in to defend her. Just as he stood by when his father kidnapped Lilly all those years ago.

His anger waned like a dying storm, leaving him feeling small and useless. Composing himself, Tern unscrewed the bottom half of his lamp. The container was full of fresh carbide. The upper chamber held water. He checked the lever on top of the lamp that, when open, allowed the water to drip onto the carbide, releasing a gas that would ignite when the flint striker sparked. Satisfied, he affixed the squat lantern to his soft-billed cap. Suddenly he couldn't wait to get back to the cool, dark depths of the mine.

Obviously Lilly was fine. She didn't need, nor would she ever want, for him to champion her. He was twice a fool to even consider it. Best lose himself in his work—forget the past and forget the girl who would never be his. Unwittingly, Stanley James had given him the perfect opportunity to see what came first in the Skip Rock operation: safety or money.

It wasn't as if he didn't understand Stanley's quandary—he walked a line as dangerous as a tightrope over a chasm. Understanding didn't change Tern's mission, however. Ultimately he would turn Stanley in if need be. He was here to study the safety of the mines, and Number 4 was decidedly unsafe. His responsibility was to the government and to the safety of all miners, not just the ones at Skip Rock.

Tern cast his personal feelings aside as if they were little more than a ragged coat. He passed by the huge wooden tipple just as a load of coal thundered down the long chute into waiting railcars. He stopped to watch. A chunk of the black magic popped over the side of the chute and landed with a thunk at his feet. He jumped back, but he couldn't tear his eyes away. With its elongated, narrow body, the tipple put him in mind of a praying mantis, mesmerizing yet at the same time strangely menacing.

Walking on, he approached the boarded-up entrance to the number 4 mine. Behind those boards lay the richest seams of coal he'd ever seen. His mind whirled with possibility, and despite himself he began to feel excited. What if it could become a safe mine? That would give him some satisfaction. It would be nice to report something positive to the agency for a change.

Or if it went the other way and he had to turn Benedict Arnold, so be it. Maybe he went at finding truth in a backhanded way, but his motive was pure. Let the chips fall where they may.

CHAPTER 13

IT WAS GOING to be a hot day. Hot and busy. Lilly cracked the door to get some air as she dressed in a handkerchief-linen blouse and a camel-colored five-gored linen skirt. It was just too muggy to wear her usual dark-blue serge. She slipped her newly polished shoes on over lisle stockings.

A bowl of grits steamed on the table. Lilly didn't have an appetite for grits, but she stirred a pat of butter into the bowl and added a pinch of salt. She didn't want to hurt Myrtie's feelings. On a morning like this in Lexington, her aunt Alice's cook would have served a medley of fresh berries with a little pitcher of nutmeg cream along with bite-size bran muffins.

Lilly couldn't help but miss the convenience of living

in the city. She wondered if Boston would be anything like Lexington. By this time next year, she'd be living there with Paul.

Paul—she'd meant to reply to his most recent letter last evening. She knew he'd want to discuss her upcoming trip to meet his family. The letter had been waiting on the table when she came in from the Eldridges'. The last thing she remembered was slitting the flap of the envelope with the letter opener and sliding the one page out. She had fallen asleep before reading it, with the coal-oil lamp still burning on her bedside table.

She spooned a bite of grits and went to get the letter. She could read it while she ate. Now where was it? Maybe it had gotten underneath the cover when she made the bed. Kneeling, she ran her hand under the counterpane. There was nothing there. She was just about to lift the crocheted dust ruffle when she heard a voice calling from the yard.

"Doc! Doc!" someone screamed. "Hurry fast. Timmy's getting kilt!"

Timmy? She knew Timmy Blair. The boy was always in one sort of trouble or another. Just a few days ago she'd removed a thorn from his foot and, before that, a bean from up his nose. Timmy had a passel of cousins who'd all watched his minor procedure appreciatively. "Oh," they'd said in unison when she pulled the sprouted bean from Timmy's unusual garden.

Lilly grabbed her bag. The girl on her stoop was Timmy's older sister, Jenny. "What's he gotten into now?"

"He was holding the cow's tail while Mommy milked, and next thing you know, Bossy was towing him down the hillside," the girl said as they hurried along. "Mommy turned over the milk bucket in her haste to run after him. She caught Bossy, but now she can't get Timmy loose. Him and Bossy both are all tore up from where that crazy cow drug him straight through a briar patch."

"What do you mean, she can't get him loose?"

"His hand's caught up in Bossy's flyswatter. Hurry, Doc," the girl urged. "If that cow gets bit again, Mommy won't be able to hold her back. It'll sure enough be the death of Timmy. Bossy fairly hates horseflies."

Lilly was learning that nothing that happened in Skip Rock happened in private. She and Jenny were attracting quite a following, and more people were waiting at the farm just outside of town. You would have thought a circus had come to town the way folks were congregating on this side of the split-rail fence around the Blairs' cow pasture. On the other side of the fence a bull snorted a keep-away warning as he pawed the ground. People were shouting and pointing toward the far pasture, which seemed to agitate the animal even more.

The sight of the bull brought Lilly up short. He was solid black except for the cream-colored horns that stuck out on either side of his massive head. She wouldn't do Timmy much good from the end of one of those horns.

Mr. James and another man climbed the fence. Mr. James picked up a stout stick and faced the bull. Lilly followed Jenny along the outside of the fence to the gate. The man held it open and allowed them through, but he kept his eyes on the angry bull. There would be mayhem if the animal escaped the pen. "Don't worry," he said. "We'll keep him away."

Jenny didn't hesitate but ran straight down the hill. Lilly followed. At the fence line, shaded by a grove of trees, were Timmy, his mother, and the infamous Bossy. Mrs. Blair held a length of rope, which was looped around the cow's neck. At the business end of the animal, Timmy waited.

"Hey, Doc," he said. "Am I glad to see you."

"Bossy won't let anybody near," Mrs. Blair said. "She's about to pull my shoulder plumb out of the socket."

The cow was scared to death. Her big brown eyes rolled back in her head and she strained against the rope as Lilly slowly approached. "There, there, Bossy," Lilly said, extending her hand, palm open, to the cow. "There, there."

Lilly waited half a minute before she attempted to touch Bossy. When she did, she scrubbed hard with her knuckles in the sweet spot right between the horns. It was a maneuver she'd watched her Daddy John do numerous times with his own cantankerous bovines. If a cow could be said to sigh, Bossy did with pleasure.

"Mrs. Blair, if you'll slack the rope and rub Bossy just so, I'll see to Timmy."

Hairs from the cow's tail twined around Timmy's fingers taut as catgut on a fiddle. His hand had already turned purple.

"Gracious, young man, how did you manage to get in such a dilemma?"

"Trouble picks on me," Timmy said.

"Can you fix him, Doc?" Jenny asked. "He won't be no good to anybody tied up to the cow that way."

"Hush, Jenny," Mrs. Blair said. "Let the doctor alone."

Lilly took scissors from her bag. "Jenny, I'm going to need some assistance. Hold Bossy's tail just so—that's good—perfect. Watch out for her hooves."

"Bossy ain't a kicker, just a swatter," Mrs. Blair said.

Praise the Lord, Lilly thought. If Bossy kicked Timmy, the animal could easily fracture his skull.

Timmy's freckled face turned white as clabber. "Are you gonna have to cut my fingers off?"

"No, Timmy. You'll keep all your fingers. I promise."

"You ain't gonna cut Bossy's tail off, are you? Mommy will be mad if you do."

"Hush, Timmy, and let the doctor work," Jenny said in a perfect imitation of her mother. She held Bossy's tail straight as a yardstick with both hands.

Lilly snipped Bossy's stringy hair, leaving just a brush where it met her long tail. Once Timmy was separated from the cow, Lilly led him to sit beside her in the shade and began to unbind his fingers. After five minutes or so, all the hair was removed. She set to work on his superficial scrapes and scratches with a gauze pad and a bottle of iodine.

"Whoo, that stings like fire," he said, hopping around. "I reckon you better put some on Bossy too."

The crowd of folks had moved down the fence row to be closer to the action. Mr. James was standing beside Mrs.

Blair, and Lilly thought she saw a fleeting smile cross his face. A few feet away, the other man stood with his arms folded, serious as a sentry. He seemed vaguely familiar, but she couldn't place him.

Mrs. Blair led Bossy to Lilly. The cow was snorting and rolling her eyes, obviously still in distress. Lilly looked Bossy over and found a long gaping wound on her right flank. The animal had gashed it on something in her mad run down the hill. It would have to be stitched. As Lilly leaned in for a closer look, an errant horsefly landed on Bossy's wide rump. The cow tossed her head, flicked her stubby flyswatter, and sidestepped into Lilly, nearly knocking her off her feet.

"Whoa!" someone in the audience called out.

The sun turned its heat up a notch. Not a breeze stirred. Leaves hung listlessly on parched trees, and the birds seemed too hot to sing. Flies buzzed a fresh patty.

Sweat stung Lilly's eyes. Where was a nurse when you needed one? She patted her forehead in the crook of her arm and tucked an errant lock of hair behind her ear. Perspiration trickled down her back and stained her underarms, not to mention there was a smear of something brown and unsavory on the front of her linen skirt. She wished for a cool bath in Aunt Alice's oversize, claw-foot bathtub. What had she gotten herself into? She should be in Lexington plying her trade in the sanitary conditions of a hospital's surgical suite.

The murmuring of the folks in the background caught her attention. She supposed that now they wanted to critique her veterinary skills.

"Where's the bull?" Mrs. Blair thought to ask.

"Joe here put him in the other pasture," Mr. James said.

Now Lilly recognized the other fellow as Joe Repp, the guy she'd met in the commissary one Saturday. She wondered how he managed to look so cool and collected in the midst of the mayhem. He was dressed like a miner, but his starched and freshly ironed work shirt fit like it was tailored.

Lilly picked up her kit. She had never in her life sutured a cow. She had no idea how one as flighty as Bossy would react, but she couldn't leave the wound open. "Let's take Bossy to the barn."

Mr. James bent closer to Lilly. "You know what, little gal?" he said in a low voice. "It'd be good if you sewed her up right here."

"Mr. James, I'm not sure . . ."

"I'll help. You'll do fine." He turned to the other man. "Hey, Joe, would you fetch a bucket of feed?"

Lilly looked closely at the ragged wound. She would be a laughingstock if this didn't work.

Soon, Joe was back with sweet mash. He put the bucket on the ground. Bossy sauntered over and began to eat. Mr. James took the lead rope. If the cow decided to bolt, it would take a man's strength to hold her back. Jenny held the cow's switching tail. Timmy fanned the flies away. Mrs. Blair patted Bossy between the shoulder blades.

Lilly doused the wound with the red germicide and began to sew. Bossy paid her not a whit of attention.

"That's as pretty as any quilting stitch I ever saw," Mrs. Blair said when Lilly finished.

"Look," Timmy said, waving his hand in front of Lilly's face. "My fingers ain't purple anymore."

Jenny tugged on Lilly's arm. "I'm gonna be a doctor when I grow up."

"Hush, child. I never heard such," Mrs. Blair said with a self-conscious smile and a shake of her head. But Lilly noticed she cupped the back of her daughter's head with tender fingers.

"I do believe you'd make a fine doctor," Lilly said as she put the cork stopper back in the bottle. "Would you like to put this in the bag for me? Careful, the red will stain your fingers."

"I wouldn't mind a'tall," Jenny said. "Then I'd look like you, miss."

Lilly's fingers as well as on her shirtwaist sported red iodine stains. She hoped Myrtie could work some magic on these stains, else her outfit was ruined.

"Joe, will you take Dr. Corbett back to town?" Mr. James said. "I'll stay and get the cow to the barn, then let the bull back in the pasture."

"Sure thing," Joe said.

Lilly wondered why she needed an escort, but it was such a pleasure to hear Mr. James call her *doctor* that she wasn't about to protest. She walked to the gate with Mr. Repp. Jenny stuck to her side like a bur on a wool blanket.

"Where's Landis this morning?" Lilly could hear Mr. James ask.

"He was off to work before sunup," Mrs. Blair said. "I always fix his breakfast early, so he was long gone afore I went to milk. He'll be that grateful to you, Mr. James, and the doctor, of course. Landis is real partial to his kids."

"Mommy," Jenny said, "can I tag along?"

Her mother turned to answer. "That's up to Dr. Corbett, but I suspect she's had about enough of us Blairs this morning."

"I'd be glad for the company," Lilly said.

"Timmy! Put that slingshot away and go with your sister. You kids come right back. I'll be timing you."

Jenny slipped her hand into Lilly's. "I love me a good adventure," she said.

"As do I, Jenny. And you, Mr. Repp, do you like a good adventure?" Lilly's eyes met his as he held the gate for them. They were a curious steel-blue color—and solemn. There was not a hint of laughter there.

"Never thought about it," he said as he latched the gate with the wire loop. His voice was as grave as his eyes.

Well, Lilly thought, *this Joe Repp doesn't chat or smile. Perhaps he thinks I am flirting.* She would need to be more careful.

Lilly took extra care with her bedtime routine that evening. She brushed her hair, starting at the widow's peak and ending well below her shoulder blades—a hundred strokes with her silver-backed brush—and buffed her nails to a shine. Propping her hand mirror against the base of the coal-oil lamp, she used tweezers under the arch of her eyebrows. Her mother compared Lilly's brows to a crow's wing. "Pretty as a crow's wing," she would say.

She laughed to remember that. Only her mother would find anything pretty about a common crow. Lilly laid the tweezers aside and rested her weary head on her folded arms. She ached all over from tussling with Bossy this morning. This was decidedly not what she had signed up for—boys tangling in a cow's tail, cows running amok, folks watching her every move like she was a freak in a circus sideshow.

Sitting up, she let her head roll on her spine to loosen her muscles. She raised one shoulder and let it drop, then did the other. The top of her right foot was sore and sported a bruise the size of a half-dollar. She started to massage it with a bit of cold cream but yelped with pain. Bossy must have stepped on her. Obviously she was not cut out to be a veterinarian.

Lilly flipped through the calendar she kept with her stationery, stamps, pens, and pots of ink in her wooden traveling desk. It was July. Her rotation here would end in September. In some ways it didn't seem as if she'd been at the coal camp in Skip Rock for nearly six weeks; in others it seemed like she'd never been anywhere else.

She knew she was learning, but she wasn't sure if her new skills would serve her well in Boston. There probably weren't many cows wandering around in Hamilton Hospital, and she decidedly wouldn't be escorted to work every morning by a pack of unruly hound dogs.

She plopped down on the bed. Something tickled her

brain. Hamilton Hospital . . . Paul . . . his letter. Gracious, she'd forgotten all about it in the clamor of the day. Dropping to her knees, she lifted the crocheted bed skirt. A tiny gray mouse twitched its whiskers and scampered into a mouse-size hole in the baseboard behind the bed.

"Eeek!" she screamed, then laughed at herself. She'd wrestled with a four-hundred-pound heifer today and now she was screaming at a mouse? "Lord, You sure do keep me humble."

Laughter turned to aggravation when she saw what the mouse had been gnawing on. The envelope from Paul's letter had a jagged tear across the top, and his letter was a pile of bits and pieces. Scrambling under the bed, she saved as much of his missive as she was able. Maybe she could piece it together like a jigsaw puzzle.

She stuck all the pieces in what was left of the envelope and laid it on top of her portable desk. Her eyes grew heavy with sleep. The letter would have to wait until morning. Just before she turned out the light, she cracked the door to get a bit of air. She stood for a moment as an errant gust swirled the hem of her long cotton nightdress, caressing her ankles. She propped the door with the brick provided for the job— Mrs. James had knit a cover for it—and turned to see the envelope fly off the desk. Confetti, copious enough for any mouse-size celebration, scattered riotously across the floor.

She was certain she could hear the mice strike up a band as she climbed into bed. *They'd better have fun tonight,* she thought as she drifted off to sleep, *for tomorrow I'm setting a trap.*

CHAPTER 14

TERN PINCHED A CORNER of the corn bread sandwich from his lunch bucket between two fingers. He was so sick at heart he could barely choke it down.

Yesterday, at the Blairs' cow pasture, he'd blown his chance to have some sort of connection, if only in passing, with Lilly Gray. "Never thought about it"—that's all he could come up with when she asked if he liked adventure! She probably thought he was as dull as a butter knife.

He jerked his head to see if his headlamp would stop sputtering. Had he neglected to put fresh carbide in the bottom this morning? And did he remember to fill the water chamber? What was happening to his mind?

Lilly was happening, of course. Thoughts of her tortured his brain with a sick craving. He couldn't sleep. He couldn't eat. He was getting careless.

A lump of dry bread stuck in his craw, and a day-old beard rasped when he stroked upward on his throat. He pitched what was left of the sandwich down a hole—let the rats take it. After a long swallow of stale water, he closed the lid on his lunch bucket, stood, and stretched. Man, he was going to have to pull up some grit from somewhere.

"You should have said if you weren't hungry," Elbows said from his seat on a ledge rock. "I would have et it."

"I didn't take you to raise," Tern said as he turned away.

"You're winking and blinking like Wee Willie," Elbows called to his back. "Better fix·your lamp before you get lost back in there."

Stupid, Tern thought. He took a deep breath and blew it out though pursed lips. He didn't know why he let the man get under his skin. If he couldn't handle Elbows's mouth, he shouldn't have picked him for his team. But aggravating as he was, Elbows worked hard as a beaver building a dam. He was small built but wiry and could swing a pick in close quarters better than anyone else, including Tern. It was nothing for his tally of coal to reach eighteen tons a shift. The man never seemed to tire.

Tern walked deeper into the pit head. The reopening of Number 4 was going well so far. His headlamp wavered and then went black. He reached up to the side of the lamp lens to the flint striker and got a flare, but it wouldn't sustain.

Along with what was left of his mind, he'd left his carbide flask at the boardinghouse; now he'd have to borrow some from one of his men.

As comfortable as he now was in the black depths of the hole, he still didn't trust leaving his supplies to be tended to at the lamp house like the other miners did. Years ago, when he'd first gone down the mine, learning a trade to support his brothers and his shiftless father, he'd been tricked. He was only sixteen at the time and not expecting to meet up with tomfoolery in such a dangerous place. The fellow who was showing him the ropes, Short Jump—seemed like everybody in there had a nickname—said Tern's headlamp needed to be replaced. Short Jump thought it best if he swapped gear with Tern. He'd said for Tern to keep picking whilst he went to the front and got a different lamp.

Tern never suspected it was just a snipe hunt. Soon as Short Jump was out of sight, Tern's light went out, plunging him into darkness deep as a well on a moonless night. He still remembered the panic that overtook him that day. Like the fool he was, he'd run straight into a wall and coldcocked himself. He woke up to guffaws and knee slapping and a nickname of his own: Goose Egg. Now here he was dumb as a goose egg again, letting his lamp run out of fuel.

Tern leaned against the cool rock wall behind him. If he didn't get a minute's peace, he was liable to hurt somebody. Suddenly he was tired of being both Joe Repp and Tern Still. He wasn't sure which was real anymore.

He flicked the striker again. The light sputtered, then

caught, casting puny shadows on the rock face. Before him, Lilly danced at the edge of the darkness. Without thinking, he reached for her with no completion. He swallowed hard against the disappointment rising like bile in his throat. Would Lilly never be more than a form without substance to him? He couldn't bear the notion.

Tern took off his short-brimmed miner's hat and shook the attached lamp. The shadows skittered away like frightened children. A few lumps of carbide clattered thinly in the chamber. He could buy a little time while his men were still eating lunch. He let his mind wander where it would— a dangerous proposition.

It was not really dark that night—the night he'd rescued Lilly. She was just a slip of a girl, and he was not yet a man, but she'd made him feel like one. Even now, all these years later, he remembered the butterfly quickness of her cool lips against his smooth-faced cheek.

It had all started over a dog. A beagle dam, as he recalled. A series of circumstances had led Lilly Corbett from her stepfather's place to his family's farm that day—the day Isa Still went to the pond with a sack full of unwanted puppies.

Isa Still, his father—although Tern had stopped calling him that years before he died in a sanitarium. The man was just a loss—a not-very-smart, degenerate loss. If it hadn't been for their grandmother, no telling what would have happened to Tern's younger brothers when their mother died. An ache squeezed his heart; he didn't like to think about his mother.

He was never exactly sure what killed her. Isa had acted like he was the only one affected by her death, and Grandma put on her stoic face and shushed Tern whenever he brought it up. "Don't be stirring things up" was all she'd have to say. It seemed like the little kids forgot their mother right away, maybe because the family moved so soon after her death. And of course, the baby never even knew her.

Her name was Adie. Adie Dolores. Her maiden name was Blanton. In the summer she grew sunflowers and marigolds, and in the fall she liked to roast the sunflower seeds on the hearth. Adie—his mother—wanted Tern to go to school, but Isa wouldn't allow it, so she taught him to read from the Bible, and she taught him to cipher with pebbles picked up from the creek. His quickness delighted her, and behind his father's back, she borrowed a set of encyclopedias, one volume at a time, from the school when it was not in session.

She stowed any book she had borrowed for him in the pantry behind a lard bucket. She kept a little coal-oil lamp in there too so Tern could read at night after everyone else had gone to bed. His father never caught on.

His mother didn't speak against Isa, and she waited on him hand and foot. She said he made her laugh, and she liked to laugh. His bullying was with words and with seclusion. He had no truck with the outside world, and he hated the government with a singular passion.

That last summer, when she was pregnant with Lorne Lee, his mother seemed to just fade away. Grandma moved in and then Adie went to stay at the Pelfreys, where Lilly's mother had a place for sick people. Tern guessed Mrs. Pelfrey was a doctor or a nurse, but he didn't know for sure. And he didn't know what went on there, but his mother came back in a box. Grandma carried baby Lorne Lee home in the same wagon that carried the coffin.

Isa went nuts that summer. He was like a mad dog off his leash, plotting retribution against "all them people what minds other people's business." Tern thought it would blow over once hunting season started; Isa liked to hunt better than he liked to eat. But then Isa kidnapped Lilly.

As Tern's father told it, he'd barely pitched the squirming burlap sack full of puppies in the water when Lilly Corbett butted in. "Little smart aleck," Isa had said, "trying to run my business—tell me what I can do with my own animals! Huh—well, I showed her."

He'd shown her all right. Showed her the inside of the defunct still house, where Tern's papaw used to make whiskey. Showed her good by keeping her confined there for three days. Showed her so good that Tern's family had to flee their home for fear of the law, leaving Lilly locked away and alone.

That night was when Tern started making his own decisions. He'd loved his father despite the contrary way he did things. Isa had never used the belt on Tern or the others and he kept them fed; it seemed like love at the time. But leaving the girl unattended while they skedaddled to Tennessee was Tern's breaking point.

They'd traveled several miles that evening, Grandma berating Isa all the way, the little boys thinking it was fun, and the baby mewling for a bottle. Tern's insides were torn up like he'd swallowed razor blades. Soon as they stopped to make camp and his father stretched out by the fire, Tern had slipped away.

It was going on 3 a.m. when he'd sprung the lock and freed Lilly from her prison. He remembered she wouldn't leave the dog or the one puppy she had managed to rescue from the pond. He'd walked her home in the moonlight. She'd tucked her hand in the crook of his elbow. He thought she'd be mad at him; he was Isa Still's son, after all. But he didn't recall any anger, just the feel of her next to him, the smell of her—honeysuckle and wild roses—the way her voice pattered as welcome as rain in August to his ear, the way his heart swelled when she surprised him with a kiss.

In the years that followed, he had put the lust for learning his mother had nurtured in him to good use. His father took ill in Tennessee—heartsick, his grandma said, but Tern doubted that. Regardless, the sickness mellowed his father, and once they moved closer to Grandma's kin, he didn't kick up a fuss when Tern attended high school.

Tern took advantage of every opportunity. Mornings he studied; afternoons he chunked coal. He made just enough to feed and house Isa, Grandma, and the kids. Less than a year after the move to West Virginia, Isa rallied from his melancholy. He married a childless widow woman and moved his lot, including Grandma, into the widow's comfortable house. And just like that Tern was free. He left with his thumb in the air, hitchhiking as far north as his ride would take him. He thought he'd never swing a pick again.

So much for plans, he thought now as his headlamp sighed and breathed its last. A short burst of a laugh tasted bitter as green persimmons in his mouth.

"What's so funny?" Elbows called from just around a bend in the pit head.

Tern pushed himself away from the coal face and braced to deal with his crew. They would think he was foolish to let himself run out of light. And he was—foolish. He was right back where he'd started from, swinging a pick in a mine and longing for a girl who could never be his. *Man,* he thought as the light from the other men's lamps pierced the darkness, *I've spent my life getting back to her.*

His team was joshing and laughing among themselves like they did every day. He could hear Elbows start one of his long-winded tales. One of the men was sixty-eight and so stooped and bent, Tern couldn't discern how tall he was. Another was a youngish man with five little children. He was already coughing his lungs out; Tern didn't see how he could last the year. Tern thought they were the bravest men on the face of the earth. Even soldiers in combat could see an end to a skirmish, but the mines never rested.

Tern felt ashamed of his cowardice concerning Lilly. He felt certain she would keep his identity secret. As he dropped some borrowed rocks of carbide into the lamp's chamber, he resolved to make himself known to her at the very next opportunity. Joe Repp could take his chances.

CHAPTER 15

LILLY FURLED her long-handled yellow parasol and stuck it in the umbrella stand just inside the sanctuary door. It sat as alone as an old maid on a Saturday night. The ladies in the community favored black bonnets for church, but Lilly liked to wear a hat and carry the parasol Aunt Alice had given her to protect against the sun. So far, her face was as fair as her aunt's and she hoped to keep it that way. Her plain straw skimmer had been ruined on the trip to the Eldridges', and so today, she wore a cloche festooned with purple ribbon and gold and white feathers. She knew the hat was out of place, but sometimes a girl just had to feel pretty. Besides, she was tiring of trying to fit in.

Beside her, Myrtie James fussed like a mother hen on a rainy day. She always made a show of escorting Lilly to sit with her in her favorite pew. There were no pew doors bearing nameplates like the ones in Aunt Alice's church, but folks still sat in the same place every Sunday. As Lilly braced for the usual stares and glares that accompanied their short trip down the aisle, she felt sad for Myrtie; it was obvious she was being snubbed because she was with Lilly. Would these hardheaded people never give in? She had thought Darrell's continuing progress—he had taken his first steps just a couple of days ago—would change some minds, but it didn't appear to make any difference.

When Myrtie stood back, Lilly entered first. Myrtie preferred to sit next to the aisle. Lilly thought it was so she could keep an eye out for Mr. James, but he never came to church. Most of the seats on the men's side remained empty every Sunday, but still the women kept their place.

The backless bench they sat on was hard and unforgiving. Each time she shifted position, Lilly was reminded of her hapless dash through the woods astride the runaway horse. Would it be unchristian to pray the sermon was short today? She bowed her head.

Myrtie nudged her gently. Lilly's eyes flew open. The preacher began lining the words to one of her favorite songs, and the congregation's singsong voices followed. Myrtie had an excellent voice, and Lilly found herself harmonizing as they sang about the harvest and the time of weeping. Lilly discovered she liked the pure, dulcet sound of voices unaccompanied by a piano or an organ.

The sermon was not short—far from it. Lilly would have to get out the liniment when she got home. She followed Myrtie to the door, where they paused to greet the preacher. He gave Lilly's hand a little squeeze as if in extra blessing. The slight act of sympathy unnerved her. Her eyes shimmered with tears. Squaring her shoulders, she stepped out into the heat of the day.

Every single person in the churchyard looked her way. Smiling mouths turned into frowns or were quickly hidden behind pasteboard fans. *Sticks and stones,* Lilly thought, but the old saying didn't help. Maybe she would write Dr. Coldiron this afternoon and plead with him to hasten his search for her replacement. She was sure the inhabitants of Skip Rock would be happy to see the back of her.

A tug on her skirt caught her attention.

"You forgot your umbrella," Jenny Blair said as she swatted at her brother. "Stop it, Timmy! I'm the one who found it."

Timmy danced away from his sister's quick hand. "Can I unroll that there boomerang, Doc? Huh? Can I?"

"Timmy, you're dumb as a head of cabbage," Jenny said. "This ain't no boomerang. Fling it and see what happens."

"Why would I pitch it?" Timmy said. "It wouldn't be no good in the rain if it was broke, now would it?"

Jenny shook her head and sighed. She showed Timmy the latch that released the umbrella. "See, Timmy, this here's an umbrella. A boomerang is like a weapon. You pitch it and it comes back. I think warriors use it to knock each other out."

"Oh yeah," Timmy said. "I always get them words mixed

up." He jabbed the air with the pointed end of the parasol. "This could be a weapon too. You could poke somebody in the gut with this."

Mrs. Blair hurried over. "Children! You put me to shame. Timmy, I've a mind to wear you out," she said with a swat to Timmy's behind.

"I'm sorry, Ma," Timmy said. "Jenny started it."

"Please don't fret, Mrs. Blair," Lilly said. "I so enjoy your children. Timmy reminds me of my brother Jack."

"Then I feel sorrow for your mother," Mrs. Blair tee-heed. "I was hoping to get a word with you. I was wondering if you might make a call on Bossy. She ain't healing up just right."

"Of course. Let me go get my bag—"

"You got to eat first," Myrtie interrupted. "You can't go traipsing around with nothing in your stomach. Mrs. Blair, why don't you and the young'uns come by for lunch? You can walk Dr. Corbett to your place after."

Timmy bounced up and down. Excitement flashed in his eyes. Jenny seemed to be holding her breath as she waited for her mother's reply. Lilly thought going to Mrs. James's home would be a rare treat for them.

"I wouldn't want to put you out none, Mrs. James. You see how these kids of mine can be."

"It would be a right pleasure to have you," Mrs. James said, "and they ain't nothing wrong with children being children."

Mrs. Blair hesitated. "I should go on home and tend to Landis's dinner."

"We'll fix him a plate. You all come on now."

Lilly walked slowly back toward town. It was good to be alone for a while. It seemed like she'd been surrounded by people ever since she left her childhood home to go to university. Even the spot halfway up the mountain where she did her early morning devotionals had been breached by others' needs. She missed the solitary walks she once took along Troublesome Creek. The shallows she and Ned had crossed on their horses were nearby. Although the day was quickly waning, her heart yearned for the peace she would find there. It was only five minutes out of her way; she could already hear the rush of water and feel the cooling shade of the many trees that overhung the river.

As soon as she saw the water rippling in the fading sunlight, she could feel tension draining from her shoulders. There was not a soul in sight, so she unlaced her shoes and removed her lisle stockings. She folded the stockings neatly and laid them atop the shoes before she lifted her skirts and walked out into the stream.

"Whoo," she gasped as cold water lapped her ankles and then the back of her knees. Oh, it felt so good. The water was fast-flowing and so pure, she could see sunfish darting away. She wished for the red gabardine bathing costume that was tucked away in a bureau at Aunt Alice's house. Paired with red stockings and black high-topped bathing slippers, it was the most freeing thing she'd ever worn. And cute—it was ever so cute. If she had it on now, she could sit right down in the water. But splashing with her feet would have to suffice. Sprays arced and danced before her as she kicked.

The water made her feel clean after her turn in Bossy's stall. It had been easy to see the source of the cow's distress. The poor thing had a boil, red and overripe as a slop-bucket tomato, at the very tip of the suture site. When Lilly prodded the wound with a lancet, Bossy bucked like a rodeo bull and kicked a hole in the stall door. Pus shot out of the wound, spattering a wall and the front of Lilly's long white lab coat. The smell was horrendous. As Lilly left the farm, Mrs. Blair had been scrubbing the coat on a washboard, and the children were feeding mash to Bossy. If the cow didn't recover soon, she'd be big as a fattening hog.

Now, standing in the water, Lilly let it all go: the lack of privacy, the shunning treatment of many of the townsfolk, her homesickness, the never-ending concern for patients like Orie Eldridge. She pretended her worries had no more weight than paper boats floating away in the swift current.

Shadows were stealing the sunlight from the water as she turned back toward the bank. She should hurry; she didn't want to be caught out alone after dark. She shuddered as old fears overtook her much as they had that day in the hardwood forest.

It had taken her years to deal with what she had endured as a child; she rarely even thought about it anymore. But something she couldn't put her finger on was dredging up old memories that were as perilous to her well-being as a circus bear on a broken chain. She glanced about in the gathering darkness. The very trees had sprouted eyes. As if she were a child again, she could feel a hand clamp over her mouth.

She had to get out of the water and back to town. There was safety there.

In her fear and haste, her bare foot slid on a moss-covered stone and she fell. Finally she was doing what she wanted to do all along—sit on her bottom in the riverbed. Her skirts billowed around her, and when she tried to stand, the same slick rock cast her back down. The shock of the fall snapped her to her senses. She couldn't help but laugh at her predicament.

Then something big crashed through the underbrush. Was a black bear coming to finish her off? Did he think she was a huge trout thrashing in the stream? More likely, it was a Skip Rock resident who was going to catch her in an embarrassing situation. As she tried to right herself, a man she recognized plunged into the water, swept her up in his arms, and carried her to the safety of the riverside.

"Well, Mr. Repp," she said, "we meet again."

"Are you all right?" he said. "Is anything broken?"

She could feel the tautness of his muscles and the steady beat of his heart against her upper arm. Suddenly she was filled with the desire to stay where she was. It was all she could do to not relax against that strong chest. Goodness, she was turning into a simpering girl full of fear and longing.

"I'm fine. You can put me down now, Mr. Repp."

Even in the waning light she could see the heat rise to his face. "I'm sorry. . . . Of course . . . I was just—"

"Watching from the forest? Waiting to rescue a damsel in distress?" Instantly, she regretted the patronizing tone in her voice.

"No, no," he said as he gently lowered her until her feet touched the ground. "I was . . . Well, I've been reading, if you want to know the truth. I was just walking Apache back to the trail when I heard a commotion in the river. I thought someone had been thrown from their horse. I'm sorry if I offended you in any way."

Lilly shook her head and breathed an exasperated sigh. She was making a muddle of the moment. "Mr. Repp, forgive me, and thank you. I thought you were a black bear."

"I've been thought worse of," he said and then both of them were laughing. Lilly couldn't stop. It was if she were a schoolgirl again, giggling over a bit of foolishness with a classmate. She laughed until tears streamed down her face.

He pulled a dripping wet handkerchief from his back pocket and handed it to her.

She shook the soggy kerchief. "Goodness, what shall I do with this?"

He reached down and handed her the only dry thing in sight, one of her own stockings.

"Turn your back," Lilly said while mopping her face. Regaining her composure, she sat on the bank, pulled on her hose, and laced her shoes. When she looked his way, he was standing with his hands clasped behind his back.

Gathering her wet skirts, she stood. "I can't help but wonder what you were reading. Do you carry a book everywhere?"

"I like to keep something at hand," he said, turning to her. "I probably shouldn't let on that I like a bit of verse. You might think I'm getting above my raising."

"More likely I would think you are an educated man."
She narrowed her eyes. "If I had to guess, I'd say Thoreau."

He raised his hands in surrender. "Henry David himself."

Her eyes followed his and took in the last rays of the sun
casting diamonds across the river.

"He'd like it here," Mr. Repp said. "It's so peaceful."

"Hmmm," she sighed. "It's been a long time since I had
time to read anything not medicine related. I'd quite forgotten how much I enjoy poetry."

"All work and no play . . ."

"Makes me a very dull girl," Lilly finished.

"Hardly," he replied.

He studied her like she'd studied him, and Lilly could
barely bring herself to turn her face away. To break the spell,
she started up the slippery slope, but her foot caught in her
raggedy skirt tail and she lost her balance. As he steadied her,
a tug as strong as a river's tide willed her closer. She looked
into his steel-blue eyes and a tiny spark of recognition flared
within her. It seemed a strangely familiar gesture when he
leaned his head toward hers. She fought a sudden desire to let
him kiss her. Instead, she straightened and took a step away,
fussing with her hair.

"My, it's nearly dark," she said, hoping the shakiness of
her voice didn't give her away. "I'd best be getting back. Mrs.
James will be rounding up a search party."

"Do you want to ride?" he asked. "I'll lead Apache."

She was relieved to think he didn't expect her to share
a saddle or, worse yet, a lap. She was surely imagining his

romantic interest. The man barely knew her. She'd had a weak moment, that was all. A moment's homesickness. A moment's yearning for someone who knew her and loved her.

"I'm not much of a horsewoman, Mr. Repp. I'll walk. Maybe I'll dry out."

CHAPTER 16

TERN STILL WALKED with Lilly toward town. If she went to the ends of the earth, he would follow. Leaves rustled in a slight breeze and chased the heat of the day away. Birds quieted, except for the rain crow whose high, lonesome call foretold a coming storm. He hadn't been so comfortable in another person's silence since his mother died.

He remembered as a little boy walking with his mother to a neighbor's springhouse to draw drinking water. The neighbor had built a well over a never-dry spring, and hand over hand, his mother hauled water to the surface in a bucket attached to a long rope. Tern would carry one small tin bucket home, and she would carry two wooden ones. They made a game out of who could go the farthest without spilling a single drop. Almost always, about half a mile from home, they'd rest a spell under the shade of a tree. His mother would take a tin cup from her apron pocket and offer Tern a sip of the cold water. To him, it tasted as sweet as the nectar from the trumpet of a honeysuckle vine.

His mother made each trip seem like such an adventure; it was only in looking back that he saw how her shoulders sagged under the weight of those buckets. Once he'd spied a perfect robin's egg lying in their path. When he'd handed it to her, she laughed with delight as if the blue egg were an unopened gift. Days later, a tiny bald and ugly creature pecked its way into the world from the tea towel nest in back of the cookstove's warming oven. She'd taught him to soak segmented night crawlers in milk before dropping bits of worm into the always-open mouth of the nestling.

The day they released the robin to live its own adventure was the last time Tern remembered crying. He wanted to make it a pet, but his mother said it went against nature to pen a wild thing up. She'd pulled him to her and dried his cheeks with the palms of her work-worn hands. "Don't be a-spilling tears, Son," he recalled her saying. "This old world's full of woe, but it's pretty all the same."

Funny, he'd only seen his mother in tears one time, though he supposed she could have been in tears daily. She was carrying the last child she'd ever have, his brother Lorne Lee, but she was ill, and for reasons unknown to him she had to go away. She sobbed and sobbed into the knit shawl she'd pulled up over her face. Fourteen at the time, Tern thought he was a man, and so in perfect imitation of his father, he'd stood on the porch and watched her go. He never even told her good-bye.

The thing he most remembered was how cold and silent the house felt in his mother's absence. He'd steeled his heart against his sorrow, but now, in Lilly's presence, he allowed himself to feel a mustard seed of joy. The hard line of his mouth relaxed. He felt like he was finally home.

Lilly stopped and lifted a sprig of false sweet william that grew in bunches beside the road. "Aren't these the toughest flowers ever?" The lavender-blue blossom rested in her palm. "It takes a knife to cut one, but they last a long time in a little water."

Tern agreed it was so and resisted the urge to pull the whole bunch out of the ground for her. Every so often she'd comment on some little thing: a red-winged blackbird flitting from branch to branch, a terrapin retreating into its shell, a single tree frog's peep. It made him happy to think she was as much in touch with the natural world as he was.

Her fall in the river, just as he was leaving his favorite reading spot, was surely a sign. His resolve to make himself known to her was being rewarded. He gathered his courage. Now was the time. But his mouth was dry as a lizard on a hot rock and his tongue was thick with unsaid words.

Night had fallen before they rounded the last bend in the road to the clinic. Good—it would be easier if she couldn't see the desperate need he was sure was stamped across his face. The last thing he wanted to do was scare her off. He watched as she paused to straighten her skirts and pin an errant lock of hair into place. If he were blessed enough to witness those deeds a thousand times, it wouldn't be enough. He swallowed hard around the lump in his throat.

Lilly turned and touched his arm. The innocent contact nearly took him to his knees.

"Thank you again, Mr. Repp. It was very thoughtful of you to see me home. I'll be on my way now."

He took a deep breath. "Lilly, I have something to—"

A commotion from near the clinic where a throng of people gathered cut him off. Laughter, the *bang, bang, bang* of firecrackers, and the clanging of pots and pans set up a racket. It put him in mind of a shivaree, but he didn't see a bride and groom.

"What in the world?" Lilly said.

"I don't know, but it sounds like New Year's Eve."

"There she is!" someone shouted, pointing their way.

Lilly was pulled away from him by Landis Blair's son. The boy grabbed her hand and towed her toward a bonfire that was shooting merry sparks into the night sky. Someone struck up a tune on a fiddle. Tern spied Darrell Tippen sitting on the clinic porch with his leg propped up on an overturned bucket.

Ned Tippen walked a donkey right past Tern. The donkey's ears protruded from a straw hat. Was this some kind of nightmare?

A woman he thought was Darrell's mother yelled over the

donkey's sudden bray, "We surprised you, didn't we, Doc? We've been working on this all week. Ever since Ned here told us who you really are."

From what he could see, Lilly looked stunned. She fingered a strand of pearls at her throat.

Tern hung back with Apache. The crowd meant her no harm, and it didn't look right, him being with her as dark fell. The last thing he wanted was to stir up gossip. He'd watch the fun and wait his turn. Maybe after the folks finished whatever they were celebrating, she'd let him walk the rest of the way home with her.

Darrell beat on the upturned bucket with the bowl of a long-handled ladle. "Listen up!" he said. "Ned's got an announcement—just in case there's one of you been hiding under a rock the last few days."

"All right, folks," Ned said, beaming. "You all are going to be proud to know that our own Doc Corbett is a Tippen cousin! She's a true-blue mountain gal. Her daddy is a Pelfrey and my mother, God rest her soul, was a Pelfrey. I know you're all here to make her purely welcome."

Darrell's mother circled Lilly's waist with one arm. "That's why we called you all together. We wanted to surprise the good doc here. You all treat her like family—or you'll answer to me!"

As folks reacted to the news, the donkey Ned held by a lead shook his head like a dog with a bone. The straw bonnet popped off one long ear and slid down over the donkey's face. He bared his yellow teeth and nibbled on the rim.

"My beautiful hat," Lilly cried. With a laugh, she pulled it away from the donkey and set it on the crown of her own head.

Tern marveled at her aplomb as people clapped and hooted.

"We've arranged to have Slow Poke here—" Ned indicated the donkey—"in service anytime you need a ride. It won't be so far to the ground next time you get thrown."

Tern knew some people were reserving judgment until they saw if Lilly could take a joke. It was the mountain way to laugh at your own self as hard as you might laugh at others. She didn't fail the test. Quick as a cat's sneeze, and with a boost from Ned, she was sitting sidesaddle on the animal's back. The Blair boy led the donkey through the crowd. His sister—Tern couldn't remember the girl's name—skipped behind, carrying an umbrella as bright as a daffodil against the dark sky.

Mr. James stepped out then. After helping Lilly down from the donkey's back, he turned to face the audience. "You all know we got off to a rough start with the doc here, her being a woman and all, but I do believe we're of a like mind now. Anybody who feels different, speak out once I've finished my piece." He turned to Lilly. "What I'm beating around the bush about, little gal, is that we're proud you came. You've turned out to be a right good sawbones. If things was different, if the power was in our hands, we'd ask you to stay on."

People were smiling, and heads were nodding.

Lilly's hand was at her throat again. She worried the strand of pearls as if it were a rosary. You'd have to be blind not to see the confusion on her face. Tern held his breath against her reply. He prayed she'd say yes.

Suddenly a man Tern had not noticed before strode out of the shadows. Decidedly a stranger, he was well dressed in a high-buttoned navy-blue frock coat and linen trousers. Tall and thin with ginger-colored hair and a clipped mustache, he held a black bowler at his side. With a tidy gesture, he nudged a pair of wire-rimmed spectacles up the bridge of his nose.

"Dr. Corbett, I presume?" he said in a familiar way.

Lilly's eyes widened with surprise. "Paul," she squealed as she flung herself into the man's open arms. "Am I glad to see you."

Obviously no stranger to Lilly, the man lifted her off the ground and spun her in circles. She was laughing when he put her down. "Gracious," she said with a smile, "forgive my lack of manners. Mr. James—everyone—this is Dr. Paul Hamilton, my fiancé."

Tern's heart plunged with the sickening speed of a runaway elevator. Well, that was that. It was almost with relief that he faded into the night. His secret was safe; he'd never have to take the chance of being rejected by Lilly.

His heart turned hard as stone. Soon enough he'd finish his assignment in this desolate place. He couldn't wait to be shut of it.

CHAPTER 17

"REALLY, LILLY, A DONKEY?" Paul Hamilton asked as he held one elegant hand over his nearly empty coffee cup.

Lilly shook her head the tiniest bit, hoping Paul would catch the signal and Myrtie James would not. Of course he didn't understand the significance of the donkey or the test she'd passed at the celebration last evening. So giddy with delight at him surprising her there, she hadn't thought to explain. It was difficult enough to justify to him why she hadn't known he was coming or why she'd let his letter become mouse fodder and why she was living in a shack in back of a shack.

Myrtie picked up a squat pitcher. "More molasses?"

"No thank you," Paul said.

Myrtie hovered at his side. Paul had barely touched the pancakes or the thick-sliced bacon on his plate. "Can I fix ye something else?" she asked.

Paul seemed to notice her for the first time, though they'd been sitting at her table for the better part of an hour, long after Mr. James had left for the mine. "Perhaps a coddled egg and a slice of wheat toast?"

"Coddled?"

"Never mind, Myrtie," Lilly said. "I expect Dr. Hamilton's never had blackstrap molasses on his pancakes before. It takes a little getting used to. Don't you think?"

Myrtie removed Paul's molasses-soaked plate. "I've got just the ticket," she said, marching to the stove.

"You better hope it's not pickled pigs' feet," Lilly murmured.

"Pickled what?"

Lilly laughed. It was rare to see Paul confounded. "Pigs' feet. They're yummy. Pour a little molasses over and it's better than chocolate ice cream."

"I never heard such," Myrtie said, sliding a fresh plate of pancakes and bacon in front of Paul. "Dr. Corbett's pulling your leg. Nobody eats pigs' feet with molasses. Here. I made you the special syrup my mommy used to make for me." Myrtie tipped a small saucepan. Thin, maple-colored syrup streamed over the flapjacks.

Paul forked up a bite. "Very good. Excellent. You'd think this syrup was from Vermont."

Myrtie beamed. "Ain't a thing but brown sugar melted with a dollop of butter."

With knife and fork Paul set about slicing the thick jowl bacon. His knife grated against the plate. "I've met my match," he said.

"Watch and learn, Paul." Lilly picked a piece of bacon from her own plate and bit off the end.

"You'll make an excellent surgeon, my dear girl," he said. "Nothing stymies you."

They laughed and teased their way through the rest of the meal. Lilly hadn't realized until now how much she'd missed him and how long it had been since she'd laughed at anyone but herself.

"Come," she said as soon as they finished. "I want to show you the clinic."

Dogs sniffed Paul's ankles and raced circles around them, kicking up clouds of red clay dust.

"So much for the shoe shine at the station," Paul said. "I should have saved my money."

Lilly saw the town as Paul must have seen it. Tiny, weatherboard houses set cheek by jowl. Washtubs and stacks of kindling wood on front porches. Wide-eyed, barefoot children hiding behind their mothers, the women and old men eyeing him with the same suspicion that she had endured just weeks before.

"Poor Lilly," he said. "A rose among thorns. Boston will be better suited for you."

Paul knew she'd been raised in the mountains of eastern Kentucky, but the only kin of hers he'd ever met was her aunt Alice, cousin Dodie, and uncle Benton—and Benton Upchurch owned a bank. Aunt Alice's house was a mansion compared to the shanties they were passing. He seemed to have forgotten that her mother ran a midwifery clinic on Troublesome Creek and that she, Lilly, had fallen in love with the practice of medicine there. She might not want to live in the mountains, but she'd always have an affinity for folks living just this side of poverty. If he tried to put her on a pedestal, she'd jump right off.

Before she could explain, thunder rolled across the top of the mountains and fat drops of rain plopped into the dust at their feet. The storm that had threatened since last evening was coming on strong.

Paul pulled her close under the protection of a large black umbrella. He was always prepared.

"Those are nasty-looking clouds," he said. "Let's run for it."

Once inside the clinic, Lilly made a quick visual inspection. Shipshape as always; Ned never left it less than perfectly tidy. She knew if she opened any door or drawer, it would be perfectly stocked.

Paul paced the small outer room, then strode into the surgery. He stood with folded arms and looked about. Lilly pointed out the gas-driven autoclave and the levered operating table underneath a perfectly positioned lamp. "I did my first reconstructive surgery here, Paul. I'm sure I told you all about it in a letter."

Paul stroked his pencil-thin mustache. "What, pray tell, happened to the patient?"

Lilly's temper flared. "The young man was sitting on the porch last evening. He will soon be walking without a crutch."

"Darling girl, I've upset you. I wasn't questioning your expertise, just your working conditions."

"This is quite modern for the area, Paul. Frankly, I was surprised to find it thus."

"I suppose, but there's need for much improvement. What's on today's list of things to do?"

"Wait out the rain, then make some house calls. You may need to change your shoes," she teased.

Paul opened his arms. "Come here."

She gladly acquiesced. "I've missed you so."

"And I you," he said, tipping her chin. His kiss was gentle, without demand; his embrace warm and safe. She might stay there all day.

"I've something for you." Paul extracted a small velvet-covered box from his jacket pocket. "Mother insisted you have it."

He opened the box to reveal a beautiful pearl ring set with a glittering diamond on either side. She held out her hand and he slipped the ring on.

"There," he said. "I couldn't be happier."

Lilly kissed his cheek. "It's lovely, Paul." She put her hand to her throat. "Look how it matches Aunt Alice's pearls."

He opened his arms again and she nestled close.

"Mother is thinking of a spring wedding," he said against the top of her head.

"Umm, maybe late May. Lexington is beautiful then."

"Are you set on Lexington? Mother was hoping for Boston— so many friends and business acquaintances, you know."

A frisson of disquiet altered Lilly's mood. Paul must have forgotten they'd already talked about the matter. She didn't expect his family to travel to Troublesome Creek—to do so would be difficult—but she would not ask hers to go to Boston. That would be unfair. Lexington seemed the best compromise.

As the outside door opened, they stepped apart. Ned shook his rain slicker and deposited a stack of mail on Lilly's desk. "It's raining cats and dogs out there." He stuck out his hand. "Hey, Dr. Hamilton, good to see you again. Hope the boardinghouse met your expectations."

"It was fine, Ned. Thanks for recommending me to Mrs. DeWitt. I should have made reservations."

"No need. I can always rustle you up a bed somewheres."

The men talked—Ned offering Paul a tour of the mine, Paul asking polite questions. Lilly sorted mail. There was a letter from her mother and one from her twin sisters. Molly and Mazy would take turns, one writing in blue ink, the other in black. She would set them aside for later and enjoy them with a cup of tea. With a thumbnail under the flap, she pried a business envelope open.

The room had darkened with the rain, and so she stepped to the window, scanning for the heart of the matter.

. . . *an interesting proposition,* she read in Dr. Coldiron's bold script. *One you should carefully and prayerfully study. Whatever your decision, I remain your devoted teacher, Dr. John Coldiron.*

The men's voices faded in the background. Rain tapped against the windowpane as if begging to be let in. Lilly's shoulders sank under the weight of the letter. Dr. Coldiron posed a question she did not want to consider. A board of men at her alma mater was offering to extend her stay in Skip Rock, Kentucky. The need was great, the letter said, and they hoped she would say yes to their offer. Of course, they understood she would need expanded facilities, a house of her own, and an assistant or two. Further down the road, they hoped to send qualified residents to intern at the clinic under Lilly's direction. Her commitment would be for five years, and she could handpick her replacement. The salary he quoted was not considerable, but it was adequate.

A knot the size of a green apple formed in the center of Lilly's stomach. She wished the letter had never come. She wished Ned had dropped it in a puddle of rain. It would be hard enough to leave the people she had become close to—Ned and Darrell, Armina and Aunt Orie, the Blairs, Myrtie and Mr. James—without them knowing she was willingly leaving.

Folding it precisely, she slid the missive back into the envelope and tapped it against her chin. How interesting; even a week ago there would not have been this quandary. The folks at Skip Rock would have helped her pack her bags, they were so anxious to see the back of her. But now . . .

The words of Mr. James came back to her: *"If things was different, if the power was in our hands, we'd ask you to stay on."* Thunder boomed and shook the room. With the tip of one finger, she traced a raindrop down the windowpane. She would have to tell Mr. James about the offer, but first she needed time to think. Her answer was obvious—no way was she staying on. For though she had much regard for the people and though the place was rife with opportunity to practice her skills, she did not feel at home here.

There was something about this place—something dark and brooding that stirred old fears and tainted her emotions like ink spilled on a tablecloth. And if she stayed, there would of necessity be more forays inside the mine. Just thinking of the claustrophobic trip in the number 4 mine to rescue Darrell Tippen made the knot in her stomach tighten.

"Hey, Doc, did you see the package?"

Lilly held up a thick manila envelope and noted that the return address was from Massey's Pharmaceuticals in Lexington. When she tore it open, an amber-colored bottle tumbled out onto the desktop. "Looks like we've got Aunt Orie's medication. How soon can we get up there?"

Ned opened the outer door. Black clouds swirled ominously in a strangely greenish sky. Forks of lightning sizzled dangerously close, and sheets of rain pounded down. "We ain't going nowhere fast." He unhooked his slicker from the coatrack and put it on. "I'll be back when this lets up."

He started across the threshold, leading with his strong leg to the first step, retaining balance with his peg. The steps were slick with rain, and his good foot shot straight out. He grabbed the doorframe with both hands. The wooden peg popped off his stump and he went down. "Jiminy whiskers," he yelped.

Paul grabbed him under the arms and hauled him back inside. Ned sat down heavily on the straight-backed chair just inside the waiting room door. Resting his palms on his thighs, he doubled over in pain. "Just give me a minute."

Paul was already kneeling. "Might I have a look at this?"

Ned's mouth was a thin straight line, and his face was drained of color, but he nodded.

Lilly grabbed bandage scissors and a packet of gauze soaked in carbolic lotion. Ned had wrapped his stump with a figure-eight bandage made of a strip of sheeting three inches in width. The end of the dressing had been torn into a Y, which was fastened with a knot. She snipped the knot and rolled the bandage tightly as she unwound it. Ned had probably washed and reused it a dozen times already.

Her eyes met Paul's when she revealed the below-the-knee amputation. "Ned, do you feel feverish?"

Ned flexed his knee, wincing slightly. "No. I'm fine. It's just been a mite red the last couple of days. It'll heal right up."

"My good man, you've developed an abscess," Paul said with authority. "See how the wound has burst open with infection?"

The clinic walls shuddered in a sudden howling wind. Rain leaked from the ceiling in a steady *plop, plop, plop* onto the floor. "I should get a bucket," Ned said.

"Goodness, Ned, I'll get it." Lilly searched under a shelf in the storage room, found a gallon tin, and put it under the leak.

"There'll be another over yonder by the desk." Ned pointed to a brown stain on the ceiling. "You might as well move the trash can under there."

Lilly wanted to wrap her arms around Ned. She wished she could contain his suffering as easily as the bucket contained the dripping rain. "I'll get a thermometer."

"How long has it been since your surgery?" Paul asked.

"Three years ago, May 15. Me and the boys was shoring up the roof in Number 4." He held his thumb and index finger a quarter of an inch apart. "We was that near done."

He shook his head as if he still could not believe his luck. "Elbows—do you know Elbows? He was outside loading a cart with more timber planks when he seen a swirl of leaves shoot out the mouth of that old widow maker. He said the mule hauling the cart was fractious—that was his first sign. Animals have a sixth sense about such things. Anyways, he grabbed the mule's harness and ran for his life. They was three men killed that day, and seven kids lost their daddies." He ran his hands down his thigh and lifted the stump. "See, this ain't nothing."

"Comparatively thinking, I suppose not, but there's no need for undue suffering." Paul stood with crossed arms, surveying the situation. "There is a need for reconstructive surgery. This was finished with a bread loaf flap—much used during the war, but no longer in favor. I believe I could fix you up with a proper closure, which would allow use of a modern prosthesis."

Ned's hands gripped the chair seat. "Them's big words, Doc."

Paul waved his hand as if chasing the words away. "Simply put, you need surgery and a decent prosthesis—sorry—decent replacement of that ghastly peg."

"How long are we talking about?"

"Do you mean how much time from surgery to replacement?"

Ned's eyes sparked with interest. He nodded.

"Several weeks, according to how quickly you heal," Paul said.

"What if I just leave it be? I've got used to the pain."

Lilly listened as she gathered supplies to treat the wound: black salve, sterile gauze, a bandage, metal fastener tacks. She knew exactly what Paul would say.

He didn't put it gently. "Loss of the entire limb from gangrene and most likely the loss of your life."

Nervously, Ned unfastened and fastened the top button of his shirt. "You're saying I don't have a choice?"

Lilly poured water in a basin for Paul to scrub his hands. She could easily dress Ned's wound herself, but Ned needed to form a bond with Paul. It would ultimately help him make the right decision.

Paul undid his cuff links and began to roll his sleeves. "On the contrary, Ned, the choice is yours alone. Meanwhile, Dr. Corbett," he said, drawing Lilly into the conversation, "I hope you have some crutches." He nudged the peg with one foot. "Ned won't be using this again."

Ned moved to sit on the end of the exam table. Lilly watched as Paul applied a sterile bandage from the knee joint to the stump. He worked in oblique and circular turns, which he carried alternately over the face of the stump and round the limb. It was like watching an artist at work.

Beads of perspiration dotted Ned's forehead. "It'll heal up for a while, then break open again. This is the worst, though." He wiped sweat with the crook of his arm. "I don't see why it won't callus over."

"I'm amazed you've done as well as you have," Paul said. "Your surgical repair was rudimentary at best, but surely lifesaving." With the tiny toothed tacks, Paul fastened the bandage, then gently tapped the stump. "No weight bearing on this."

Ned slid off the table and balanced on the crutches Lilly provided. "I thank ye," he said.

Paul's eyes narrowed as he stroked his mustache with his thumb and index finger. Lilly could almost see the gears in his brain turning. "There would be no charge for the surgery or the prosthesis if you would be willing to come to Hamilton Hospital in Boston. Your case would make an interesting opportunity for my students."

Ned leaned forward, using the crutches to propel himself toward the door. "I'll think on it," he said as he carefully maneuvered over the threshold. "Looks like the storm's taking a break. Hey, look at the rainbow."

Arm in arm, Lilly and Paul stepped out into a world washed clean. The air smelled fresh as just-ironed linen. The wind-whipped trees and flattened grasses were a brilliant green against the backdrop of sunshine spearing through dark-gray clouds. A rainbow of pastels arced gracefully across the sky.

"That was quite a piece of work," Lilly said as Ned disappeared around the corner of a building.

"Well, my dear, I've bandaged many a wound," Paul said, tightening his one-armed embrace.

"Yes, I know, but that's not what I'm talking about."

"A bit of charity is good for the soul."

"You're a good man, Paul Hamilton," Lilly said.

"Do I deserve a kiss?"

"Paul! Mind your manners."

"All right—this time," Paul said. "But you don't make it easy."

CHAPTER 18

THE RAIN CONTINUED on and off all day. Toward late afternoon, the sun burst forth, chasing the clouds away and leaving the air humid and close. Paul and Lilly took a late supper with the Jameses. Myrtie had gone all out with chicken and dumplings, stewed tomatoes, creamed corn, dressed eggs, and her special potato salad made with mustard and mayonnaise dressing.

They'd just filled their plates when a knock at the door called for Myrtie's attention. "Come in. Come in," she said, ushering Tillie and Turnip Tippen into the room. "Stanley, get the extra chairs."

Turnip held up a palm to stop her. "Thank ye kindly, Mrs.

James, but we ain't staying. Another storm's a-coming in." He rolled his eyes. "But Tillie here wouldn't rest until I brung her and her cake over. It is good cake, if maybe just a little damp."

Always the perfect hostess, Myrtie would not hear their refusals. "Should we say grace again?" she asked as bowls and platters were served to the Tippens.

"I reckon the Lord heard us the first time, Myrtie," Mr. James said.

Lilly listened with some amusement as Mrs. Tippen regaled Paul with the story of Darrell's accident and Lilly's intervention to save her son's leg.

"And I told Turnip here, I says, 'For a woman, that Lilly Corbett's a fine doctor.' Didn't I say that, Turnip?"

Turnip lifted his head from the plate of chicken and dumplings. "That ain't exactly how I remember it."

"Do you want a taste of that coconut cake or not?" Mrs. Tippen stage-whispered.

Lilly caught the look on Paul's face. His tight-lipped smile said, *"Get me out of here."*

Turnip sopped gravy with half a biscuit. "That's what she said, all right." He popped the biscuit into his mouth, leaned back in the chair, and patted his round belly.

Myrtie set a crystal cake stand on the table. "Dr. Corbett, would you do the honors?"

Lilly sliced the cake, mischievously cutting Paul's extra thick as Myrtie poured fresh coffee. The dessert was surprisingly light and delicious.

Paul plowed through every bite before he excused himself

from the table. "Ladies, thank you for dinner. I don't know when I've had a finer meal, but daylight comes early. Dr. Corbett, if I could have a word."

Their footsteps squelched against the wet grass. Paul clasped Lilly's hand, moving it back and forth, forging a swinging bridge of intimacy. Lingering raindrops showered down from the branches of a tree. Laughing, they ducked and ran the last few feet to her stepping-stone stoop.

"Do they eat like that every day?" he asked.

"Hardly. Couldn't you tell you were being honored?"

"Honored to death," he said. "That meal was dangerous to one's health."

Lilly lingered at the door. She wished she could ask him in, but she didn't have a sitting room and couldn't very well have him in her bedroom. It wouldn't be proper. Besides, there was too much gossip about her already. It made her miss the city, where one's every move was not scrutinized.

Dr. Coldiron's letter was burning a hole in her pocket, but she could hardly discuss it while standing under a threatening sky. As if in punctuation to her conundrum, thunder clapped and a hundred fingers of flame turned the night sky into a Dresden plate crackled with age. Dark clouds formed and raced across the moon.

They saw the door to the Jameses' house open. "Best come in here until the storm blows over, Dr. Hamilton," Mr. James yelled from the lit doorway.

Paul squeezed her hand. "Until the morning, darling Lilly. Sweet dreams."

She returned the pressure. His hand was strong and sure. Singular, fat raindrops pelted down a warning. "Good night, dearest. Now run!"

From the safety of her window, she laughed to see him hotfooting it across the yard. "Poor Paul; I surely hope the Tippens have taken their leave."

After turning up the wick of the coal-oil lamp, she flicked the head of a sulfur match across a striking strip, held the flame to the wick, watched it catch, and seated the chimney. With her elbows propped on the table, she reread Dr. Coldiron's letter—then she read it again. A smudge of smoke cast a shadow across the pristine pages.

"Bother," she said louder than was necessary in an empty room.

On the bottom shelf of the washstand, she found one of Myrtie's cleaning cloths. Lifting the chimney once again, she ran the rag up inside the globe. Satisfied that it was spotless, she turned the wick down a smidgen, folded the rag, and settled back at the table.

Wind whined at the door like a hungry dog. Against a sudden chill, Lilly plucked a shawl from the back of the chair and draped it across her shoulders. Beyond her cozy nest, rain increased in a torrent's fall.

The wall clock struck ten. Lilly stretched her arms overhead and yawned, tired but not too sleepy to reply to Dr. Coldiron's letter.

She opened the top of her portable writing desk and perused her options: small pots of blue, navy, or black ink;

heavy vellum or light onionskin stationery with matching envelopes; two rolls of stamps; clean blotters; penholders of various hefts and colors—all waited her selection. The navy on the cream-colored vellum. She dipped the nib of a tortoiseshell pen into the navy pot.

> *My dear Dr. Coldiron,*
>
> *I hope this missive finds you in good health. I cannot begin to tell you of the blessings I have received from my internship here in Skip Rock. I owe an eternal debt of gratitude to you, my benefactor.*

Words flowed smooth as silk from her pen as she relayed medicine practiced and lessons learned. Toward the end of the second page, she realized she was putting off the inevitable. She hated to disappoint her mentor, but the words had to be written, and in all fairness, he knew she hadn't intended to stay past September.

Eleven chimes. *Goodness, how did it get so late?* She rolled her head on her shoulders to loosen up the kinks, then dipped the pen for what must have been the hundredth time and continued:

> *I have no doubt you will understand why I must decline your generous offer. Aside from the fact that I had no intention of staying here at Skip Rock, my fiancé, Dr. Paul Hamilton, would be most displeased if I accepted.*

Lilly hoped Dr. Coldiron would sense the humor in the last sentence. He of all people knew that she was much too headstrong to let a man, even Paul, deter her from her goals.

She closed with the usual obligatory sentiments, set the inked pages aside to dry, addressed the envelope, and pasted a stamp in the upper corner.

There—finished. She slapped her hands lightly as if dusting all her cares away. But doubt niggled at her conscience. She studied the flame in the lamp as if it could burn away any lingering guilt. The flame reminded her of the gay bonfire from the night before and of Mr. James's words: *"If things was different . . ."* Therein lay the doubt and the guilt. Things were different. Dr. Coldiron's letter made it so.

Lilly shrugged. Really, she had no debt to these people. Nothing was owed except finishing out her tenure. It wasn't as if she would leave them in a lurch. The college and the coal company would work in tandem to find someone more than willing to practice here. Her desire was to be where she could make a difference; Skip Rock, with all its prejudices and backward ways, was not that place.

She reached to turn down the wick, but something stayed her hand. She had not prayed about this. She had not searched the Scripture. She cupped her chin in her hand and idly flipped through the pages of her Bible.

As a girl, she had collected words. She smiled to remember that she had once determined to name her children Verily, Inasmuch, and Cipher—just because she liked the way the words tripped off her tongue.

Closing her eyes, she let chapter and verse glide past before stopping her index finger to mark a place. She had watched her mother do this many times when she was seeking God's direction. She opened her eyes. Oh, dear; she'd turned to Job—not the happiest of books. Job 40:14 to be exact. She read aloud: "'Then will I also confess unto thee that thine own right hand can save thee.'"

Whatever could this mean? The rain drummed on the roof like a mantra leading her to a quiet place, cleansing her of every thought, every worry. She would be still and wait upon the Lord. When she was perfectly calm, she opened her eyes. At her right hand was a pot of ink and a pen, the letter, and the envelope addressed to Dr. Coldiron. *"Thine own right hand can save thee."*

She put the ink and the pen back into her writing desk. The letter she studied. With a sigh, she slid it under a short stack of stationery before closing the portable desk. She would wait a few days to put it in the mail.

Lights off, she dressed for bed, knelt for prayer, and slipped between freshly ironed sheets. Sleep came quickly if not sweetly.

Dark and depressive memories, masquerading as dreams, darted like bats through her sleep. Her younger self dwelled in an unreal world where dogs could talk, houses had no walls, and tin roofs slammed open and shut, open and shut, open and shut, like an unlatched door in a high wind. The noise was so loud, she woke with a start.

"A dream, it's just a dream," Lilly said with relief as she

searched with her feet for her slippers. But *bang! Bang! Bang!* The noise persisted.

Tying the belt of her dressing gown, she went to answer the knock at the door. The dark stoop was empty. Puzzled, she stepped outside, minimally protected by the roof's overhang. The washtub thumped against the wall. As lightning rent the eastern sky, the tub popped loose and wheeled down the road. The big snowball bush beside the overflowing rain barrel writhed in the squall. Beneath her feet, Lilly could feel the ground rock in harmony with the rolling thunder. A sudden rainy gust nearly sent her scooting off the porch. Grabbing the doorframe, she pulled herself inside and with effort pushed the door closed. She leaned against its smooth surface, catching her breath.

The house groaned and shuddered around her. Hurriedly, she stripped off her soaked nightdress and pulled on the clothes she had laid out the night before. Fingers thick with fatigue, she fumbled with the clasp on her pearls. The darkness seemed suffocating. She lit the lamp; her claustrophobia dissipated in the yellow glow only to be replaced by true alarm at what the lamp revealed.

Curtains billowed at the closed windows. Soot and gray ash spouted from the potbellied stove, filling the room with the lonely smell of fires long dead. She stared in disbelief as a ball of mouse-colored fluff tumbled out from under the bed and skittered across the floor. Hitting the wall, the fluff broke apart; it was every mouse for himself then as the creatures ran like long-tailed demons along the baseboards.

Lilly yelped and was reaching for the broom when the earsplitting sound of a sawmill made her cringe. Thinking to save the most valuable thing in the room, she dove under the table with her doctor's satchel. As the wind peeled the tin roof like a ripe banana, she wished she had grabbed something else instead. Covering her head with the satchel, she darted up and seized her Bible. "Sorry, Lord," she said.

After venting its wrath upon her roof, the storm waned. Through a gaping hole in the ceiling, she could see stars through the thin clouds. *Amazing.* The house was in shambles, but she was intact. Lilly tucked the Bible safely inside her case and hurried to the door. Anything could have happened during the storm. People might be injured—the clinic might have blown away.

The inside door was who knew where, but the screen door angled drunkenly across the threshold. With hardly any effort, she jerked it free. She spotted Mr. James walking across the yard. "Are ye of a piece?" he asked.

"Gracious, I'm fine. Do you know if anyone is hurt?"

"Looks like the town took the brunt of the storm. We'd best hasten that way."

Her heart took a tumble. Paul was staying at the boardinghouse. "Yes," she said, nearly running beside him, "let's hurry."

CHAPTER 19

STANLEY JAMES AND TERN STILL spent the better part of the morning assessing the damage to the coal camp. Though many homes were missing some shingles or sported busted windows, no lives had been lost.

"That's a miracle in itself," Stanley said as he and Tern watched men unroll tar paper atop what was left of Mrs. DeWitt's boardinghouse.

Tern nodded. He knew what Stanley meant. There had been many anxious moments that morning as he and his crew searched the wreckage for survivors. At the Poors' house in particular, he'd witnessed a true miracle. The house had pancaked, the roof sitting on the foundation. They heard

Mrs. Poor screaming from what used to be her kitchen. It took six men to heft the roof so that she and Mr. Poor could scramble out.

A bone poked through Mrs. Poor's arm, but she wouldn't hear of going to the clinic until somebody found her baby. Elbows found the little fellow under the debris of the front porch. He was still in his crib—still sleeping and sucking his thumb. There wasn't a scratch on him.

Ugly as the destruction was, a body couldn't help but admire the finesse of the storm. At the boardinghouse, which had one wing ripped off, Tern found eight forks from Mrs. DeWitt's silver service stuck in the wall over the mantel. He pulled them out one at a time as if from a tough piece of meat. Landis Blair had come and asked some men to help him get his cow off the roof of the barn. The very cow that had caused little Timmy such trouble. He said she was bawling her head off. Landis also reported the storm sucked all the water from his farm pond. And then a small thing, but telling: the house where Lilly boarded had no front door or roof. Mr. James said the storm left the screen door but took the other. It was hard to figure the strangeness of it all. It was like the storm had fingers that picked and chose what to demolish and what to leave alone.

Mr. James hadn't needed to tell Tern about Lilly's door. He'd seen it for himself. As soon as the wind allowed, he'd dressed and run out into the dark to check on her. He was thankful to see Mr. James was already there. As usual, Tern hung back, watching, making sure she was truly all right.

"Paul?" he heard her ask. "Mr. James, have you seen Paul?"

He could have answered the question easy enough. He could step right from behind the tree where he lurked and say, "I've seen him. He's fine." But he didn't. It wasn't his place.

⁂

Lilly spent the morning stitching and mending. One more gash and she'd be out of suture supplies. Somehow, Paul had commandeered the more interesting setting of bones and molding of casts, and he'd commandeered Ned to help him.

Her face flooded with shame. What difference did it make who did what as long as folks were taken care of?

"That's it, then?" Paul strode to the door and looked out into the yard. "Everybody's put back together?"

"Appears to be so," Lilly said as she filled out a supply form for Ned to take to the pharmacy in town. She waved the paper to dry the ink. "It was wonderful to have your help today, Paul."

"Glad to be of service," he said with a droll smile. "Say, might we get away from here for a moment? I feel as if I haven't had a minute with my girl."

Lilly hesitated. She really didn't have a second, much less a minute. She turned an amber vial of medication over and over. Her mind was miles away with Aunt Orie.

"Seriously," Paul said, reaching out to her. "I didn't come all this way just to practice medicine." His clasp was sure and strong as he pulled her out of her chair and sang, "All work and no play makes Lilly a very dull girl."

Lilly couldn't help but laugh. "Let's walk back to my place. I saved my kit and my Bible; everything else might have been blown away for all I know."

"Does it really matter? You won't be here much longer anyway."

True enough, Lilly thought.

Due to flooding, the mines were closed for the day, but the camp was still a beehive of activity. Men scampered across roofs with hammer and nails, pried broken glass from window frames, and hauled off trash. Women toiled over roiling tubs of water, arms bent like chicken wings, scrubbing the storm away on ribbed washboards. The clean smell of the lye soap they used perfumed the air. Raucous boys ran up and down the road, shouting and chasing each other as if a circus had come to town. Serious-faced girls kept to the shade of porches, corralling younger siblings, often as not with a fat baby brother or sister perched on their skinny hips. Lilly felt a stitch in her heart. When had it all become so achingly familiar?

As they passed by the Jameses' house, Myrtie waved them over. Lilly recognized several of her own dresses and shirtwaists flapping on the clothesline in Myrtie's side yard. "Some men are a-working on the little house," she said. "I took the liberty of moving your personal things outen the way."

"Did you have any damage here?" Paul asked.

"No, ain't it amazing? That storm cloud was playing hopscotch—a hit here, a miss there. Weren't God good, though? Sparing everybody's lives?" She gave a satisfied grin. "This'll swell the church coffers come Sunday morning. Ain't nothing like a good storm to set folks on the right path."

Paul nodded.

Myrtie caught Lilly's eye as if she needed a private word.

"Paul, would you excuse us for a moment?" Lilly asked.

"I'll just walk over to your place—see if I can be of some service."

"Thank you. I'll be right there." As soon as he was out of earshot, she turned to her landlady. "What is it, Myrtie?"

"You'll be wondering about your unmentionables. Everything was soaked," Myrtie said as she drew Lilly through the front door and out the back. "I washed them out and hung them here on my private line." She indicated a wire clothesline strung between two posts on her back porch. "I couldn't very well tell you that with your fellow standing right there."

Lilly's chemises, petticoats, knee-length pantalets, and cotton hose dried on the line. Truthfully, Lilly hadn't given them a passing thought, but now Myrtie's act of kindness made her eyes brim with tears. "Myrtie, this is so thoughtful."

"I never liked to hang my drawers on the side-yard line for prying eyes to see. Stanley strung this up for me." She rubbed the skirt of a petticoat between thumb and index finger. "Still a bit damp. I'll have them done up in no time."

Before Lilly could properly thank her, Myrtie was rushing through the door and heading for the cookstove. "Oh, my aching back, if I let these beans boil dry . . ." The pot of pintos steamed as she lifted the lid and stirred with a long-handled spoon. "Thank goodness. My head's not on straight today."

Myrtie looked over her shoulder as she poured water into the pan from a granite pitcher. "Your sundries are there on the table. I'll put them in the back bedroom directly. You'll be staying there until the little house is all fixed up."

Lilly looked through the few things she'd brought with her from Lexington: some photos and her dresser set. She opened her writing desk, afraid of what she would find, but all was tidy and dry. Flipping through the stationery, she saw the letter from the night before. She took a moment to fold the pages with sharp creases and put it in the envelope. She could give it to Paul to post for her when he left to go back to Boston in a couple of days. It would be a rite of passage—marking the end of one part of her life and opening the door to another. She ran a ribbon of mucilage along the envelope's flap and closed it—sealing her fate.

Unbidden, the perplexing Scripture stole into her thoughts. *"Thine own right hand can save thee."* She supposed that meant she had saved herself through the writing of the letter—with her own right hand—but she needed time to think about it and time was in short supply.

"Myrtie, did you find my galoshes in the mess?"

"Yes, ma'am, you'll find them on the front porch, setting in the sun." Myrtie put her spoon on a cracked saucer and turned from the stove. "Whereabouts are you going?"

"I'm going to the Eldridges'. I've had Orie on my mind

all morning. I'd really like to consult about her case with Dr. Hamilton while I have the opportunity."

Myrtie poured cornmeal into a yellowware mixing bowl and cracked an egg in the center. "I heard tell that when Dr. Hamilton leaves, he's taking Ned Tippen with him—heard he's going to make Ned a new leg. Is that so?"

Goodness, Paul had seen Ned only yesterday. How did this get spread so quickly? "I don't know what has been decided. I'm not sure what Ned wants to do."

Myrtie plopped a dollop of bacon grease on the bottom of a cast-iron skillet, smeared it around, slid the heavy skillet onto the top rack of the oven, and closed the door. "Reckon what a body would make a leg outen? China would smash, and cast iron would be so heavy Ned couldn't drag it around." Myrtie shook her head ever so slightly as she stirred buttermilk into the bowl. "Seemed like he did fine with his peg."

Lilly could imagine the chatter that had taken place over scrub boards and clotheslines this morning—as if the storm wasn't fodder enough for gossip. "Are folks worrying about Ned?"

"I wouldn't like to be putting words in other people's mouths, but you know what they say 'bout them big-city hospitals."

"No, what do they say?"

Myrtie looked around. She answered in a low voice. "They experiment on people—especially poor people. Ned might go away and come back with no legs—or four legs. A body never knows."

Lilly shook her head. Experimentation—that old saw again. "Now, Myrtie, you know folks said the same thing about me when I first came here. They said I would experiment on Darrell, remember?"

"Yeah, but that was before we knew you was kin." She wrapped her hand in the tail of her apron, using it as a potholder to pull the smoking skillet from the oven. The bacon grease popped when she poured the cornmeal mix in. "You can't trust nobody but your kin unless they's somebody else's close kin." The oven door slapped shut on the unbaked corn bread. "And that's the Lord's truth."

Myrtie handed Lilly a brown paper sack with a folded-over top. "You better take this if you're heading to Orie's. And you'd best stop at the shed and get Stanley's hip boots for your doctor friend. That old Swampy Creek's liable to be fractious."

Lilly sat on the top porch step and pulled sheets of rolled newsprint from her galoshes. They were nice and dry. She put them in her carryall along with the sack of food and the quart jar of tea Myrtie had provided. She'd get the waders and Paul, return to the office for Orie's medicine, and hope to find Ned there.

The screen door squeaked open. "You all try and get back in time for the fish fry tonight."

"Fish fry?"

"Yeah, over to the schoolhouse. Landis Blair's supplying the fish. There were hundreds of them flopping in the mud of his pond that got sucked dry. I'm taking beans and corn bread and maybe a couple apple pies."

"I might be bringing Mrs. Eldridge back with me."

"That so? Is she that bad off?"

"Yes, she is. But this is the perfect opportunity to try a new treatment, while Dr. Hamilton is here." Lilly stood and slung the linen carryall over her shoulder. "Something just occurred to me, Myrtie. If Mrs. Eldridge comes, it's likely her niece will come also—along with two little ones. They'll need someplace to stay."

"Bring them babies to me. Orie Eldridge is a fine Christian woman. I'd be tickled to help out any way I can."

CHAPTER 20

SWAMPY WAS INDEED FRACTIOUS, although not too deep to cross on horseback. Clumps of tattered cattails, tangles of poison ivy, felled decomposing tree trunks oozing slime mold, and no telling what else dotted the sloping banks. The beating sun reflected prisms of dull color from circles of oily slicks. A heavy, rank odor exuded from the water.

The party—comprised of Lilly, Ned, Paul, and three other men—paused on the banks of the creek, waiting for Ned's direction.

"It's already gone down, praise the Lord," Ned said as he nudged the horse pulling a wagon out into the creek. "Watch for snakes."

Lilly was amazed at how well Ned was doing despite the loss of his peg. He had pitched his crutches into the wagon bed and pulled himself onto the bench seat as if he did it every day. She needed to talk to him about accepting Paul's offer as soon as she could. She was praying he would say yes.

Soon after they crossed, they caught Armina coming out of the henhouse, a woven basket on one arm and Bubby in the other. A rusty black bonnet protected her face from the sun and a long feed-sack apron covered her dress. She was barefoot.

"Let me go up first," Lilly said. Nudging her horse forward, she raised her hand in greeting. "Armina—hello. We've come to check on you all. I see you made it through the storm."

"And I see you brung an army with you." Armina stared at the entourage of men and horses.

Lilly dismounted and wrapped her mount's reins around the low-hanging branch of an apple tree. "I only brought folks who already know Aunt Orie. They've come to help us get her to Skip Rock for that treatment we talked about."

Armina lifted one freckled arm to point at Paul. The egg basket scooted down to rest in the crook of her elbow. "That ain't the teetotal truth. For certain sure, he ain't from these parts."

Lilly backtracked. "You're right, of course. I wasn't thinking. That's Dr. Paul Hamilton. I've asked him to consult on this case."

"Aunt Orie ain't a case. If you was in the need of a consult, whatever that is, ye should have asked me first."

Lilly's temper flared. Armina was like dealing with a distempered dog, all growl with a bite. "Shouldn't whether she sees Dr. Hamilton or not be Aunt Orie's decision?"

Armina's shoulders slumped. She barely caught the egg basket before it slid off her hand. Suddenly she looked like the vulnerable girl she was. "She's real sick, Doc. She took a bad turn last night. I was just going to fix her some custard."

Lilly touched Armina's arm ever so gently. "Let us help you."

"Don't be bringing in all them men."

"No, just Dr. Hamilton and me."

"All right then. They's a water trough beside the barn if the horses need water." Armina gave Lilly the egg basket, then looked toward the riders. "That'un knows where the well house is if the men need refreshment."

Lilly caught the ghost of a smile on Armina's face. She couldn't resist a tease. "You mean Ned? I'm surprised you even recall him."

"Humph. It ain't every day you come across a one-legged man."

Heading back, Ned halted the party at the near edge of Swampy. It was upstream from their previous crossing. Ned was looking for the flattest, least rocky of places. They'd decided Aunt Orie would have to be carried down the mountain on a canvas litter. They'd brought a wagon in hopes, but it proved too jolting for a body in her condition.

Instead, Armina and the babies rode in the back of the

wagon that Ned drove. Lilly stayed on horseback while Paul insisted on helping the other men carry the litter.

Ned hopped down and walked to the sloping bank of Swampy. He poked the ground in various places with one crutch. Ahead of his probing, bullfrogs plopped off the bank and a sunning water snake slithered away. Ned seemed to be studying the way the holes filled with water, but Lilly couldn't figure why.

Paul took advantage of the wait to pull on the hip-length rubber waders Myrtie had provided.

"Looks safe," Ned said. "I'll go across first."

After the wagon crossed, the stretcher bearers chose to traverse a sandbar where the footing was shifty but the water level low. Standing in the stirrups, Lilly watched her patient for any sign of distress. The men struggled to keep the bulging stretcher higher than the level of the stagnant water. Flat on her back, Aunt Orie held on so tightly that her knuckles were white.

The party was nearly onshore when Paul lost hold. He seemed to be struggling against the current, although Swampy was anything but fast flowing. The other men heaved the litter up the low bank.

Lilly directed her horse toward Paul, but Ned turned in the wagon seat and yelled to her, "Get out. Get that horse out of the water!"

Despite her instinct to assist Paul, Lilly did as she was bid, leaving him fighting an unseen force. "Paul! What is wrong?" Was he having a heart attack brought on by the exertion of carrying the three-hundred-pound patient over uneven ground and slippery creek rock? Was he being attacked by a turtle or bitten by a snake? She slid off her horse. She had to go to him.

One of the men jerked her back before she got a foot in the creek. "You'll make it worse, ma'am," he said.

The scene burned into her brain with the intensity of a bad dream: The bleached-white stretcher on the ground, Aunt Orie propped in a sitting position against a wagon wheel, her head and shoulders protected by a blanket roll. Ned racing to the bank, his crutches flying across the ground. The two babies peeping over the gate of the wagon with round, frightened eyes. A single high-flying crow cawing a raspy warning.

Paul was trapped by something unseen, already up to his lower chest in the dirty water. "I can't breathe," he wheezed.

"Quicksand!" Ned yelled. "Don't move a muscle, Dr. Hamilton."

"Somebody fetch a stick," Armina hollered.

One of the men found a barren poplar branch and stood on the bank with it, not sure what to do next.

"I'm the slightest," Armina said. "I'll take it."

"Easy . . . easy," Ned instructed as Armina removed her shoes and apron and cautiously waded into the slimy pool. Leaning forward, she propelled one end of the long pole Paul's way. "Don't lose hold of your end," Ned said.

Armina paused and shot Ned a look. "Do I look like I ain't did this before?"

Lilly sank to the ground. Ragweed prickled her nose and rye grass cushioned her knees. As a child she'd heard stories of people who were forever lost to unexpected swirls of quicksand that sucked the life from its hapless victims. It was well known that once it caught you in its bizarre vise, any movement made the situation worse. She could barely stand the look of fear on Paul's face. And to think he was here because of her.

Without taking her eyes off Paul, she began to pray. "Heavenly Father," she bartered, "please save Paul. I'll do whatever You want, go wherever You want—just please, please, save him from the quicksand."

While Lilly prayed, the men clasped hands and formed a chain, linking the last hand with Armina's. Armina pushed the slim poplar branch forward until it brushed Paul's fingertips. Frantic, he lunged for it. With an obscene slurp, the deep mass of mixed loose sand and water swallowed his body up to the armpits. Thankfully, he had managed to keep one arm free.

"Don't move! Don't move!" people yelled.

"Them waders has filled up and got him trapped," one man said.

"I once saw a pool of quicksand take down a heifer—like it was nothing more than a soda cracker," another commented.

"Cheese and crackers," the first replied.

Lilly sucked in her breath and held it. Her sweetheart was going to drown before her eyes, but for the life of her, she couldn't turn away.

Armina strained against the murky water, nearly losing her slippery grasp on the living chain that kept her safe.

After several thwarted attempts, Paul clutched the branch and hung on. The chain began to inch him forward. Emitting a huge glop of a sound, the quicksand gave up its prey. Paul was hauled to the bank. His lungs heaved for air as his body rested on a matted carpet of prickly catbrier and creeping three-toothed cinquefoil. Tattered and torn, he'd lost the waders, his socks, and his glasses, but he was alive.

Tears of thankfulness shimmered in Lilly's eyes as she hurried to his side. Gathering her skirts around her, she knelt beside Paul and wiped grit from his face with the embroidered hankie from her pocket. His eyes were even greener when seen without his spectacles.

Her heart shifted for the barest moment as a pair of mesmerizing blue eyes replaced the green ones before her. She shook her head to clear her vision. Why would she be thinking of another man, a veritable stranger, at a time like this?

"Oh, Paul, I'm so sorry."

Stunned, he lay there for a long moment, gasping and spitting up brackish fluid. Finally he found his voice. "Darling Lilly, Boston is looking really good right now."

It was nearly suppertime before Lilly had Aunt Orie settled in the clinic's back room. The poor old woman sounded worse than Paul had when he coughed up sand and creek water. Armina flitted around like a bird out of the nest. She rearranged the pillows behind her aunt's back, raised, then lowered the window, added a blanket, then decided it wasn't needed. The two babies slept at Aunt Orie's feet, exhausted from the excitement of the day.

"After a night to get acclimated, we'll start her treatment," Paul said, peering nearsightedly at the patient. He was dapper as always, having found a change of clothes and dry shoes among his things in the undamaged wing of the boarding-house. All he lacked was his prescription spectacles.

A light knock at the door caused them all to turn. Myrtie and two ladies Lilly recognized from church stood at the threshold.

Aunt Orie raised a trembling hand in greeting. "Myrtie," she said, "it's been ages."

Myrtie went to the bedside. She smoothed wispy strands of hair from Orie's forehead. "Tell us what you need. We're here for you."

"Rest," Orie managed to say. "Just rest."

"How about us ladies stay with Orie for a while?" Myrtie asked, looking first at Lilly and Paul and then at Armina. "Ain't no reason you young folks shouldn't go to the fish fry. After the happenings around here today, you all could use a little fun."

Lilly watched Armina closely. She wondered how long it had been since the girl had had anything resembling fun.

"I wish you'd go, Mina," Aunt Orie whispered. "It'd do me good to think on it. These ladies are my friends from long ago."

Confusion clouded Armina's features. "I could take the babies."

"You'll do no such thing," Myrtie said. "We'll watch these young'uns."

"We could go for just a minute maybe," Armina agreed.

Myrtie removed her bonnet and unpacked the valise she'd brought along. She put a stack of cotton fleece diapers, a shaker of talcum powder, and a small tub of Vaseline on a side table. Matter-of-factly, she shook out an apron and tied it around her waist. "That's settled then. You young folks go along. We'll be fine."

CHAPTER 21

TERN STILL BALANCED a dinner plate and a full cup of coffee as he took a seat at a sawhorse table. The community supper was in full swing. Landis Blair manned the huge iron skillet suspended over an open fire while various women ladled side dishes from an abundant supply.

Tern felt a little guilty for not bringing anything. He could have picked up a couple loaves of light bread or something from the company store. He hadn't intended to come, but Mrs. DeWitt was busy putting her kitchen to rights following the storm. There'd be no supper at the boardinghouse. A man had to eat. He was bushed after a day repairing roofs and glazing windowpanes. It wasn't too bad, though. Only three buildings were a total loss, and half a dozen others needed patching, like Lilly's place, where the roof was rolled up like a scroll. He and Elbows and another guy had put it to rights. When the other men moved on, he'd stayed to rehang the door, which he found in the backyard of the James place. It was crazy how the wind had taken the door but left the screen.

He forked up a bite of the best coleslaw he'd ever tasted and considered what a mistake that had been—being there by himself with even the essence of Lilly. It reminded him of the first time he'd gone into the kitchen after his mother died. There was her apron on a peg behind the door, there the shoes she wore to the garden, there the sweet-potato vine she'd started in a fruit jar, winding lushly down the window. He remembered taking the fruit jar from the sill and hurling it against the wall. The crumpled vine had lain on the floor like a silent reproach.

Once the doors were secure, he'd gone inside Lilly's house to open the windows and find a doorstop. Without the benefit of fresh air and sunshine, mold would soon take over. The room was stripped. He supposed Mrs. James had come for Lilly's things. Still, he could feel Lilly's presence, and he couldn't help but linger for a moment. He wished he were a praying man. Maybe that would give him some comfort.

"Father God, maybe You could give me just a little something to ease the ache in my chest," he'd started reverently, the words choking like dry dust in his throat. Why would God answer such a selfish request? Besides, it had been too long. Too long? It hadn't ever been. He supposed he'd never prayed. Not even standing beside his mother's grave when the preacher exhorted them to turn to the Lord in their time of need. He'd turned, all right—turned and walked away.

The window by the door was swollen shut. He'd struck the frame several times with the heel of his hand and shoved it open. The doorstop was just inside the door. It had some sort of fancy frilly covering that was soaked through, but the sun would dry it. He propped the door and stood on the stone stoop wondering where to go next—maybe he should check out Number 4, see if it was flooded. He hoped not.

A bit of something caught his eye. A ribbon—a long white ribbon rippled breezily from the wind-whipped snowball bush beside the porch. Tern retrieved it. It was Lilly's; he was sure of it. That day in the store when he'd first come face-to-face with her, her hair had been caught up with a white ribbon. He'd looped the length of silk around his fingers, making a tight package, before he slipped the tiny bit of comfort into his jacket pocket.

A woman with a big bowl of good-looking potato salad brought him back to the present. "Don't mind if I do," he said as she spooned a dollop onto his plate.

Elbows jostled him as he slid onto the bench. "So, Joe, did ye check out Number 4?" he asked around a mouthful.

"Not yet," Tern said, scooting over to give room. He couldn't believe he was getting used to the aggravating banty rooster of a man. Just went to show . . .

Elbows bit into a hunk of corn bread. Butter greased his chin. "Think we'll be working it tomorrow?" he asked.

Tern surveyed the sky. The setting sun lit up the horizon with a blaze of color. "Red sky at night . . ."

"Sailors' delight," Elbows chimed in, punctuating his every word with his fork. Flakes of fish dropped like snow onto his shirtfront. "Red sky in morning, sailors take warning. Say, did you find that little lady's door?"

Tern's eyes followed the direction of Elbows's pointing fork and saw Lilly Gray just a stone's throw distant. He thought Mr. James said she'd gone off with a party of men to help some real sick woman. But there she was with Paul Hamilton. He looked different somehow, but Tern couldn't put his finger on what the difference was.

"You hear what happened over to Swampy?" Elbows asked.

Tern forced himself to keep his interest on his plate. Someone had served pickled beets, not a favorite, but he ate them anyway. "Uh, no. That's that polluted creek everyone talks about, right?"

"Yeah, years of mining upstream took a toll on old Swampy. When I was a boy, you could seine there all day and never run out of fish. It was a black bear's haven."

Tern bit into a beet. The tart taste made his eyes water. "So what happened?"

"The way I heard it, the doc there and that other doc and Ned Tippen and some other fellows were bringing Mrs. Eldridge—do you know of her? She's the heftiest woman you ever seen—down the mountain to the clinic. Anyways, the whole company got caught up in quicksand. I heard they had to hitch a horse to Mrs. Eldridge and drag her out of the creek. I knowed her husband—used to work with him. God rest his soul. They're good folks."

Tern nodded. He was sure they were. But it was becoming impossible to keep his eyes off Lilly and looking at her sideways was causing a crick in his neck.

"Say, I'm going for a piece of pie. You want some?" Elbows stood and stacked Tern's empty plate on top of his. "I seen apple, blueberry, and chocolate."

"No, I'm good," Tern said. He was glad to be rid of the man.

The music started up before Elbows was halfway to the pie table. Stanley James tuned a fiddle, Ned Tippen brought out a battered dulcimer, and Darrell Tippen balanced a washboard between his knees. *This should be interesting,* Tern thought.

He was about to make his getaway when a girl positioned herself right in front of him.

"I know you. You're the one that helped save my brother from our crazy cow, Bossy." She pointed at his chest. "You got beet juice on your shirt."

Tern blotted the spots with a handkerchief. He was no better than Elbows.

"You want to dance?" she asked.

Tern recognized the indomitable Timmy when he bounced up behind his sister.

"Mommy's looking for you," he said with a tug on her pigtail.

"Can't you see I'm busy? Go away or I'll swat you one."

Timmy dodged her hand. "I'm just trying to keep you out of trouble."

"A likely story, Timmy. Go eat some pie."

"Pie? I didn't know there was pie! I'll be right back."

"That's the trouble," the girl said. "He always comes back."

Tern felt like he'd been attacked by a swarm of mosquitoes. What was the girl's name? Janie? June? It was something with a *J*.

"So do you?"

"I'm sorry. What was the question?"

"Do you want to dance?"

Tern shook his handkerchief like he was expecting the bloodred spots would fall to the ground. All he'd managed to do was spread the beet stains and soil his handkerchief. Yeah, that's what he'd do—go dancing with a girl. Not like that would call attention to himself. "I don't think so. But thanks for asking."

"I reckon you're just going to give up without so much as trying."

"Excuse me?"

The girl stood on tiptoe and whispered, "I saw you looking at Doc Corbett and I saw her looking back at you."

Tern looked around as if for help. He had to get out of this conversation. "Young lady, the doctor has a gentleman friend."

"I know, but he ain't right for her."

"And why is this any of your business?" Tern figured he'd finally lost what was left of his mind to be exchanging words with a girl who couldn't be more than ten years old.

"Don't you see, if she goes off and marries him, she won't never come back here. That would be a terrible thing."

Timmy ran up with a slab of chocolate pie balanced on his palm. A rim of meringue mustached his upper lip. "Mommy says you'd better get yourself over to her right now, missy. She says if you don't mind her, I get to cut a switch." He spread his hands wide apart, making his dessert wobble. "And I'm gonna cut a big one—with thorns."

"You're silly as a goose, Timmy. Mommy wouldn't switch me with a thorn tree."

Timmy's pie plopped to the ground. "Oh, shucks," he said. "I've got to get another piece."

His sister shook her head in a see-what-I-have-to-put-up-with? motion and turned her attention back to Tern. "You wait right here."

Before Tern could take in what she was doing, the Blair girl was towing Lilly his way. Now he wanted to dance. He wanted it in the worst way.

The band struck up an old-fashioned waltz, and next thing Tern knew, Lilly Gray was in his arms.

"Mr. Repp," she said, "we meet again."

"Where's your friend?" Tern asked. He could have bitten his tongue.

"Paul lost his spectacles today and now he has a raging headache. He excused himself."

"Too bad," Tern said, guiding Lilly onto the patch of ground that comprised the dance floor.

He was careful to keep a proper distance between them

and to hold her lightly. She followed his steps easily. He wished the dance would go on forever.

"You've obviously danced the waltz before, Mr. Repp."

"Please, call me Tern."

"Pardon me?" Lilly said quizzically.

"Joe, I said. Please call me Joe."

Lilly cocked her head and looked at him with a puzzled expression. "There's something very familiar about you, Joe."

"I look just like a thousand other guys—"

"Perhaps not a thousand," she demurred. "Are you from here?"

He didn't have to think about the answer. He was used to deferring attention from himself. "I've lived a lot of places. How about you? Is Kentucky your home?"

Her cool gray eyes studied his. "Yes," she said, "for now. My family lives in Breathitt County. Are you familiar with the area?"

She was getting too close, but he couldn't bring himself to lie outright to her. He could feel sweat beading his forehead. "Vaguely," he said.

As the strains of the waltz faded, Turnip Tippen cut in, claiming Lilly for the next dance. Feeling like a coward, Tern took the opportunity to bow out. He could feel Lilly Corbett's stormy gray eyes on his back as he walked away.

Once out of sight, he blotted sweat from his forehead with his beet-stained handkerchief. Man, he'd almost spilled his guts. What relief it would have been to simply tell Lilly everything. He was nearly sure she wouldn't betray him, but he couldn't take the chance. One word could give him away. If the men he worked with found out who he was, he'd be branded as a scab. No way would they understand that he was there to make their jobs safer and more secure. All they would see was that he was a pretty good liar. They'd likely beat the tar out of him or worse. He needed to pull up stakes soon and get out while the getting was good.

❧

Over Turnip Tippen's meaty shoulder, Lilly watched Joe Repp walk away. Her mind was awhirl and it wasn't from Mr. Tippen's fancy footwork. As soon as Jenny Blair deposited her into Mr. Repp's arms, she'd begun to enjoy the dance. Perhaps she had enjoyed it a little too much.

When the tune ended, Lilly fanned her face in a mock of female distress. "I believe I must sit this next one out."

In a gentlemanly way she didn't expect, Turnip Tippen took her elbow and led her to the bench seat beside the schoolhouse. Within seconds, several ladies were waving church fans in her face. She accepted a cold glass of lemonade.

"Are ye ill, Doc?" Tillie Tippen asked.

"Goodness, no," she replied, hoping Mr. Repp was still about. She twisted the pearl ring on her finger, the antique ring so lovingly put there by Paul. "I'm sure a night's sleep will put me to rights. It's been a long day for all of us."

That set the ladies to talking about the strangeness of a day that began with mayhem and ended with a dance. "It's for certain sure," one lady said, "our kind of folk bear up under what can't be set aside."

One by one the ladies left, leaving Lilly alone on the bench. She sipped her drink, relishing the sweet-tart taste of it. She saw Armina standing in front of the small band, swaying to the beat of the music. A young man stepped in front of her, obviously asking for a dance partner. Armina shook her head. *Too bad,* Lilly thought. *It would do the girl a world of good to have some fun.*

Fun? How long had it been since Lilly had fun? It seemed she'd left silliness behind her when she'd left her home place for Lexington. While medical school was interesting and challenging, it most decidedly was not fun. She had pleasant times with Paul. He could be a funny man, but he was as serious as she was.

Thinking about Paul made her think about his mother. Lilly's brow furrowed with the beginnings of a tension headache. Why would Paul's mother think Lilly's family would come to Boston for the wedding?

"Dr. Corbett?"

So deep in her own thoughts, Lilly was surprised to see Mrs. Blair standing before her. "Can I beg a favor?" the woman said.

Lilly patted the bench beside her. "Certainly."

Mrs. Blair took an envelope from her pocket, then took a seat. She removed a letter and handed it to Lilly. "This is from my sister in Virginia. It came in the mail yesterday. I recognize her signature, but I can't read the rest. I didn't want to ask Jenny to read it, for it might be bad news."

"'Dearest Sister,'" Lilly read in a low voice and then continued through the closure. When she finished, she put her arm around Mrs. Blair. "I'm so sorry."

Mrs. Blair tapped her lips with two fingers as if holding back a sob. "Ah, Mommy has been sick a long time. I kept thinking I should get somebody to help me pen a letter to her, you know? Something personal from me to Mommy." Her shoulders shook but she held back tears. "It would have given her something to hold on to."

"Should I find your husband?"

"No, I kindly want to think on this by my own self for a while," Mrs. Blair said as she stood and slid the letter back into her pocket. "I ain't quite ready to share it just yet."

How sad, Lilly thought as she watched Mrs. Blair walk away. It reminded her of Lynn, the woman who had served her sumac-ade after Lilly tended to her toddler's ears. She had noticed that many of the women she cared for here in Skip Rock could not read. Their children fared better because of the schoolhouse behind her, but it seemed as if it was too late for the Mrs. Blairs of the community.

Lilly placed her empty glass on the bench, then stood and regarded the brick school building. Curious, she turned the doorknob and stepped inside. Chalk dust and the smell of well-oiled floorboards reminded her of her own school days. She walked between two rows of double desks, dodging the potbellied stove smack in the middle of the room, to the heavy oak teacher's desk.

A dictionary, several manila file folders, a ruler, a compass, and a wooden paddle were neatly displayed on the desktop. Lilly lightly slapped the palm of one hand with the paddle. She'd never felt the swing of it, but oh, she'd pitied the boys. Neatly arranging the paddle, she picked up the teacher's handbell. She rang it lightly as if calling a room full of students to order.

A picture of George Washington hung from a nail in the wall. Lilly studied a selection of penmanship papers, which were displayed along the top of the blackboard. She looked for Timmy's and smiled when she saw he'd erased his *T* so many times that he'd nearly worn a hole in the paper. Jenny's, on the other hand, was letter perfect.

School was in session from late summer to Christmas. Although the coal camp children could have attended year-round, the students who lived outside the town wouldn't be able to get to school in really inclement weather.

Suddenly, she was weary. She hadn't stopped since being awakened by the storm.

The door cracked open and Armina slipped in. "I thought I seen you come in here," she said.

"Are you ready to go? We should check on Aunt Orie."

"One of the ladies fixed a plate for me to carry to her," Armina said, holding it out for Lilly to see. "Folks are nice hereabouts."

Lilly held the door for her. "Yes, they certainly are. Give me a second to take my lemonade glass back to the table."

"Oh, I did that already," Armina said, leading the way to

the footpath. "Say, who was that fellow you were dancing with? He was right easy on the eyes."

Amused, Lilly couldn't resist a tease. "That was Ned's uncle Turnip. He's quite the dancer."

"You know full well I ain't asking about anybody what's named after a vegetable. I'm talking about that tall, good-looking man. He don't act like he's from these parts. Plus, why ain't you dancing with your doctor friend?"

"Dr. Hamilton is resting after the vigor of his day. You know, I should take him a plate also."

"He can have this one. Aunt Orie can't eat like this anymore. I just didn't want to offend the ladies by not accepting it."

"You're a kind soul, Armina. Did you do any dancing? I noticed you were enjoying the music."

"That was pretty—that dulcimer music. Say, what happened to Ned's wooden leg?"

Lilly smiled to herself. Armina was paying attention to Ned. She didn't know whether to be happy for him or to warn him to flee. Of course, it wasn't up to her whether they became sweethearts or not. Love found its own course.

She relayed Ned's accident as well as Paul's offer. Somehow she knew Armina would keep her confidence—she wasn't the type to blather.

Midway to the clinic, Armina caught her elbow and brought her to a stop. "Look," she said, pointing to a meadow where thousands of fireflies displayed their diminutive lights in the dusk of the evening. "Don't that make you sad?"

"It takes me back to my childhood and evenings spent

catching fireflies in a fruit jar. I kept them on my bedside table. What about them makes you sad?"

"They're just so hopeful—you know? Spending what little time they have on earth pining for something they probably ain't going to get." Armina held the dinner plate close to her chest. A light breeze ruffled her long skirt. "There's something mournful about this time of day. Aunt Orie calls it the gloaming, when the sun's setting and everything gets real still—makes you lonesome like. Was you ever setting on the porch on a night like this and heard a train's low whistle or the coo of a mourning dove? It'll flat out give you the shivers."

"Goodness, Armina, you should write poetry."

"Like anybody would ever read it . . ."

Lilly touched her lightly on the arm. "I would read it."

They walked on in companionable silence. They were nearly to the clinic before Armina spoke again. "So you never answered my question. Who was that fellow?"

"You know, Armina, I don't really know anything about him."

"Maybe you should try finding out. You looked like you was made to be in his arms."

"Armina—"

"Don't fret. I ain't gonna say anything to anybody, but you don't want to spend your life like them lightning bugs, flitting all around looking for love when it's right in your face."

Lilly was flustered by Armina's suppositions. How ridiculous, thinking she would fall for a man because of his looks.

After all, Paul was handsome in his way and successful. Besides, Lilly was not the type to go from one man to another.

Truthfully, she had not been attracted to Paul when they'd first met. As a beginning student, she had no social life to speak of, and besides that, she found Paul brilliantly intimidating. She often felt he was talking down to her.

When he began to single her out, first for study sessions and then as an autopsy partner, she was guarded. As she got to know him, she learned he really was as smart as he seemed, and he was also a kind and gentle man.

The engagement ring on her finger slid out of position. It needed sizing. "Paul is my best friend," she felt compelled to say. "Don't you think it is important to be best friends with the person you marry?"

"I don't know. I've never had a best friend. I figured I'd know the right one when I saw him."

Lilly couldn't resist the chance to turn the tables. "Have you seen the right one, Armina?"

With one hand, Armina held Aunt Orie's supper; with the other, she caught a lightning bug and let it walk the plank of her thumb. Its tiny lantern flashed brightly before it flew away. "I'm still figuring," she said. "It's a right smart harder to discern than I thought it would be."

CHAPTER 22

LIGHT SHONE from one window of the clinic. Lilly caught a glimpse of Paul bending over the sickbed.

Beside her, Armina caught her breath. "Do you think Aunt Orie's taken a turn? Why else would that doctor be there with her?"

"I expect Dr. Hamilton is just checking on her," Lilly said. Hiding her own surprise, she opened the door.

Armina rushed past her. "I knowed I shouldn't have left her!"

Aunt Orie rested on the operative bed. It was up as high as it would go. A metal rolling table was pushed up to the side. Wearing gloves, Paul was attaching a long needle to a hypodermic syringe. A surgical packet wrapped in heavy brown paper lay open on the cart.

Myrtie James, her face as lined as tablet paper, stood across the bed from the doctor. She held Aunt Orie's hand.

"Stay back!" Paul barked.

Armina stopped, but her narrowed eyes and jutted chin threatened a coming storm. "Who said you could go operating on her without me being here?" She put a hand to her heart. "She looks like she's already passed on."

"She's mildly sedated. Young lady, you need to wait outside."

"But I don't understand. What are you fixing to do?"

"I'll explain to you when I've finished. Mrs. James—if you'd escort Miss Eldridge out."

Myrtie wrapped an arm around Armina's waist. "Let's take this plate to the front room," she said, peeking under the wax paper cover. "What did you bring her?"

"Paul, what happened? What are you doing?" Lilly couldn't keep the exasperation from her voice. He had no right to treat her patient without her present, and he had no right to speak harshly to Armina.

"Her heart has been compromised. I've got to drain some fluid or she's not going to make it through the night," Paul said matter-of-factly while undoing the packet of sterile surgical drapes. "How was the shindig? Did I miss anything?"

Lilly was flummoxed. Paul might as well have been dressing a side of beef. She opened her mouth to correct him but didn't. This was not the first time she'd accompanied him in a surgical suite, nor the first time she'd witnessed his change of personality. Paul didn't like to immerse himself in his patient's world. He was all business, and he was the best. Aunt Orie was blessed to have him, and so was she.

Hours later, Lilly woke with a start. She'd fallen asleep in a chair at Aunt Orie's bedside. Armina sat across from her, alert as an owl at midnight.

"She's turned a corner," Armina said. "She ain't slept this sound in a coon's age."

Lilly put two fingers to one side of Aunt Orie's throat to check her pulse. "I'm sorry you were so frightened earlier, Armina."

"It was the shock—that's all. I appreciate everything Dr. Hamilton has done for Aunt Orie."

Lilly looked around the small room. "Where is Paul?"

"You were so beat, you fell asleep setting up," Armina said, rubbing her eyes. "The doctor is in yonder sleeping on a gurney, and Ned Tippen is a-setting on the porch." She barked out a laugh. "I reckon they don't think you and me can take care of her without their aid."

As if he'd been summoned, Ned appeared in the doorway to the surgery. "There's a fellow on the porch, says you told him to fetch you when his wife's time was near."

Lilly searched her memory for who it might be and remembered the couple who lived in the meadow, Hiram and Lynn. She could nearly taste the too-sweet sumac-ade.

Paul entered the room. How he could look so together after the day they'd had puzzled Lilly as she neatened her hair with pins and combs.

"What now?" he said.

"Want to help deliver a baby?" she asked, pulling two walking sticks from a tin umbrella stand.

Paul threw his hands up. "Why not? It will be the perfect ending to a perfect day."

"Will you be okay, Armina?" Lilly asked. "I might be gone awhile."

Ned slid into the chair Lilly had just left. "I'll stay."

Armina cut her eyes sideways at him. "I reckon we'll be fine—fine as frog's hair."

The hardwood forest was vastly different at night. A breeze whispered hauntingly through the treetops, and the ground murmured with the sound of small creatures scurrying about in the dead leaves and fallen branches. A high yellow moon beamed through the interstices of the towering trees, but it was not enough light for a person to note landmarks. One tree looked like another in the near pitch dark. One could get very lost very quickly in such a place, Lilly thought. She marveled at Hiram's sure-footed progress through the woods.

"We seen a panther here once," the man said, pointing with his ever-present shotgun. "Black as the ace of spades. Hit was crouched yonder on that high boulder. I drawed a bead, but I couldn't pull the trigger—thing was just too purty for killing."

Paul nudged Lilly with his elbow. She knew he didn't believe Hiram's story. "How did you manage to keep the wildcat from jumping on you?"

"Throwed a rock," Hiram said. "Thing took off like Snyder's hound. We ain't ever spied it again."

It was daybreak before Lilly had the newborn and her mama tucked safely in bed. Hiram had constructed a bed frame to hold the corn-shuck mattress since Lilly had last visited. He ran his hand over the headboard, proud as punch, as he told Lilly of his handiwork. Lilly was proud of him. He was trying very hard to provide for his family.

Paul turned down Hiram's offer to see them back to the footpath that would lead them to Skip Rock. "Thank you, but we'll manage quite well," he said, striding across the yard as if Lilly was going to follow in his wake.

Lilly lingered on the porch. There was an art to taking your leave—Paul just didn't know that. "Take good care of Lynn and the children, and fetch me if need be."

"I aim to pay you for your service," Hiram said.

"No need to think of that today. Maybe bring me some sumac grapes next time you have some."

Cleve pulled on his daddy's arm.

Hiram bent over to allow the boy to whisper something in his ear. "That's a good idea, boy. Go fetch one."

Lilly was nonplussed. She supposed she would have to carry something like a chicken tied up by the feet or half a bushel of shelled corn back to town.

The boy slid under the porch and came back with a coon-hound puppy.

Lilly rubbed the little fellow's head. "Oh, my, I couldn't take the children's pet."

"Take him," Cleve said. "We got more."

The puppy's fur was silky smooth, his eyes brown and sparkly, but his belly was as round and tight as a pumpkin.

"He ain't been wormed yet," Hiram explained.

"Lilly?" Paul called from across the yard.

"Just a minute, Paul," Lilly said, holding up her index finger. "What do you use for worming?"

"A drench of linseed and spirits of turpentine should turn the trick," Hiram said, depositing the wiggling pup in Lilly's arms. "Ye can repeat in three days if need be, but I ain't never had to do it but once."

"Thank you. He's a beauty." Lilly nuzzled the top of the dog's head with her chin. "May I have permission to name him Cleve?"

"That'd be all right," Cleve said with a grin.

"What do you say to the lady, Son?"

"Please and thank you, ma'am."

"You're welcome, Cleve. Come and visit your namesake anytime you want."

Paul was out of his element. He led Lilly around in circles for half an hour—Lilly biting her tongue, not wanting to penetrate the hot air of his pride—before she heard the splashing spring and spied the tulip poplar. "It's a straight shot from here, Paul," she said, shifting the heavy pup from one arm to the other. The puppy kissed her chin with his petal-soft tongue.

"You know that thing's full of parasites," Paul said.

"An easy fix. Isn't he the sweetest?"

"You're not thinking of keeping the dog? What would we do with him in Boston?"

"I would like nothing better than to keep this puppy, but I won't."

The dog squirmed in her arms. She set him on the forest floor and let him explore for a moment. He tried to climb over a fallen limb but rolled over instead, lying like a turtle on its back. Laughing, Lilly scooped him up. "I know the perfect home for you, Cleve," she said as they continued on. "Mr. James is going to love you."

On the outskirts of Skip Rock, Paul slowed his step. "What's on your agenda, Lilly?"

"Agenda?"

"Any other patients at death's door? Any other women due to give birth?"

"No, nothing pressing. Why do you ask?"

"I'm taking the first train out tomorrow, darling girl." He caught her free hand and brought it to his lips. "I've taken the liberty of securing a ticket for you also."

"But . . . but, Paul," she stammered, "I thought you would stay longer."

Dropping her hand, he pinched the bridge of his nose between his thumb and index finger. "I can't continue without the proper spectacles. Besides, I think I've had quite enough of Skip Rock."

Her head whirled. She needed time to think. "I can't just leave on a whim, Paul."

"Hardly a whim, Lilly. I am to be your husband, after all."

She rested the puppy in the crook of one elbow and laid her free hand against Paul's cheek. "I know, but who will care for these people? I can't leave until the coal company provides a replacement doctor for the clinic."

"The clinic is little more than a first-aid station."

Lilly's anger boiled over. "How can you say that after you saw what I did for Darrell Tippen? After Aunt Orie?"

"I'm not saying you are a poor doctor, sweetheart—far from it. I am saying you're wasting your considerable talent in this backward, forsaken place."

"I've told you my history. I was raised in a place much like this. I am one of these people."

He circled her with his arms. She didn't resist, but she didn't put the puppy down; he provided a needed barrier at the moment.

"But you rose above. You are no longer a part of them." Paul leaned back so he could tip her chin. "You belong in Boston with me." He chuckled as if he was trying to lighten the moment. "Besides, the sooner you come, the sooner you can help Mother with the plans for the wedding. It's going to be quite the social event."

Lilly stiffened in his arms. "Were you not listening when I explained about the need for my family to have the ceremony in Lexington? My aunt Alice has her heart set on it."

"A small detail," he said, "one we can work out with

Mother. But first things first. I'm sure Mrs. James will pack your things . . . and, let's see . . . we'll need to leave for the depot at six in the morning. I'll have Ned procure a carriage."

Lilly broke from his embrace. She had to stop this runaway train. "Paul, I will not leave these folks in a lurch. I can't think you would expect me to do such an unprofessional thing. I have a letter of intent already prepared to post to Dr. Coldiron. It states I will finish my time here as planned."

They'd reached the clinic door. She walked up the steps, but he didn't follow.

"Why, Lilly, I thought you'd be more than happy to leave. I don't understand."

Setting the puppy across the threshold, she turned to face him. "I'm not sure that I understand myself."

"Ah, well, I shouldn't have pushed you. We have plenty of time. I only want what's best for you, dear."

She was touched by his sweetness and reminded of why she'd agreed to marry him in the first place. "It will all work out; you'll see. Now go and pack; then come back to take the noon meal with me."

He held his arms up in mock surrender. "Between the storm and the quicksand, I have little to pack, not to mention I'm leaving my dearest behind."

Lilly threw him a kiss. "I'll see you at lunch. We'll have some time together, I promise."

Inside the clinic, Lilly sank into the rolling chair, folded her arms on the desktop, and rested her head on them. She'd never been so weary, not even following long days and nights on duty during medical school. Like liquid lead, the tiredness seeped into her very bones. She needed to check on Aunt Orie, but her legs refused to lift her from the chair. Perhaps she could catch a quick nap where she sat.

But her mind was in too much turmoil to let her rest. It should be easy to leave this place like she had planned. What was keeping her here? And why did every decision seem so daunting? She twisted the ring on her finger as a sinking feeling settled in her chest. Paul would not be happy, but she wasn't ready to leave, not even in September. This place, these people, had kidnapped her heart much like she had been abducted so many years ago.

Her mind hiccuped on the word *abducted*. As a girl she'd liked learning the meanings of words, and she would often repeat a new one many times a day. In medical terms, *abduct* meant to carry away from the median. That's what had happened to her when she was kidnapped. She had been carried away from the median, the nucleus—her family.

Irritated, she chastised herself. Why was she obsessing on that worn-out theme again? It was years ago, and no lasting harm had come to her, after all.

She'd best be thinking about how she would explain her change of heart to Paul. The very thought filled her with dread.

The puppy growled and tugged on one of her shoelaces. Lilly laughed despite herself. She'd check on her patient in the surgery room, then carry her furry gift to the Jameses. Sleep would have to wait.

CHAPTER 23

A COMMOTION IN THE HALLWAY of Mrs. DeWitt's boarding-house disturbed Tern Still's Thursday morning slumber. He groaned and threw an arm across his eyes. Since the storm of day before yesterday, there had been no peace in the house. With one wing closed down, many of the men were double- and triple-bunking. There was a constant coming and going up and down the stairs and in and out the doors. Despite Mrs. DeWitt's request, he had refused to go halves with his room. All he needed to finish him off was the good Dr. Hamilton sharing his space. That wasn't about to happen. He thought the doctor was sleeping in the pantry off the hastily repaired kitchen, but he didn't much care. Since she'd accepted his extra five-dollar bill, Tern didn't think his landlady did either.

Elbows had been all abuzz at supper last night. The man blathered like a schoolgirl, and for once Tern had been glad of it. If Elbows's wagging tongue was telling the truth and not just a version of it, Paul Hamilton was leaving on the first train this morning. Tern fumbled on the bedside table for his pocket watch. He flipped the case open—6:30 a.m. Chances were the man had already left for the depot.

He scrubbed his face with his hands before throwing his legs over the side of the bed. Outside the door, he found the usual bucket of hot water waiting. He splashed a quart of it into the china basin and poured the rest into the matching pitcher. He lathered soap and began a shave. In the mirror he saw his face stretched in a rictus. He looked like he'd been dead three days—kind of felt like it too.

The blade of the straight razor swept neat as a scythe in overlapping strips across his cheeks and chin. Finished with his shave, he wet his toothbrush before pouring a bit of tooth powder into the cup of his palm. The familiar rhythm of his morning rituals soothed him.

There was only one clean shirt in his clothes cupboard. The rest were stuffed in the laundry bag, with the arm of one hanging out of the sack. It was his favorite white one—well broken in and softer for the wear. He tugged it free. Man— he'd forgotten about the beet juice stain. He should wash it out; no telling when Mrs. DeWitt's hired girl would get around to it. He could soak it in the basin, but why not take it with him? He aimed to go to the river for a break from his hectic week.

Dressed, he cut a sliver of soap from a new bar, stuck it in the stained shirt's pocket, rolled the shirt in a ball, and put it in his saddlebag. Problem solved, he was out the door and to the kitchen for a quick bite.

❧

Lilly stood in the train station and waved until her arm ached. Paul leaned out the window by his seat and waved back until finally distance swallowed him up. He had been unexpectedly blasé about her staying on in Skip Rock for the near future. "You're just betwixt and between, darling Lilly," he'd said when she broached the subject. "You'll get your fill soon enough. Boston will be waiting." Coward that she was, she hadn't pressed the issue. Besides, maybe he was right. Maybe she'd feel differently come winter.

She had always loved a depot. The train's warning whistle, the screech of giant brakes, the smoke and cinders flying, folks arriving and departing—the ladies dressed in their finest and the men hailing porters to load luggage on carts.

"All aboard!"

She heard the call from another track. *All aboard*—those might just be the most exciting words ever. Just for fun, and to prolong the experience, she bought a paper cone of salted peanuts from a vendor to share with Ned. They found an empty bench and sat knee to knee.

"Thanks for bringing us, Ned. It was good of you."

"Sure, I was glad to do it."

"I've not had a chance to ask you about Paul's offer to fit you with a prosthetic leg. Have you been thinking about it?" She pinched a hot peanut from the bag.

"Haven't thought of much else." Ned rattled the peanuts in the container. "Funny thing—I resented that peg leg . . . until it was gone. Now I miss it in the worst way." He lifted one of the crutches lying against the bench beside him and then let it go. It fell against the other crutch with a soft thunk. "These things are killers. They slow me down something terrible."

"Paul's the best, Ned. He would take good care of you."

"I reckon you miss him already." Ned shook peanuts into his palm.

Did she? Miss him? Lilly pondered. Well, not yet. He'd only been gone a moment, and he had seemed so out of place in Skip Rock that she felt relieved to have him gone. She was sure that given a little time, longing for him would overtake her. She twisted the pearl ring on her finger. Yes, she was sure she would miss him soon enough.

A family walked in front of them. A girl clutched her hat to her head in the wake of a departing train. The straw hat was trimmed with a blue silk ribbon. The girl reminded Lilly of herself when she was younger. She liked fashion even then.

"See that girl?"

"The one with the hat?"

"I had a hat like that when I was eleven. My aunt Alice sent it to me to wear on a train trip." Try as she might, Lilly couldn't help comparing her own eleven-year-old self with the pretty young girl in the ribbon-bedecked hat. She'd been dressed for a trip to Lexington, the first time her mother had allowed her to travel alone. She remembered it was a hot summer day and she'd gone searching for a dog she thought was in distress, disobeying the instructions she'd been given to stay put. She'd found the dog and the meanest man she ever hoped to meet.

The man, Isa Still, kidnapped her that summer day and kept her locked up in a room made of tin. Even now she could feel the heat of that place; funny how it made her shiver. Mr. Still had a son who had rescued Lilly. She might not be sitting here today if not for that boy.

She popped a peanut into her mouth, savoring the salty taste. She remembered the boy's odd name, Tern, and his icy-blue eyes.

A tiny frisson of unease tiptoed up her spine. She had heard that name recently . . . and she had looked into those eyes.

"I bet you were pretty as a speckled pup under a red wagon in that hat," Ned said, leaning back and crossing his arms across his chest. "I wish I'd known you then, Cousin."

"It's probably a good thing you didn't." Lilly tossed the remaining nuts to a red squirrel scouting the perimeter of the platform. She was ever so glad for Ned's company, which kept her rooted in the present. "Can you imagine the trouble we would have gotten in?"

"Do you still have the hat?"

"No, it got lost."

"Huh," Ned said in that dismissive way men have. "Can I ask you something, Cuz?"

"Surely."

"Would Armina step out with me if I was to ask her?"

Lilly balled her fist and lightly punched Ned's shoulder. "Going to stick your head in the bear's mouth again, Ned?"

"I kindly like this bear. She's got enough of a growl about her to keep you on your toes. A spunky woman makes life interesting."

"Armina's interesting all right."

Ned kicked an errant peanut toward the scavenging squirrel. "So should I? Ask her?"

"I think you should bide your time and let Armina do the asking."

Ned stood and hopped about, picking up his crutches and seating them under his arms. "Sounds like a plan."

During the ride back to Skip Rock, they both fell quiet. Lilly was thankful for the silence, but should she tell Ned of her suspicion that Joe Repp was not who he purported to be? For she knew, as sure as she knew her own name, that he was Tern Still, the boy who'd rescued her many years ago. But how had he come to be in Skip Rock at the same time as she? Was he following her? Why would he? He'd never been less than a gentleman the few times she'd been in his presence.

"You seem a thousand miles away," Ned said finally as the wagon passed the turn to the river. "Anything you want to share?"

Lilly was reluctant to tell him what was really only a

suspicion. It was easier to let the cat out of the bag than to put it back in. "I'm just woolgathering, Ned. Would you mind to let me off here? What I need is a walk."

❧

At the river's edge, Tern shook out his white dress shirt and doused it in the cold water lapping at the sloping bank. The stains didn't fade much. Looked like it was going to take some labor—didn't everything? He worked soap into the stains and around the perspiration mark at the neck of the shirt. He couldn't bear a ring around the collar—a sure sign of slovenliness, as far as he was concerned. He rubbed and scrubbed with poor results. Man—he should have left it to Mrs. DeWitt. He was going to ruin it.

"My goodness, Mr. Repp," a soft voice from behind him said. "You are a man of many talents."

Shocked, he nearly pitched headfirst into the river. He didn't have to turn his face to know the speaker was Lilly. That voice was etched on his heart like a tune on an Edison gramophone cylinder.

"A man's work is never done," he said, chagrined.

"And a woman works from sun to sun."

Still crouched over his laundry, he looked at her over his shoulder. She wore a dress of lavender-blue and a funny little flowered hat perched like a nest in her lovely dark hair. He swallowed hard against the desire to take the combs from her hair and watch it fall.

"You know anything about beet stains?" he asked.

She looked at him oddly, as if he'd spoken in a foreign language. "My mother would say spread the wet shirt to dry in the sun. You could try that."

"Thank you." He carried the dripping wet shirt up the bank and draped it over a rock in a patch of sunlight.

"What a beautiful day for doing one's laundry," she said.

"I don't usually. It's part of room and board, but with all that's going on . . ."

Mercifully, his words sputtered out. Unfolding from his crouched position, he walked up the bank, keeping his distance but staying in her presence. It was enough for now.

"Are you always this serious, Mr. Repp?"

"It's just . . . Well, you caught me off guard. I wouldn't have thought there was another soul between me and town. It's so peaceful here, you know."

"Yes, I do." One finger at a time, Lilly removed short white gloves. "I was actually coming back from the train station. I had Ned drop me off here so I could walk the rest of the way. My mind has been so crowded the last few days that I needed a bit of a break."

"There's been a lot going on in Skip Rock; that's for sure." With the tip of his boot, Tern kicked at a pebble embedded in the dirt. He couldn't bear to look at her for longer than a second—he'd for sure give himself away. "So did Dr. Hamilton get off okay?" He hoped his voice sounded as nonchalant as he meant it to be.

"Poor Paul. I nearly got him killed twice over—first the

storm and then quicksand, of all things. Whoever thinks they'll be swallowed up by quicksand?"

"That's a rough one, all right."

"We were all so surprised, scurrying around like a bunch of ants, all our plans to bring Mrs. Eldridge safely to the clinic gone horribly awry. Oh, but you should have seen Armina—do you know her? Mrs. Eldridge's niece? The way she took charge was amazing. She was barking orders like Mr. James does. Funny thing is, all the men obeyed."

She stared at him in an appraising way as she talked. Her words were chatter, full of nothing, as if she were gentling a wild horse. He was suddenly uncomfortable in her presence.

She knew. He could see it in her eyes. She *knew*.

Tern's heart dropped. "How did you figure it out?"

"Mr. Still, you had a slight slip of the tongue at the dance. It didn't register at the moment, but today at the station, it came to me. I want to know why you are here in Skip Rock, Kentucky, of all places. I want to know if you are following me."

He took a step forward.

She put up her hand to stop him.

"I'll keep my distance," he said. "I don't want to scare you."

"I am most decidedly not afraid of you, Tern Still," she said, raising her chin and fixing him with a stare. "Oh, indeed I am not."

Giving credence to her words, she took a seat on a fallen log. A muskrat clambered down the bank at her back, startled by the human intrusion. He slid into the muddy water and paddled away, using his black, scaled tail as a rudder.

Tern wished he could paddle away too. Instead, he lifted his arms in supplication. "Would you give me a chance to explain myself? Do you remember me with any favor?"

She shook her head as if denying something she didn't want to hear. "It was all so long ago. I thought I'd put it behind me. Then I came here and the nightmares and strange fears started up again. Now I know why."

"The last thing I ever wanted was to hurt you, Lilly. I should have left here after I saw you that first time in the mine."

"Why didn't you?"

He raised his shoulders and let them drop. "I needed to be near you. You hold me in your sway. You wanted to forget the past, but I wanted to live in those memories of you. I've loved you for the longest time."

Two perfect tears spilled from her eyes. He'd have given anything to wipe them away; instead he dared to take a seat beside her on the fallen tree, careful to leave a space between them.

"I had my life all planned," she said. "And now . . ."

He leaned forward so that he could see her face. "I can't tell you why I'm in this particular place and working in these mines. But I'll be finished soon. I promise you I'll leave then. I'll go and never bother you again. All I need is to know you're happy." He tapped his knee with his fist, willing himself to be strong. "Well, that's not entirely true, but I'll make it work. You'll see."

She placed her hands on the rough bark of the fallen tree. He thought she was going to rise and walk away from him. He wouldn't blame her if she did.

"I hope you don't hate me," he said.

Lilly gathered her trembling hands in her lap and clasped them tightly. She took a deep breath and held it. Tern could feel the exhale pass his face, soft as a feather in the wind.

"I used to write your name on the covers of my Big Chief paper tablets," she said. "It drove my mother batty."

"I never said your name aloud. I didn't think I deserved to."

"I've often wondered about your family. I prayed no harm would come to any of you—or to your father."

"Ah, Lilly, how can you be so kind?"

She didn't answer for a minute, letting a certain peace settle over them. Finally she said, "I remember a boy who was very kind to me. Don't you remember that boy, Tern?"

He stood and walked to the water's edge. He couldn't bear her seeing the tears in his eyes. Selecting a small, flat rock, he skipped it across the surface of the river. It sank halfway home.

She came up beside him. The rock she flung leaped lightly through the water, leaving perfect ring after perfect ring all the way to the far bank.

"Man," he said, "you always were a challenge."

They both laughed then, but the laughter held a touch of sadness.

"Why do you use a false name?" she asked. "Are you in some kind of trouble?"

"I don't have any right to ask you this, Lilly, but would you trust me? Would you let me be just plain Joe Repp for a little while longer?"

She looked at him so guilelessly, so sweetly. He felt absolved.

"When we were children and I was captive in that little house high up in the trees, you rescued me. I trusted you then with my very life. I guess I can trust you now."

They stood so close he could have easily pulled her into an embrace. But he held back. He was not going to ask anything of her she wasn't ready or willing to give. He meant what he'd said—the only thing that mattered to him was her happiness.

The crack of a rifle broke the tenuous connection between them. The first shot was followed by a second and then a third. Faintly, they could hear the warning whistle.

"What could be happening?" Lilly asked. "I thought the mines were closed today."

"Yeah, they were supposed to be. Listen, you take Apache and ride back. That'll be quicker for you. Nobody will notice if you leave him tethered in that grove of trees by Mr. James's office. I'll fetch him later."

❧

Tern was right, Lilly thought as she looped Apache's reins over a low tree branch as close to the office as she could get without being seen. No one was looking her way. They were all rushing toward the portal of Number 4. The whistle continued to shriek like a banshee.

She saw Ned at the edge of the gathering, rifle in hand.

Heat rose to her face. Had he seen her at the shallows and then shot the gun to save her from embarrassment? Well, it mattered little now. Why had the whistle gone off? Who might be inside the mine? She tucked her hair up and smoothed her skirts.

"Ned," she said, touching his elbow to get his attention. "What has happened?"

"Oh, you're here. I hoped you'd hear the gun. I didn't know how far you might have wandered along the river." The emergency supply kit from the clinic was on the ground at his feet. "We'd better hurry on up there."

Ned pushed through the crowd. "Give way!" he shouted. "The doc's here."

Lilly was relieved to see Mr. James on this side of the portal. He waved her over. Dozens of miners milled around the site. The mine opening belched dust like a smoke signal.

"Somebody's in there," Mr. James said. "We don't know who—nor why. I need you and Ned to stand by."

He turned back to the men. "Everybody cue up in teams and see if we can figure out who's missing. Has anybody seen Joe Repp? More'n likely it's someone from his crew."

"I'm here, Stanley."

Lilly's heart skipped a beat. Her world was upside down, but now was not the time to think about it. Inside the mine a man could be dead or gravely injured.

"Did you send anybody in there, Repp?" Mr. James said.

"No, sir, my guys had the day off like everybody else."

"I should have never tried to reopen this widow maker," Mr. James said. "I knew this was likely to happen."

Lilly watched as several men gathered around Tern. His team, she surmised. "It looked good to go, Mr. James," one said. "We were being careful."

Others agreed.

"So who's missing?" Tern said. "Did we get a count?"

"It's Elbows," a guy said. "He's the onliest one not accounted for."

CHAPTER 24

LILLY WENT TO THE CLINIC to wait for Mr. James's directions. It could be hours yet, or it could be days before they knew if anyone was indeed trapped inside the mine. And Lilly had other patients to care for in the meanwhile.

Aunt Orie was sitting up in bed, eating scrambled eggs, when Lilly checked on her. Armina was washing windows.

"Did Dr. Hamilton get off okay?" Orie asked. "I feel I owe that man my life."

"His train pulled out right on time," Lilly said, searching for a way to change the subject. She wasn't ready to think about Paul. "Where are the babies?"

"Mrs. James insisted on keeping them at her house,"

Armina said. "I told her it was too much on her, but she wouldn't hear of me packing them away." She doused her rag in soapy water and rubbed at a fly speck. "Poor woman, now she's got them two plus that dog you drug in."

Gracious, Lilly thought, *don't spare my feelings.* "Mr. James is taken with Cleve. I'm sure he's not too much trouble."

"I'm just saying your timing was a little off."

Lilly left Armina to her scrubbing and Aunt Orie to her eggs. In the front room, she pulled out her desk chair and sat down. Armina had hit the nail on the head. Her timing was off—way off. But what she had felt with Tern this morning was like nothing she had ever felt before.

She looked at the ring on her finger, thinking of the life she and Paul had so carefully planned. It had been her desire to work in a big city hospital. Her hope had been to practice for a few years until they had children. And even then, Paul had said, they'd get a nanny and Lilly could do research, another strong desire.

Something irritated her neck. She swatted an ant to the floor, then unclasped her necklace, feeling around for another bug. She stretched the cream-colored pearls across the desktop, bumping her finger slowly over each small hump. The life she was supposed to lead was like that string of graduated pearls—each step leading to the next in an orderly fashion. There was much comfort in the thought.

She took a square of soft flannel from a desk drawer and began to polish her pearls. If only she could find a quiet place to think, but outside her door the warning whistle blasted off and on, and inside Armina clanked the bucket. Lilly lingered at the center pearl. Then, as if she'd snapped it on purpose, the necklace broke. Pearls bounced like hailstones across the floor.

Lilly gasped and fell to her knees, gathering precious beads one at a time. Dismayed, she watched as two pearls rolled like marbles across the slanted floor, pinging off chair legs and the wastebasket before disappearing down a knothole by the baseboard. Scrabbling to the corner, she stuck her fingers into the hole. If a mouse bit her, she would wring its neck. But no use; she couldn't find the pearls.

She laid the ones she did find in a line across the desk, searching for the most important and largest pearl. It was missing, but at least she still had the silver clasp.

She slumped back in her chair. Aunt Alice had been so pleased the day she presented that string to Lilly. They'd climbed the stairs at her aunt's house in Lexington together. Lilly had followed Aunt Alice into her bedroom and watched as she lifted the heavy, velvet-lined jewelry casket from its place of honor on the polished cherry dresser.

"Now sit," Aunt Alice said, indicating the bench in front of the mirror. She swept Lilly's hair away from her shoulders and fastened the lovely gift around her neck. Lilly remembered the reflection of her aunt's face, proud and happy, in the looking glass.

She would be so disappointed if Lilly didn't go to Boston.

Lilly's mind was awhirl with competing emotions. How could one moment change her life so completely? Were years of study all for naught? Yes, she could practice anywhere, but it seemed God had led her here to Skip Rock. And it seemed He meant for her to stay despite her well-laid plans. Medicine practiced here would be rudimentary at best, just like Paul had pointed out. And what of Paul? He wouldn't leave Boston even for her, but her feelings for Tern had cheapened all they had meant to each other. She had been sure Paul was exactly what she wanted in a husband.

She gathered the pearls, the clasp, and the broken string and put them in an envelope. When things had settled down, she'd get someone to search under the building for the missing pieces. Aunt Alice could have them restrung.

With a tug, she removed the engagement ring from her finger and added it to the envelope. It was a family heirloom. She would return it via Ned when he went to Boston for his treatment. Lilly knew he would go just as she knew Paul would treat him with courtesy. Paul was nothing if not a gentleman and a man of his word.

Lilly's emotions flipped like a fish on the line. Someone was going to get hurt—Paul for sure and more than likely Lilly herself. How could she do this to the man who loved and trusted her? The moments with Tern had seemed so right, but she still couldn't believe she had put herself in such an awkward position. If she'd learned anything in medical school, it was the danger of letting emotion overrule common sense. She needed to see him again, but she needed to be careful—careful of his feelings and of her own.

Opening the desk drawer, she laid the jewelry-laden

envelope inside, then closed the drawer with a decisive slam. "I can only hope Paul will forgive me," she said.

"Are you talking to me?" Armina asked, coming from the back room and whipping a feather duster around the corners of the ceiling. "When can Aunt Orie go home?"

"Before he left this morning, Dr. Hamilton left instructions to watch her for the rest of the week." Lilly rattled round white pills in an amber-colored bottle. "We'll start her on these diuretics this evening and see what happens."

"Dyer-whats?"

"They'll help her lose some fluid—keep her busy . . . and you too, Armina."

"Well, that's all right. I like busy."

Lilly went to the door and looked out toward the mines. "I'm going to walk up and see what's going on. Surely they know something by now. I don't know whether to wear my overalls or not."

"Put them on. If ye don't, you'll need them certain sure."

Myrtie James and one of the church ladies came walking in, arms full of food and babies and the puppy. Bubby and Sissy clambered over everything. The puppy, a red bandanna around his neck, sniffed and knocked over a wicker basket full of papers. It was a welcome diversion.

"Have you heard anything?" Myrtie asked. "We've been having a prayer session—praying God's mercy over whoever's trapped in there."

"I'm just going to walk over. Do you want to come along?"

"Go on, Myrtie," the other lady said. "We'll be fine here."

Lilly saw Armina start to puff up with righteous indigna-
tion at the very thought she needed help. Lilly caught her eye
and Armina backed down. "Yes," she said, "you all go along.
We'll find something to keep us busy."

Many more folks had gathered at the mine's opening. A stocky
gray mule pulled a cart loaded with supplies up the road.

Mr. James approached. "It's Elbows. He's in a pickle
for sure."

Myrtie put her hand over her heart. "Don't give up hope,
Stanley. God is in the miracle-making business."

The sun beat down. Mud puddles, lingering since the
storm, steamed like watched pots in the rutted road. Dust
drifted by in sheets of grit. The jarring sound of pickaxes
and shovels waging war against the fallen rock just inside
the portal grated like fingernails across a blackboard. On the
sidelines, under the trees, women murmured and children
played.

"You ain't going in this time, are you, Stanley?" Myrtie's
face pursed with anxiety.

Lilly was touched when she saw Mr. James squeeze his
wife's arm. She rarely witnessed overt expressions of affection
between the two.

"Go on back to the house now, Myrtie. Bake me up a
chocolate pie for supper."

"He's always like that," Myrtie said, watching her husband's retreating back. "But I always worry just the same."

Lilly understood. She didn't want to think of Tern being

in there either. It didn't help that she had been back in the dungeon during a cave-in herself. The miners were truly brave to face such peril each working day.

"The worst I ever heard tell," Myrtie was saying, "happened over to Lynch. One poor widow woman lost ever one of her sons in one day. Can you imagine six coffins in a line and each one holding a piece of your heart? She surely felt as bad as Job's wife that day."

"No, I can't imagine such sorrow," Lilly said.

Lilly could tell Myrtie was twisting her hands under cover of her apron. "I don't know what's kept Stanley alive. He's always the first one called on. I pray the Lord will keep him safely in the palm of His almighty hand."

"You should go roll out a piecrust, Myrtie. It will be suppertime before you know it."

"Yes, you watch. Long about three o'clock you'll see the women yonder start to fade away. They'll head home to start supper, and if their men don't come home to eat, they'll bring vittles over here."

"The waiting is a hard thing for the families," Lilly said.

"A rescue squad will have to go in there. That's several more men in danger. One roof fall often leads to another." Myrtie rolled her arms in the apron like a window shade. "That Repp fellow will go first—it's his outfit, Stanley said. He'll check the forewarning bird to see if the air is poisoned. If it ain't, then they can go ahead clearing the way. You know what I hope?"

"What, Myrtie?"

"I hope he ain't stuck so bad they can't get to him, and if he is, I hope he's already dead."

Lilly put her hand to her heart. What a terrible wish.

"Why don't you stop by the clinic on your way and see if Armina will let you take the children with you?"

"I will do just that," Myrtie said, brightening. "I've got to fetch Cleve anyway. You made Stanley's day with that dog."

"I'm glad you didn't mind, Myrtie. I should have asked permission first."

After a while of waiting on the sidelines with the other women, Lilly checked the watch pinned by a fob to the bib of the overalls Myrtie James had tailored to fit her. Two o'clock. If she had an apron to hide under, she would have wrung her hands as Myrtie did.

As time dragged by with no news, tension sparked like live wires from person to person. Rumors flew about like frightened doves. One person whispered that thirty men were trapped inside, that the company was keeping it quiet. Another said it was a trysting couple caught unawares as the roof caved in upon their love nest.

Lilly had to shake her head at the last one. As far as she was concerned, the least romantic place on earth had to be the inside of a mine. And as for thirty men, she knew better, but she kept her own counsel.

Finally Ned came for her. "Mr. James is asking for you."

A hush fell over the crowd. Everyone listened intently; even the children ceased their games.

"Who's going in, do you know, Ned?" Tillie Tippen asked. "Have you seen your uncle Turnip?"

"Sorry, Aunt Tillie," Ned said. "I ain't at liberty to say the crew that's scouting inside."

Ned escorted Lilly to the site. Her mouth was dry as the grit that blew around their heads, and her stomach clinched painfully.

"Doc," Mr. James said, "the men are in. It might be an hour; it might be three days. You should go and wait it out at the clinic. I'll send Ned for you when the need is nigh."

Lilly acquiesced, although it would be harder to wait away from the scene. At least here she had a sense of being useful. Was Tern inside? Words formed into complete sentences on the tip of her tongue only to be discarded unspoken. She couldn't ask without raising suspicion, and he had begged her trust. Of course he was inside. The man, Elbows, was part of his crew.

With a nod, Mr. James walked away. It hurt Lilly to see how his shoulders slumped under the weight of the day.

She rested her hand in the crook of Ned's elbow. "Let's wait a little while, Ned. I can't bear to leave just yet."

They moved out of the way, and Lilly sat on the tailgate of an empty wagon. Ned stood alongside.

A short stump of a man carrying a slatted-wood birdcage approached Mr. James. Lilly couldn't hear what they were saying, but she saw Mr. James take the cage.

"He's brought a new bird," Ned said.

Lilly's heart thumped. "But that must mean the air is poisoned; else why replace the other one?"

"Dust has probably got to him," Ned said. "Are you thirsty? I'm going to fetch some water."

"Yes, I could do with a drink." She was thirsty and maybe hungry. It was hard to pinpoint what she was feeling. And it was becoming increasingly hard to retain a professional detachment from the chaos that surrounded her. Of course, she cared about all the miners and their families, but it was fear for Tern that made her palms sweat and her stomach hurt. She might as well admit it, if only to herself.

CHAPTER 25

TERN STOOD BESIDE the three men he'd chosen to help in
the search for Elbows: Turnip Tippen, because he'd survived
more cave-ins than a cat had lives; Bob Hall, because he
knew the course of Number 4 like the back of his hand;
and young Billy, because he was slight of frame. The boy
had no shoulders to speak of. He'd be more valuable than
gold if they needed someone to squeeze through tight spaces.
Stanley James had approved the crew. Tern knew Stanley was
champing at the bit to come along, but he had to supervise
the whole affair, not just the inside job.

Billy carried the replacement bird in one hand and a coal-
oil lantern in the other. "What should I do with this other'n?"

he asked, his voice cracking midsentence. He opened the tiny door of the hanging cage and the dusty canary hopped onto his finger.

"Fling it off," Turnip said. "It won't live long with all this dust in its throat."

"What do you want to do?" Tern asked. It wouldn't hurt to indulge the boy, considering what he might face when they found the missing miner.

"It ain't but a short ways back. Cain't I put it outside?"

"Make short work of it," Tern said.

"We shouldn't tarry over a dumb bird," Turnip said and spat on the floor.

"We won't," Tern said. "Billy can catch up." The light from the young man's lantern was already fading.

The men rolled a rock that must have weighed a hundred pounds out of the path.

"We need to give Billy Boy a nickname. I think I'll call him Fleet," Turnip said, huffing for breath.

Tern cast lumps of coal and rock to the side. "Fleet?"

"Yeah, Fleet, like fleet of foot. A moniker makes you feel like you belong—like you've been initiated into the club. The boys have been tossing around a name for you, Joe."

"Yeah, what's that?"

"Drifter."

"Why Drifter?"

"You don't seem to light anywhere for long, I guess is the reason."

"Fair enough," Tern said, hefting a rough-hewn truss

and laying it aside. He was rewarded with a splinter big as a matchstick in the meat of his hand.

They reached a fork in the tunnel. The lamps attached to their caps barely penetrated the darkness. They also carried lanterns. Billy caught up to them, holding his high.

"Which way, Bob?" Tern asked, sucking on his palm.

"Hold up a sec." Bob made a megaphone of his hands. "Elbows!" he shouted. "Elbows!"

Tern strained to hear a reply. Silence amplified the utter darkness of the mine. If you stayed still long enough, you'd find that even silence had a sound. Tern always thought it sounded like hopelessness felt—like a rushing sadness filling one's soul. He guessed that must be what hell was like.

Bob pulled at his chin, thinking. The men's faces were black with coal dust. All Tern could see was their eyes. They looked like strange, disembodied creatures. Tern knew he looked the same. He wished Bob would hurry. Elbows, if he was even in here, could be bleeding out or drawing his last breath while Bob dithered time away.

"He would have gone this way." Bob pointed to the right. "This'n to the left was blocked before the fall."

All right, Tern thought, *a plan.*

Every few feet there was another pile of debris to move. And every few feet one or another would call out, "Elbows! Elbows!" Like an aggravated mother calling her recalcitrant child to supper.

"Listen," Bob said after a dozen rounds of calls. "I hear something."

Sure enough, a strange mewing sound could be heard far off in the distance. But where did it come from? The tunnel forked again, but Bob said they were both true avenues. Elbows could have taken either one.

"Which one would have filled a gunny sack fastest?" Turnip said.

"You don't know he was stealing," Tern said.

"He wasn't in here on no picnic. 'Sides, maybe he thought he was owed something more than the miserly wage the company doles out for sixteen tons a day."

"He'll get fired on the spot if that's the case," Bob said.

Turnip spat again. "And what if'n he's splattered like a june bug on a window glass back in there? Is the company gonna feed him if he's so busted up he cain't work no more?"

"Shut up and listen," Tern said. "We need to find him before we judge him."

The men leaned first one way and then the other, cupping their hands behind their ears. The pitiful, bleating sound seemed to come from all directions, like an echo when you shouted down a well.

"Here's what we'll do," Tern said. "Bob, you and Turnip take the right. I'll take the left. Holler out if you find him. Billy, you stay here with the lamp. That'll help us find our way back."

After a short but tedious hike over ankle-twisting rubble and chunks of breakdown big as ice chests, Tern came upon a space in which he could stand upright. What a relief. The cave was black as pitch. Holding a lantern high, he examined the area for the threat of shifting rock. There was no shoring timber in the chamber nor any broken castoff tools, no rusty bean cans with jagged lids or empty amber-colored whiskey bottles littering the floor, no sign this place had ever entertained men before.

Water trickled through fissures in the rock face like dozens of tiny waterfalls. A sightless salamander clung with suctioned feet to the limestone. Tern poked the soft, moist skin on the creature's back, and it dropped soundlessly to the floor. Cave crickets bounded about in the searing light of the lantern like grasshoppers before a threshing machine.

Tern could have stood there all day taking in the ancient splendor of the place. He wasn't a man who often talked to God, but if it hadn't been for the fact that he could hear Elbows calling, this experience would have moved him to do so. "Later," he said, feeling foolish—as if God was waiting to hear from him, Tern Still.

He could clearly hear a voice somewhere off to the right and about five feet off the cave floor. Finally, by crawling about the perimeter of the cavern, Tern found Elbows in a crawlway so narrow he had to slide inside with both arms overhead, like a swimmer poised for a dive. He was stretched out flat, his feet just barely inside the duct-like corridor, when the tip of his index finger touched the tip of Elbows's own. The trapped man's digit jerked like he'd touched a live wire.

"Elbows, it's Joe Repp. Can you speak?"

"Cain't I always?" Elbows said around a rusty little laugh.

"What happened?"

"Was you a curious boy, Joe?"

"I guess, a little."

"I was always exploring—caves, sinkholes, lairs—didn't matter what. It started with one time my brother dared me to go in a fox's den. I was ten or so. I went in there and wound up here. Ain't life grand?"

"Listen, I've got to holler for the others. You hold on. We'll get you out of here."

Tern backed out one clammy inch at time. It felt wonderful to be free. "He's found!" he shouted toward the glowing light of Billy's lantern. "He's found."

Soon the other men were gathered round, except for Billy, who stayed where Tern left him. Tern bet the boy hadn't moved an inch. He bet he'd stay there until Beelzebub's nose dripped icicles or until Tern granted permission for him to leave.

After assessing the height and width of the opening to Elbows's prison, Bob scratched his bald pate through the soft cloth of his cap. "You say his head's facing us? That means he was coming this way when he got trapped. I've got a feeling this passage goes through to where me and Turnip were at. It's more than likely wider and easier to access on the other side. Let's go have a look-see, Turnip."

Once the other men had left, Tern felt compelled to shimmy back to Elbows. "Bob Hall's looking things over. We'll get you out straight away."

"I wonder, could you spare a sip of water?"

Tern slithered out, slid back in with his canteen, and tucked the strap under the fingers of Elbows's outstretched hand. The man's nails scrabbled against the rock floor like a dog on an ice-covered pond, but he couldn't seem to grasp the woven belt. The effort set off a paroxysm of coughing followed by wheezing rales. Tern caught himself holding his breath, the sound was so painful to hear.

"Ah, me," Elbows said, "it's like I ain't had a drink all day."

Tern cupped his hand and poured a drab of water into it. Try as he might, he couldn't get the water to Elbows without spilling it. And he couldn't give him water straight from the canteen because it was too big to pass between the stone that formed the ceiling and the man's head.

"Try filling the lid and passing it in," Elbows said. "If I can work this one hand free, I can manage a drink."

That worked well enough, but it took a lot of lids and a lot of effort before Elbows's thirst was quenched. Most of the water dribbled down his chin. This was the most pitiful thing Tern had ever seen.

Tern's leg knotted with a fierce charley horse. He scooted out of the tunnel, walking straight-legged until the cramp wore off. If a few minutes in the hole did this to him, what must Elbows be suffering?

He crouched by the opening. He should keep the injured man talking. "Can you tell me what's got you trapped?"

"I reckon the rock fall shifted something down on me."

"Are you flat on your back then?"

"No, I'm sort of twisted in my middle part. My feet are turned kindly sideways. My tailbone's caught on something, but I cain't tell what."

"Are you hurting?"

"Some. Mostly I'm thirsty, and I need to stretch my legs."

Time dragged by. What were Bob and Turnip up to on the other side?

"Listen, Elbows, I'm going to send Billy back to keep you company for a while. I won't be long."

"Could you do me a favor before you leave off out of here?"

"Sure thing," Tern said.

"Would ye scratch my back?"

"That's not funny, Elbows," he said, but he was more than glad to hear Elbows's mirthful cackle. He was quite sure he would not be able to crack a joke if he were in such dire straits.

"There is one little thing you could do for me. It ain't a joke, though."

"Spit it out. I'll do anything I can."

"Is there anyone out there but you, Joe?"

"Just me."

"Would you mind to say, 'Leroy, your mommy loves you'?"

"Huh?"

"My mother would always say, 'Leroy, your mommy loves you.' She said that ever time I left the house, from the time I was just a tad."

Tern dashed a bit of moisture from his cheek. "That was nice."

"So would you say that to me? Say, 'Leroy—'"

"Leroy, your mommy loves you," Tern said, hearing nothing but a sniffle in reply. He was desperate to get away for a moment. "Now listen, you hang on. I'll be back in a jiffy."

After warning Billy not to go in the aperture with Elbows, Tern sent the boy back to keep company. He went to the fork that bore to the right and walked down to where he figured he'd find Bob and Turnip. The men had hauled a pile of debris from the opening of a lateral shaft so wide Tern could walk in.

"I believe you're right, Bob," he said when he reached them, "but we need more men, especially the shoring crew, and we need tools. You'll never dig him out this way."

"Did you figure what's got him stuck? Do you know what position he's in?" Bob asked.

"Face up. He's twisted at the waist, the knees, and the feet. Something's pressing on his backbone. He can't seem to move himself below the waist."

"Poor soul," Turnip said.

"Maybe we could rig a harness and pull him out. He ain't that far in," Bob said.

"I don't know about that," Turnip said, "Remember what happened to Pike Chapman when he got trapped down Mammoth Cave way? They about pulled him apart with a rappelling rope. He didn't live but two hours after he was freed. His internals were all a mess."

"This ain't that bad, Turnip," Bob said.

"I hope not, but this setup puts me in mind of that time in '97—was you here then, Bob?"

"Nah, I was over to Benham in '97."

"Well, in '97 we had a situation much like this one, except there was three men died in a tunnel squeeze then.

It was a rainy season that year too, much like this one has been, and then to make matters worse, we'd been blasting at the site. Unluckily, these three were in the wrong place at the wrong time when the ceiling collapsed and trapped them in a stricture much like what's got Elbows in a tether. After days of shoring roofs and hauling rock to get to them, the mine walls weakened and hydraulic pressure forced the floor up toward the ceiling. It worked just like a vise. There weren't a thing we could do but save ourselves. I can hear them screaming yet."

"It don't set well to listen to all that right now, Turnip. It's like you're only thinking of the worst."

"Forewarned is forearmed is all I'm saying."

Bob rubbed his chin. "Ayuh, there's truth to that."

"Well, here's a truth for sure," Tern said. "We're not helping the situation by standing around here jawing."

Bob and Turnip hustled to the mine entrance to update Mr. James. He'd decide what the next step was. Tern returned to Elbows's hidey-hole and sent Billy back to the Y.

"You still in there, Elbows?" he said.

"How many days have passed?"

"Days?" Tern shook his head. "It's only been a few hours."

"Ah, me, it feels like days."

"I'm coming in," Tern said. "We can talk better that way."

Tern settled in as best he could, stretched flat on his belly, head to head with Elbows. "What's the first thing you're going to do when you get out of here?"

"I always wanted to get me a job with the railroad. My

daddy used to be a tie hacker with the L&N. He'd bring home a passel of juggles nearly every day."

"Juggles?"

"You know, big splinters from the railroad ties. Daddy could hew twenty-five ties a day with his broadax. The juggles was just leavings, but they made the best kindling. What we didn't need, I'd take up and down the pike to the widow women."

Tern's hand ached. He knew all about splinters.

Elbows coughed, and Tern gave him more water.

"You don't have to talk anymore if it's too much effort."

"So many memories crowding around me; if I keep them in, I'll suffocate. Besides, talking helps me forget my predicament."

Man, Tern thought, *I can't take much more of this. I'll be bawling like a newborn calf taken from its mother.*

"Anyways, my favorite of all the widow women was Miz Rella Montgomery. She was a tidy woman and real nice. I'd fill up the wood box by the cookstove, and she'd give me a fried apple pie still warm from the oven. Doggies, I wish I had me one of them tasty treats right now. A fried apple pie and a glass of cold buttermilk would go down good."

After a trying time of listening to several more stories, Tern felt a hard tap on the sole of his work boot. He slid out.

"What's your take on this, Joe?" Stanley James asked. The other men stood around, listening.

Tern relayed what he had learned of Elbows's predicament. The men then took turns peering in to have a look.

Stanley agreed with Bob. It would be best to go in from the other side. If they tried to pull Elbows out, they risked breaking his back.

"Someone should stay here with him—keep his spirits up," Stanley said.

Tern resigned himself. "I'll stay."

CHAPTER 26

WOODSMOKE DRIFTED through the screened window in the front room of the clinic, where Lilly waited. In the gathering darkness, campfires up and down the hillside looked like the twinkling lights of a city. She sat by the window waiting. Her full doctor's kit was sitting by the open door.

With Armina's help, everything in the clinic had been aired out and scrubbed. Lilly was prepared to treat one man or a dozen, whatever presented. Aunt Orie had been moved via a rolling chair to Tillie Tippen's house to make way for the injured. Bubby and Sissy were with Myrtie. Mrs. DeWitt had set up a canteen at the base of the operation, where she served cold sandwiches, slabs of pie, and hot coffee. People milled about eating and talking. It was a macabre carnival.

Armina poked her head in the door. She'd taken up a station on the stoop, where she could watch the comings and goings. "Want to go get a cup of java?"

Lilly agreed and followed her outside. "How was Aunt Orie when you left her?" Lilly asked as they waited in a short line for drinks.

"Mrs. Tippen was chewing her ear off."

"I hope she doesn't get overtired. Maybe we should have transferred her to Mrs. James's house."

"She seems to be enjoying herself now that she's feeling better. Mrs. Tippen's put me a cot by the bed, so I'll go over there tonight."

"You seem to be enjoying being here too, Armina."

"I never in all my born days liked to come to town. Every three weeks or so, Uncle Bud will get the wagon out, whether we need anything or not. That man likes to run the roads, and we'll come down here to the commissary for coffee and sugar and such, maybe a tub of lard—you know. If we need a lot, and if we've got the money extra, we'll go to the county seat instead.

"Bubby likes it. I always bring him. Uncle Bud gets a sack of stick candy—about makes Bubby jump out of my lap. Always before, when we came down, folks acted like we had the German measles or something—like they were better'n us. I never liked to come to town."

"What is different this time?"

"Only thing different is I'm with you. People respect you, Doc, and some of that respect is rubbing off on me."

At the front of the line Armina poured cream into two cups of coffee and handed one to Lilly.

"Help me watch for Ned," Lilly said. "I can't believe he hasn't come for me yet."

Armina untied her apron strings, rolled the apron up, and stuck it in the pocket of her dress. "Ain't it hard to imagine being under the ground, trapped like a mole on a pike? Gives me the willies."

"Surely they're making progress. Oh, look, there he is." Lilly waved.

Armina sipped her coffee, looking at Ned over the rim.

"I was just coming down to the clinic," he said.

"Did Mr. James send you for me?"

"No, they ain't got him out yet. It might be all night, but Joe Repp's asking for soda straws. Do we have any?"

"Soda straws?" Lilly asked.

"Sounds strange, don't it?"

"There's a half-dozen invalid straws in the back room. The last time we used one was when Darrell was hurt."

"I know where they're at. I'll run and get one," Armina volunteered.

Ned watched her go. "I'm taking a shine to that girl. But I'm trying to be patient like you said."

"You're doing the right thing. She's starting to come around."

"Yeah?" Ned said, his face stretched in a grin. "How do you know?"

"She took her apron off when I mentioned you were coming."

"You don't say? Well, that there's a sign for sure."

One of the canteen staffers handed Ned a steaming mug. He balanced expertly on his crutches as he took a swallow. "You know what else?"

Lilly added more cream to her cup and a little sugar. "What else?"

"She ain't bit my head off all day."

"Ha. Just don't give her reason, Ned."

He gave Lilly a sage wink. "As my daddy always said, 'Don't ever corner anything that's meaner than you are.'"

"Your father was a wise man."

A boy ran down the road, steering a hoop with a stick. Lilly and Ned moved to stand under a tree with long, drooping branches.

"Listen, Doc, I don't want to speak out of turn, but that Joe guy? There's talk about him among the men. The fellow seems to be straight up, but you need to be careful."

Lilly touched his arm. "Am I that obvious, Ned?"

"Only to somebody like me. Somebody that knows you. Mostly, I've been watching him watching you."

Feeling a chill, she held her cup tightly for warmth. "Thank you, Ned. I appreciate you."

"I'd take a stick to anybody I thought was going to hurt you, Lilly."

Suddenly Lilly's burden seemed too big to carry alone. "I'm breaking my engagement to Paul," she confessed.

He nodded. "When I took you to the station this morning, I could feel there was a distance between you and Dr. Hamilton."

Lilly felt a sting of tears. It felt so good to have a confidant. "As much as I care for Paul, I was never in love with him. Marrying him just seemed the logical thing to do, like the right next step."

"There ain't no logic to love, Cuz. You want to hear something else my daddy said?"

"Surely," Lilly said.

"He used to sing these lines just to aggravate my mother. 'When love is new, it's magic; when love is old, it's tragic.' If the feeling's not there in the beginning, it won't come later when the new wears off."

"I don't want to hurt Paul. He's a really good man, but all of a sudden it seems a far piece to Boston."

"You know you're doing the right thing." Ned adjusted his crutches. "But I wouldn't mind to tour that place—that Boston. See the historical markers."

Lilly held her skirt aside and poured what remained of her coffee out on the ground. "I hope you will take advantage of Paul's offer. He meant every word of it."

They could see Armina coming up the path. "I was thinking a honeymoon in Boston might be just what the doctor ordered."

Lilly laughed, delighted. "Wouldn't that be something?"

Ned patted her hand. "I'm just thinking is all."

Lilly looked around, making sure no one was eavesdropping. "Ned, what are you hearing about Joe Repp? Are you at liberty to say?"

"Some think he's a spy for the company—that he's here gathering information so they can fire people. It's happened before. A few years back they laid all the men off and put prisoners to work in their place." Ned finished his drink and Lilly took his cup. "They took us back quick enough when the convicts didn't pan out, but still . . ."

Ned pulled a leaf from the tree and chewed on the stem. "Why else would the company insist on opening Number 4, except to give the men trouble? And why else would Repp be supervisor, and him a veritable stranger, except for the company's orchestration?"

"What do you think?" she asked, unsettled.

"I don't rightly know. There's something different about the man, but I can't put my finger on it."

Silently, Lilly had to agree. There was something about the man. She wished she could tell Ned what she had just learned about Tern, but she couldn't. He had asked for her silence.

Ned scraped the ground with the tip of a crutch. "If the men find out he's spying for the company, someone's liable to shove him down an abandoned shaft," he said in a low voice. "I don't want to see nobody come to harm."

Lilly hungered to ask him more, but Armina hurried up with invalid straws. "I brought two because if ye have just one of anything, it breaks."

Ned offered his arm. "Care to walk with me?"

Armina looked to Lilly.

"I think that's a lovely idea, Armina. Take your time."

She was amazed to see Armina tuck her hand in the crook of Ned's elbow as he hitched his way on crutches up the road toward the mine. The Armina she thought she knew would have sent him packing. She shook her head. There was no figuring love.

Well past bedtime, Lilly paced the floor of the clinic. Every few minutes, she went to the door and looked toward the mouth of the mine. One by one the campfires winked out. She watched as women leading sleepy children, young couples holding hands, and old folks hobbling from rheumatism straggled by. The canteen closed down.

What was taking so long? Why hadn't Mr. James sent for her?

Ned's words concerning Tern's safety kept coming back to her. Was Ned confiding in her so that she could warn Tern? Mr. James was in charge, and Lilly doubted that he was unaware of the men's suspicions. Surely he would see that there was no violence.

She looked at the clock for the umpteenth time. She wasn't doing anybody any good just waiting. After picking up her ever-ready kit, she headed out the door.

The warm night air was thick with humidity. In the weeds at the side of the road, locusts thrummed hoarsely in an unmelodious chorus. From a quarter mile away, Lilly could hear the sound of men working into the night. She supposed the darkness made no difference to miners. It was always midnight in their world.

Drawing closer, she saw they had strung lanterns across the foreboding, beetle-browed portal of Number 4. Suddenly she felt vastly unprepared for what was going on behind that gaping wound in the face of the earth. A man was trapped, and probably dying, inside that mountain. Inside! She could hardly take it in. She wished she could do something—anything—to help. She was not trained to stand and wait.

Mr. James stepped out to meet her. His shoulders seemed more stooped than they had been this morning. His face was black with coal dust. He made a motion as if to tip his hat, and she was filled with pain for him.

"I'm sorry," she said. "I couldn't stand just sitting around."

"It's a bad one, Doc. But there ain't nothing you can do right now."

"I'm ready to go in, anytime." She pulled on the strap of her overalls and saw him smile at her attempt at humor.

"You're a good gal, but I wouldn't chance it right now."

"The men don't want me in there, do they?"

"In truth, no, and it ain't a good time to push it."

"I understand," she said. "Have you eaten? I promised Myrtie I'd keep an eye on you."

"Soda crackers and some of them little canned weenies. I'm eating high on the hog, tell Myrtie."

One of the lanterns flickered, casting them in and out of

shadow like a celluloid picture show. "Mr. James, I wish there was something I could do."

"I expect we'll have him free by morning. You might as well get some sleep for now." He wiped grit from his face with the blue bandanna from his back pocket. "Say, that bird you liked is around here somewheres. I saw Billy bring it out."

"You don't mind if I take it?"

"No, but keep it away from Cleve." He chuckled. "That dog's a killer."

"Do you like him?"

"Gal, I wish I was setting on the porch with him right now."

Lilly couldn't help herself. She threw her arms around the neck of the man who had become her hero. "Please, please be careful."

Clumsily he patted her back. "Don't fret over me. Just say a prayer for Elbows."

CHAPTER 27

IF TERN STAYED STILL long enough, he could feel the earth shifting beneath him. Most of the time, he was on his knees, leaning his upper body inside the crawl space, keeping Elbows company. But right now, he was sitting outside the narrow tunnel, resting his cramped legs and working the splinter out of his hand. *Man,* he thought when at last the sliver was free, *that feels better.*

Somehow, Elbows had decided Tern was his long-lost brother or something, the only one who could placate him. Tern thought the man was losing touch with reality. Maybe he was thirsting to death. No matter how many lids full of water Tern scooted in, he was still asking for more. His plaintive begging was driving Tern nuts.

Mr. James, and sometimes Billy, came and went, checking on them, but the real work was on the other side of Elbows's crook-legged, rock-jagged prison. Bob figured the whole thing to be less than half a mile long—wide as a doorway on one end and tight as a coffin on the other. The big problem was the rock slide smack in the middle of the burrow.

Tern thought the problem was Elbows and why he would try to maneuver through a squeeze that tight in the first place. He'd told Tern he didn't want to take the time to turn around. He figured if he scrunched his shoulders, he could slip through. Tern figured he thought he was a mole.

"I'm thirsty," Elbows called down the tube.

Billy had brought a couple of straws. Made of glass and bent on the sipping end, one might be just the ticket for getting more fluid into Elbows. Tern had a thermos of coffee now also and a plate of food. The temperature in the mine was a cool fifty-four degrees year-round. Welcome when a man was busy working but a chill to the bones if he wasn't. Besides which, Elbows didn't have a bit of fat on him. He would get cold faster than most. Coffee would probably be good for the scrawny man.

"Do you want a bite to eat?" Tern asked.

"I could try, but don't you reckon I'll be out by suppertime?"

Tern wasn't about to tell him it was well past supper. Elbows had lost track of time. He didn't seem to know if he'd been for trapped days or hours.

Sliding the plate of food and a folding cup half-full of

coffee ahead of him, Tern made his way in. The trick was getting the food and drink to the man's mouth. Plus, with the way Elbows was lying, Tern was afraid he would choke. Then what would he do?

"That sure smells good, but I don't think I can eat. Is that coffee?"

Tern put the straw in the liquid and touched it to the other man's lips. "Go easy. It's hot."

Elbows drank it down, then sighed like he'd died and gone to heaven. "Ah, me, that was good. What kind of taters you got there, Joe?"

"Looks like mashed, and there's baked chicken, biscuits with butter, and green beans with fatback."

"I could maybe try a few taters. My belly's so empty it's talking to my backbone."

Tern tore a hunk of chicken into bits and stirred it into the potatoes. Many years ago, he'd seen his mother do the very same thing for his younger brothers. That was in the good old days.

Elbows was able to eat a few spoonfuls. Tern felt like he'd accomplished something major, but man, the situation was nerve-racking.

When Tern emerged from the tube, Stanley James was waiting.

"How's he holding up?"

"He's eating a bit and drinking. It's bad in there, though, Stanley. How's it going on the other side?"

"Slow but steady; they've removed a ton of rubble. I figure

we should be to him before morning." He crouched and looked in the hole. "I'll bring Elbows up to date. You go catch a break."

Tern stood at the mouth of the mine, gulping breaths of air that was stale as pond water. He couldn't seem to get enough. You wouldn't think it would be so since he spent every working day in the deep. It was like his lungs had tensed while inside, like they were trying to hold on to every breath, like each one might be the last. He walked outside for a bit. He had hard questions to ask himself.

Number 4 was no less dangerous than it had ever been. It was time to shut it down. His dream of finding a way for the miners to work it in safety was gone. Plain and simple, he had failed.

He kicked a rock and it bounced out of sight like a startled rabbit. He had to remember why he was here in the first place. It wasn't to change things or try to make this a secure place to work; it was to observe what was already in place and report that back to the agency. He should leave right now. Pages of evidence waited at the boardinghouse. The very best thing he could do for these men was to report the violations committed by the company who owned the mine against the men who worked it. His goal through the agency was long-term improved working conditions for the miners, not their short-term paychecks.

He clasped his hands behind his back and stretched. Who was he kidding? He couldn't leave until this present situation was resolved. And then there was Lilly. His arms ached to hold her again.

A slight wind kicked up. Dark clouds moved ominously across the face of the moon. Heat lightning flashed impotently, burning out before it even came close to touching the ground. Tiredly, Tern hunched his shoulders. All they needed now was another storm.

A rustle from the other side of a stack of timber caught his attention. The shoring crew had just gone inside with a new stack. The boards must be shifting. He'd set them to rights before he went back in. That would help work the kinks out of his back.

He couldn't believe his eyes. There stood Lilly, bathed in lantern light, dressed in overalls, with a battered birdcage in her hand.

"Forevermore," she said. "Do you spend your days figuring out new ways to startle me? I almost dropped the forewarning bird."

The bird sat huddled on the floor of his dirty cage. "Looks like somebody needed to warn him," Tern said.

"I know, poor little thing. The least I can do is feed him." She set the cage down and turned her attention to Tern. "I'm glad to see you're all right. Do they have the man out?"

"No, but we're working on it." He looked around to be sure no one was within earshot. "Lilly?" Her spoken name was as appealing as the golden flower that bloomed in wild abandon along the mountain trails. He was lost in her.

She put her finger to her lips. "Shhh, someone might overhear."

"There's no one back here but us." Looping his thumbs in the shoulder straps of her overalls, he drew her closer.

She tiptoed up, but it was not for a kiss. "Listen to me," she whispered in his ear. "There's talk among the men. They're onto you."

"There's always suspicion and talk. They have no proof."

"They don't need proof. You need to tell Mr. James about whatever it is you're up to."

He tightened his arms. Her hair smelled like sunshine. "I don't care about that right now. Just let me hold you for a minute."

Her body relaxed against his, but not for long. "This isn't right," she said. "I haven't talked to Paul."

"You're not rightly his."

"But, Tern, he doesn't know that."

"Ah, but, Lilly, I've never kissed a girl wearing overalls. I might not get the chance again."

She tossed her head. "Do you have a checklist, Mr. Still?"

He pantomimed crinkling up a bit of paper and tossing it over his shoulder. "Not anymore." Then, becoming serious, he asked, "Will you promise me something?"

She shrugged. "I can't promise you anything after what I've done to Paul. Obviously, my word is easily broken."

"Don't be so hard on yourself. You didn't make a rash decision."

"Don't you think it's rash to throw the love of a good and

kind man away and walk right into the arms of a stranger? Isn't that exactly what I've done?"

In his estimation, she didn't really want his answer to that. He was not fond of the fellow, but he did feel sorry for him. Tern's whiskers rasped when he drew his hand across his chin. "Well, I'm sorry if the man is upset, but you were always meant for me. He just got in the way for a while."

She nodded and put her palm to his face. "I want to be. I want to be meant for you."

"I'm not letting you go again. I mean to marry you."

"I'm not the usual woman who lives for a man, Tern. If we are to be together, you would have to be willing to go where I go. And right now I'm not sure where that would be."

"Honey," he said, "I would live on the moon just to be with you. You are home to me."

She brushed his cheek lightly with her lips. "I think I love you, Tern Still."

"Joe!" he heard from the mouth of the mine. "Joe Repp."

Please, he nearly moaned aloud, *not now.* Not when she'd said the most precious words he would ever hear.

Billy clambered over the stack of lumber. A plank skittered off the top of the pile, nearly striking them.

"Thank goodness I found you," the young man said. "Elbows is crying out, and I don't know what to do."

"Give me a minute," Tern said. "I'll be right there."

"Hurry up," Billy said. "He keeps asking for you."

"In a minute!"

Billy went back the way he had come, leaving planks

skewed every which way. It wouldn't have taken him any longer to walk around.

"He's scared," Tern said of Billy, as if it were important to make excuses.

"You'd best go," Lilly said.

"Lilly, I need to know that you've forgiven me for all that happened to you."

"Tern," she said, "I never blamed you."

With mercy and grace, she absolved him of the guilt he'd carried in his gut like a stone. What would happen if a grown man cried?

"I wish I had time to explain what I'm doing. I want you to know it's nothing illegal."

"I wouldn't be standing here if I thought you were capable of anything like that."

"So can I have that kiss?"

A smile toyed at the corners of her mouth. "Maybe someday soon."

"Maybe?"

"I'll be waiting for you, Tern. Be careful in there. Don't risk your life."

"Joe!" Billy yelled again.

"All right! I'm coming!" He tucked his knuckle under her chin and lifted her face. "Say you love me, not that you think you do."

"I love you."

"I can live a long time on those words," he said. "I love you, Lilly. You stole my heart so long ago."

He walked away backward, looking at her for as long as he could. It was the hardest thing he'd ever done.

Nearly around the corner of the stacked wood, he turned back. "Don't throw those overalls away."

"I thought you chucked that checklist," she said.

The image of her in the moonlight was all he needed to keep him company through another treacherous night. He forced himself back inside to where Elbows waited.

CHAPTER 28

DAY TWO of Elbows's entrapment and Lilly was still shut out. She stood on the Jameses' porch with her hands on her hips, looking toward the mine. This was exactly why it wouldn't work out for her to practice in Skip Rock. She'd been here for weeks and thought she had allayed at least some of the prejudice she faced when she first came, but it seemed not as far as most of the miners went.

Oh, the people liked her. She was welcome in nearly every home, and at church all she saw was smiling faces. But this was a coal camp and she was its doctor. She wasn't here just to deliver babies and untangle boys from cow rumps.

"Come in and eat," Myrtie said from behind the screen door.

"Were you up all night, Myrtie?" Lilly asked, cutting into her eggs and sausages.

"No, I slept a little. A body can't hardly rest thinking about what's going on up there. I started a fire about four o'clock so's I could get a hamper of food fixed to send to Stanley."

"Who took it for you?"

"The neighbor's boy; he was going anyway. Everybody's being real nice through all this—first the storm and now that poor man." She fed Sissy a bit of egg-soaked biscuit. Bubby was in a high chair, his face smeared with oatmeal. He dropped a piece of biscuit off the tray of his chair and laughed when the pup pounced on it.

"Do you want me to start some corn bread, Miz Myrtie?" Armina asked from the cookstove.

"Might as well while the stove's hot." Myrtie turned to Lilly. "That's the hardest-working girl I ever did see. I think she's practicing setting up housekeeping with some handsome young fellow."

A blush colored Armina's cheeks as she greased the bottom of a heavy twelve-inch cast-iron skillet. She was changing right before Lilly's eyes, becoming a softer version of her hard-as-a-pine-knot self. Some good was coming from Aunt Orie's illness.

"Do ye reckon your aunt would want to come over here today?" Myrtie asked. "You've been running your legs off taking care of everybody."

"She's doing all right," Armina said, stirring buttermilk into a corn meal mixture. "Miz Tippen says taking care of

Aunt Orie is keeping her from going crazy with worry over her husband."

Myrtie wiped Bubby's hands and face with a wet rag. "I understand that. I feel the same way about these two babies."

"I'm kindly glad Ned ain't able to go inside where the trapped man is," Armina said.

Myrtie gave Lilly a told-you-so look.

"When were you going to tell me you and Ned are an item?" Lilly asked mischievously.

"Humph, I figured you could tell by looking, you being a doctor and all." Armina opened the oven door using her apron as a potholder. She slid the skillet into the oven and shut the door with a soft bang.

Lilly had overstepped Armina's mercurial bounds. She wondered how hard she would have closed the door if it had been her own oven.

The dog stood on his hind feet, stretching up on the high chair. Bubby banged Cleve on the head with his spoon.

Lilly stacked her plate and silverware before walking to the door.

"What do you reckon is going on over there?" Myrtie said, coming up behind her.

"I don't know. I keep thinking there's more I could be doing, though."

"Old Doc used to take his tent up yonder whenever there was an incident in the mines." Myrtie made a vague motion toward the mountain. "That way the men didn't have to come all the way down here if they needed aid."

"Why did no one tell me that?" Lilly said.

"I seen that tent in the back room when I was looking for them straws," Armina said. "It's mildewed."

"There's nothing stopping me from doing the same thing," Lilly said. "It makes perfect sense. Armina, I'll need your help."

"Soon as that corn bread's done, I'll pass the word," Myrtie said. "See if I can't get some extra hands. Tillie will watch the young'uns."

Armina went ahead to the clinic. Lilly stopped to check on Aunt Orie and on Mrs. Poor, the woman who had broken her arm during the storm. Aunt Orie was so much better; Lilly hardly recognized her without her puffy face. Mrs. Poor was staying with her in-laws. Lilly checked her cast and taught her mother-in-law how to adjust the sling around her neck. Stopping by the livery, she rented her sweet friend Slow Poke for the day. The donkey nuzzled her pocket for the sugar cubes she'd brought for a treat.

Armina had the tent canvas spread out in the sunshine when Lilly arrived. Several women were attacking it with brushes and brooms. The smell of borax wafted on soap bubbles around Lilly's head. Within the hour more women showed up, along with any child old enough to walk. If the reason for using the tent hadn't been so dire, it would have been an enjoyable event.

They loaded the tent and poles, the medical supplies, quilts and blankets, folding chairs, hammocks, orange crates, and other various items into the cart.

One little boy pulled on Lilly's skirt. "I want to pack something," he said. Lilly gave him the rescued canary in its cage. He clutched the wire handle to his chest importantly. Every time he took a step, the cage banged against his knees.

Timmy Blair fell in beside the boy. "Let me help," he said, taking one part of the handle. "Boy, was I glad preacher called off Bible school today. Seems to me, church once a week is aplenty. That hard bench makes my backside tired when preacher gets to telling it like it is."

"Timothy Blair," his mother admonished.

"Well, you said always tell the truth," he replied. "'Sides, the Bible says faith without works is dead." He lifted the cage high, causing the smaller boy to stand on the tips of his toes. "This here is works."

A smile chased a frown from Timmy's mother's face as she nodded in agreement.

"Well, I didn't like it," his sister said emphatically. "I love Bible school and we only have it once a year. Besides, I didn't get to say my memory verse."

"You can recite it for me, Jenny," Lilly said. "I'd love to hear it."

Jenny straightened her pigtails until each hung precisely over her shoulders. "It's a good one."

"Jenny—"

"Sorry, Mother," Jenny said.

"She's taken to calling me *Mother*," Mrs. Blair said.

"Spit it out, Sis," Timmy teased.

"'Multitudes, multitudes in the valley of decision: for the

day of the Lord is near in the valley of decision.' Don't you just love the sound of that verse, Doc?" Jenny swung her shoulders in a satisfied way. "We're studying Joel."

"My favorite verse from Joel is where the bugs eat the worms," Timmy said as he shifted his hand on the wire handle.

"Nobody in their right mind cares about worms," Jenny said.

"You two, hush now," Mrs. Blair said with a sigh.

Lilly thought Joel might be the appropriate book for Skip Rock at the moment, considering what was taking place inside the mountain.

It was quite the parade going up the road. Lilly led Slow Poke with the cart of supplies. A dozen ladies with assorted children and the usual entourage of dogs followed the cart.

The excited carnival atmosphere of the first night was replaced with grim resignation. None of the women thought the trapped miner would be brought out alive. They feared for the safety of the men who risked their lives trying to save the one. From what Lilly had learned, his mother and father were old and frail, unable to come to the site. The preacher had gone to the house to inform them of the accident. Lilly decided to visit with them as soon as she had the opportunity. The shock of hearing their son was in such terrible straits could affect their health.

They pitched the large tent on a broad terrace. In front of the tent, a long, flat rock served as a porch. The tent flap was lifted on poles and anchored just beyond the rock stoop, where a huge sugar maple spread a welcome shade. A natural spring burbled out of the ground a few dozen feet away. Just past the clearing, a grove of sturdy trees would provide a perfect place to string the hammocks.

Before they began to assemble the rest of the supplies, the women and children clasped hands and formed a prayer circle. Myrtie James led them in asking God to sanctify the area.

For Lilly it was an amazing experience. She felt sister-bound to each woman there and very grateful for their help.

"What are we gonna do with these?" Timmy asked, toeing one of the orange crates.

"We'll use them like cabinets," Lilly said. "They'll keep things off the ground."

Timmy carried two of them inside the tent. He stacked one on top of the other; then, unhappy with his design, he put them side by side. "I've an idea," he said and tore outside.

"That boy always has as idea," Mrs. Blair said. "I hope that head full of schemes gets him a job as far away from these mines as can possibly be."

"Doc?"

Lilly heard the inquiry from outside the tent. She stepped through the opening to find a man with a deep cut on his upper arm. Blood dripped like raindrops onto the rock porch. "Can you fix this so I can get back to work?"

Her heart leaped with gratitude. She wasn't even finished setting up and already she had a patient.

"You're going to need stitches," she said, pressing a wad of gauze to the wound to stanch the bleeding.

"Have at it," he said.

"Armina, would you bring a chair, please?"

"I don't need a chair," the man said.

Lilly knew he didn't want to appear weak in front of her. Sometimes a man's strength was all he had. "I know, but it will make it easier for me."

He took a seat on the chair Armina shoved behind his knees and stretched his arm atop another upended orange crate. Lilly filled a syringe with a weak solution of one part carbolic acid to sixty parts water, flushed the cut, aligned the separated flesh, and inserted a suture needle. With looping stitches she closed the wound and finished by forming a knot. After dressing the area with strips of lint covered with eucalyptus salve and rolled gauze, she pulled his shirtsleeve down and buttoned the cuff.

"I thank you," he said.

"You shouldn't be swinging a pick or lifting anything heavy until this heals."

"My hurt is small compared to the plight of the man in there."

"I appreciate that, but you won't be of use if you pop those stitches."

"Yeah, okay, I'll find something else that needs doing," he said.

The women had gathered around, listening. "Can you give us any news?" Myrtie asked.

The man held his miner's cap in his blood- and coal-stained hands. Lilly wished she could wash them for him. At the moment, he represented every man who had gone down the mines to provide lumps of black gold for the comfort of others. She wished she could wash his feet to show him how humbled she was in his presence.

"They was another collapse," he said.

One of the women gasped. Others murmured fearfully.

"It wasn't in the mine proper," he hastened to add. "It was inside the narrow tunnel, but it set us back considerably."

Tension drained from the women like dirty bathwater from a tub. Lilly had to admit she felt the same. It was unbearable to think she might lose Tern before she'd really found him. No matter the situation, the burden was easier to bear if it didn't involve someone close to you—human nature, she supposed.

"Poor Elbows," she heard one lady comment.

"Yes, poor fellow," another replied.

After thanking Lilly again, the miner turned to leave.

"Let the others know I'm here," she said.

"Oh, they know," he said.

"You done a good job, honey," one of the ladies said as Lilly put her supplies away.

Honey. Lilly liked the endearment. She was plying her trade but also becoming one with the women. She felt a deep sense of satisfaction.

"Come and see, Miss Doctor," Timmy said, his eyes beaming.

"Timmy, that's very clever," Lilly said when she saw how the boy had placed a thin board across two orange crates to make a rickety ledge. His sister Jenny was setting up shop on the shelf. "I hope you asked permission to take the board."

"Yes'm, I did. I minded my manners."

"That would be the first time," Jenny said.

"Timmy, would you open the tent flaps on the side walls?" Lilly said. "It's heating up in here.

Women came and went all afternoon, setting up housekeeping and having a grand time doing it. Staying busy and being close to their menfolk lifted their spirits. Every so often, Ned came by with news of the rescue effort. No one could believe Elbows was still trapped. It didn't stand to reason.

Mrs. DeWitt had followed Lilly's lead and moved her canteen within easy walking distance of the first-aid station. She and her hired girl had prepared enough food to feed Coxey's army.

By suppertime, when the last of the women and children had departed for home, the station was complete, and Lilly had treated three more men, including Bob, who was resting in a hammock while Lilly watched him for signs of a concussion. A good-size rock had fallen from the ceiling, striking him on the back of his head and knocking him unconscious. Thankfully, he was alert now and could track the movement of her index finger with his eyes.

Lilly was satisfied with the day's work. Taking on this task had brought the women together in a way Lilly had not seen before. She walked the perimeter of the terrace, stopping to admire someone's ingenuity. A chicken coop was nailed to a tree. Through the slats of the coop, she could see a quart jar holding wildflowers. Only a woman would do this. It painted a pretty picture and gave the temporary station a touch of home.

Mrs. James had also thought to send Lilly's traveling desk to the site. Lilly retrieved her Bible from the case and took it outside. She'd sit in one of the folding chairs to read. Her mind looped with emotion like a length of yarn unless she disciplined her thoughts. Thumbing through the Good Book would help her to do that. It never failed to soothe.

The Bible opened on the marker she'd placed in Job on the night of the storm. "Thine own right hand can save thee." What could the verse mean? What was God revealing to her?

From where she sat, she could see some men queuing up for a late supper at the canteen. They were weary but not beaten by the mountain that savagely embraced one of their own. The last one in line was the man whose arm she'd stitched that afternoon. She saw him nudge the man in front of him and that one nudge another until all the men in line turned and tipped their miner's caps to her.

Lilly was overwhelmed. And though she'd fought so hard against it, she knew exactly what God meant for her to do. It concerned her right hand—her writing hand.

CHAPTER 29

TERN SCRUNCHED HIS SHOULDERS, preparing for the slide into the confining chamber. Elbows lay within easy distance from the opening, but it felt like ten miles. Tern's elbows and knees were ragged from the process of propelling himself in and out. He went in belly up this time, just to give his joints a rest. Being on his back with the breakdown blocks mere inches from his face made him queasy—like he was in a crypt—even though he'd been a miner off and on for years. The position forced him to leave his light off, but it wasn't that dark anyway. Mr. James had left a lantern at the end of the tunnel to shed a light for Elbows.

Smelling strongly of rat droppings and creaking ominously

with the dry rub of rock against rock, the crawlway was a distinctly unpleasant place. The tunnel constricted considerably just before the area where Elbows's body rested. If the man had only made it a few more inches before the troublemaking rock loosed from the ceiling, he would have been scot-free.

They had been so close yesterday—so close you could taste it. Tern couldn't believe the luck—or more rightly, the lack thereof. He had been in the tunnel holding a folded cloth loosely over Elbows's face, to protect him from the fine sifts of rock dust, as Bob and his team worked just yards away. They aimed to widen the narrow space so they could reach in and remove the stones that held Elbows as twisted as the coils of a copper distillation tube.

Turnip was chipping the rock face with a mason's hammer and chisel when Tern heard Bob cry out. The roof was falling again. Instinctively, Tern had tried to cover his head with his hands. Then the men on the other side were scrambling to save themselves and Bob, whom Turnip had pulled out by the shoulders.

Now it was the third day, and Tern was once again earthworming to the man he seemed to have inherited, like a bad debt on the family farm.

"Buddy, can't you see your way clear to get me out of here?" Elbows said when Tern reached him. "I knowed you would come to save me; I knowed it for a fact. I told my daddy at breakfast this morning, 'My buddy's gonna save me today.'"

Elbows was becoming increasingly disoriented. Last night he'd had supper with President Roosevelt. He and Teddy had

dined on quail's eggs and buttered toast in the presidential dining room of the White House. And now he'd had breakfast with
his father? He was cracking. Tern was cracking too. With but a
few brief breaks, he'd been with Elbows for three days. The dark
and the damp and the confining spaces were getting to him.

It had been a long night, but now he heard the sound of
the men working at the other end of the tunnel. Stanley had
made the crew take last night off. He'd told Tern he would
stay the night with Elbows. "Go catch some shut-eye" was
the way he'd put it, but Tern couldn't get himself to leave for
long. It just didn't feel right to leave until Elbows was safe.

As men called out one to the other and tools banged and
screeched, Elbows fell quiet. Despite the din, Tern dozed. An
argument between Stanley James and another man whose
voice he vaguely remembered startled him awake.

"Keep your voice down. The man can still hear," Stanley
said.

"James, give me one reason you're not working this mine."

The strong scent of a Cuban cigar wafted into the tunnel. Evidently Stanley had motioned toward the crawl space,
because the other man answered with a dismissive "Humph."

The cigar smoke melded with the brusque tone. It was
the big shot from the Black Lump Coal Company, the man
who'd threatened Stanley's job before.

"It's not like I'm saying leave him in there, James. Work
around him is all I'm asking."

"You might as well sign his death warrant if you start pro-
duction again. That tunnel will collapse like a house of cards."

The air in the tunnel hazed with smoke. Tern could imagine the short, stout man puffing furiously.

"Stanley, Stanley, Stanley—you're becoming a liability. You've got until tomorrow morning to get this outfit up and running again."

"My men won't cross the line. They won't put a paycheck above another miner's life," Stanley said.

"Your men?" The company man gave a mirthless laugh. "They aren't yours, James. They're mine, and they'll do what I say. Like I told you before, there's plenty more men where they came from, and some of them are real hungry."

There was a sound like one man slapping another man's back just a little too hard. "Buck up, Stanley. The poor slob's probably gonna die anyway."

Tern waited, holding his breath, praying Elbows was sleeping. He should get out of there, hop the next train to DC, and report the intolerable conditions imposed on the workers by the Black Lump Coal Company. Maybe he could put a stop to this madness before it was too late for everyone.

"You won't leave me in here to die alone, will you, Joe?" Elbows asked.

Tern choked on coal dust and cigar smoke. He released a breath of resignation. "No, buddy. I won't leave you. But listen, you're not dying. I can tell by your voice you're still as strong as ever."

Hours later, Tern had time to grab a meal. He washed his face and hands at the wash bench. He wished he could go to the bathhouse for a shave. Leaning against a stack of lumber, he ate the plate of supper Billy had brought him from the canteen. Although he generally liked Mrs. DeWitt's cooking, the ham steak, redeye gravy, and collard greens tasted like so much sawdust. He guessed the gravy and a few greens would be easy for Elbows to swallow. He wouldn't chance the ham.

Poor Billy was in there now. Every time Tern came back from a break, the kid was pale as white bread.

Down the mountain, Tern caught sight of Lilly. He'd heard Bob bragging about the care with which she'd stitched his scalp. She'd insisted he take a rest in a hammock. The stitches made his head look like a baseball.

What would the men think if they knew she was promised to Tern? Or sort of promised, anyway; she hadn't exactly said she'd marry him. She had said she loved him. That was enough for now.

An assembly of women, children, and a few old men trailed up the road toward the portal of Number 4 but stopped well short of the entrance. What sort of uprising was this? Tern wondered.

"Page 426, 'The Lord Is Good to Them That Wait,'" said the man Tern recognized as the local preacher, and the group joined in as he began to sing:

"Thou fountain of bliss, Thy smile I entreat.
O'erwhelmed by distress, I mourn at Thy feet.
The joy of salvation, when shall it be mine?
The high consolation of friendship divine!"

The melody sailed up the mountain on a breeze. Tern was enthralled. In all the places he had worked over the years, he'd yet to see anything like this offering of testimony in the midst of such a difficult time.

"Page 102, 'On the Mountain's Top Appearing,'" the minister instructed.

Tern needed to get back inside, but something about the music kept him in place. He would listen to one more song.

"On the mountain's top appearing,
Lo! the sacred herald stands.
Welcome news to Zion bearing,
Zion, long in hostile lands:
Mountain captive, God Himself shall loose
    thy bands."

Tern longed to stay, but his duty called. As he picked up the bowl of gravy and greens he'd fixed for Elbows, the choir's next choice of song stopped him in his tracks. They sang, "'Zion, beautiful, beautiful Zion, We're marching upward to Zion, that beautiful city of God.'"

Tern couldn't believe his ears. He'd marched up the aisle to the beat of that song when he was nine years old. His mother took him to church every chance they got, and although his father had declared it hogwash, his mother stood on the banks of Troublesome Creek with tears in her eyes when Tern was baptized into the Lord.

Shame heated him from the inside out. How had he

gotten so far away from the tender, longing hopefulness his mother had held for his soul? When he turned thirteen, he began to emulate his father, going hunting with him and fishing with him side by side at the farm pond. Looking back, he could see how he must have hurt his mother. And then she up and died before he could become her son again. It was easy to blame his nefarious father, but he was a grown man now. He had made his own choices for a very long time, and none of them had led him closer to the Lord.

He'd never been a praying man, rarely even throwing out a selfish request, much less praying for someone else. His mother had a simple prayer that Tern had heard her say many times. "Thy will, Father," he repeated now as he turned up his lamp. "Thy will be done."

Later, after Elbows had had his supper, and after he grew quiet, Tern slid back out of the crawl space. He hunkered down just outside the entrance with his forearms resting on his knees.

Stanley came by and squatted beside him as Elbows's tortured snores filled the air like thick dust.

"He's sleeping," Tern said as if Stanley couldn't tell.

Stanley got right down to business. "I figured you overheard the earlier conversation, if you can call it that."

Tern nodded. "I did."

"What's your take?"

"Pardon?"

Stanley cleared his throat. "There's talk about you, Repp.

Some say you're a pawn for Black Lump. They say the company embedded you in our midst as a spy."

Tern fought the impulse to hang his head. It made him sick to think he had lost Stanley's respect. "What do you think?" he asked, meeting the other man's eyes with a direct gaze of his own.

"I ain't a stupid man, Repp. Simple maybe, but not stupid."

"I never thought you were, Mr. James."

Though Elbows's snores continued, Stanley lowered his voice. "I've watched you close ever since you first came to Skip Rock, and I've formed my own opinion."

Tern's heart sank. *Here it comes,* he thought.

"No skunk of a company man would do what you have done for that man in there." Stanley punctuated his words with sharp jabs of his index finger toward the tunnel. "My opinion—and don't worry; I ain't voiced this to nobody—I think you're one of those union guys. Maybe a government man."

"What makes you think so?" Tern asked.

"Them shirts you always wear," Stanley said with the shadow of a smile. "Ain't a miner I ever knew wears such fancy shirts. And just for the record, next place you go, don't shine your work shoes."

"You got me there, Stanley."

"Here's the thing, Joe, or whoever you are. I've been in this business a long time. I can feel change in the air. The companies have gotten too big for their britches—it ain't just here it's occurring. It is past time somebody spoke out for the little man—the one who slings the shovel. My opinion, I think you're that man."

They both stood. Tern offered his hand. "My name's Tern Still," he said in a low but steady voice. "I'm sorry to have deceived you."

Stanley shook his hand with a clasp as strong as a blacksmith's vise. "I never felt deceived. Perplexed, but not deceived. I'd not have put up with that."

"Someday, Stanley, I hope we can meet on different terms—maybe go fishing or something."

"Anytime," Stanley said. "But for now, listen up. You need to get on out of here. Mr. Big Shot was spouting off out where the men could hear him. He told them the company would hold last week's pay unless they were back on the job in the a.m. No pay, no scrip, no nothing." He tapped his cap against his leg. "They're agitated as a swarm of bees with a bear's nose up the hive. They got neither a word of encouragement nor one word of thanks from the company for all their work to get Elbows out. Things could get ugly in here real fast."

The lantern glow emanating from the tunnel flickered and went out. "Hey, buddy, you out there?" Elbows cried. "It's dark in here. Joe! You out there, Joe?"

"I can't leave him in there like that," Tern said, feeling for the number 10 tally markers he'd pinned to his shirt. Maybe his luck would hold.

"You understand I can't protect you—"

"Best leave it be, Stanley. I've been on my own for a long time now. I know when to fold 'em."

Stanley jerked his head toward the tunnel. He kept his voice low. "Come hell or high water, I'm not shutting this team down. Do you think he stands a chance?"

"We've got to get him out soon, or we're not going to get him out alive."

"Aggravating little varmint," Stanley said with a despairing shake of his head. "I should have thumped him on the head a long time ago."

"I know," Tern agreed. "He grows on you, though."

"It's a terrible thing—terrible." Stanley put his cap back on. "Well, I'll send Billy back with some lamp oil—try to keep his spirits up."

After Billy brought the can, Tern filled the lantern with coal oil and took it in to Elbows. He kept the wick trimmed and turned down as low as possible. Elbows would probably die from huffing kerosene fumes, Tern thought with a macabre sense of humor. His own head pounded from the oily smoke, and when he ran his tongue over his teeth, he tasted the grit of rock dust.

Elbows tipped his head back as much as the ceiling would allow, looking upside down at Tern. In the lamplight the ensnared miner's eyes looked like black marbles suspended in space, and his whiskered cheeks were hollow as gourds. "I'm cold, buddy," he said.

Tern massaged the one extended arm, then rubbed his shoulders. "I'll go get a blanket."

"No, don't go," Elbows said. "I'd druther be cold than lonesome."

Tern fell asleep stretched out in the tunnel with his left cheek resting on the back of his left hand. His palm sank up to the knuckles in the malleable mud of the cave floor. He could track his own prints when he went in and out of the crawlspace.

"Joe. Joe? Are you sleeping?"

Tern banged his head on a slab of breakdown. Stars bloomed behind his eyelids. He couldn't even reach up to rub the bump. "What's wrong?" he asked. "Sorry, that's a stupid question."

"That's okay. It ain't your fault."

"I'm going to get you a drink. Be right back."

"Be right back. Be right back," Elbows mumbled.

Tern staggered out of the hole. His legs would barely hold him. He walked stiff-legged to where Billy kept watch.

"Hey, Joe," Billy said, "how's Elbows? You don't need me back there, do you?"

"Maybe for just a little while. I've got to walk around; my legs are seizing up."

Billy blanched. Tern hated to put the boy through this, but he would learn that a man's gotta do what a man's gotta do. And maybe because of this experience, he'd learn a trade and get as far away from the mines as his feet would take him.

"All right," Billy said with resignation. "There's coffee brewing in the pot."

Outside, Tern grabbed a tin cup from a stack. At one time he would have wondered if it was clean but now he didn't even pause before he took a swallow. The coffee was thick and tasted of scorch. It would probably eat the lining of his stomach.

The full gold moon looked like a hot air balloon rising over the tip-top of the mountain. The stars were so close, they blurred in silvery streaks. Would Elbows ever see such a beautiful sight again?

From where he stood, he could make out the outline of the aid station set up near a grove of trees. A lantern hanging on a tent pole revealed someone sitting in a chair just outside the tent. The front flap was closed. A pair of crutches leaned against the chair. It had to be Ned Tippen.

Someone had said that Ned and Lilly were cousins. He wondered if she was sleeping safely inside.

God, he prayed, *please watch over her. Guard her as she sleeps.*

Tern spooked himself. He had prayed without thinking it through, as easily as he would tie his shoes or button his shirt. Was it really that simple to talk to God? As if he'd asked an out-loud question, the melody of the song from this evening filled Tern's soul as though the choir stood right before him. *"We're marching to Zion, beautiful, beautiful Zion—"*

Falling to his knees, Tern closed his eyes, raised his arms heavenward, and let the spirit of the Holy Ghost fill him. All of a sudden, it was clear as a mountain stream why he was the one in the hole with Elbows, a man he had nearly despised. It was his chance to make it up to Isa Still. It was his offering of redeeming love to his father, who had died of tuberculosis without as much as a visit from him. God was giving him a second chance. Tern was wrenched inside out.

Lord, show me the way. Give me strength for whatever comes, for I don't know what the next day holds. Let me be as forgiving to others as You have surely been to me. I pray this in the name of Christ Jesus. Amen.

His strength was restored. With God's help he could handle whatever came.

Back inside, he approached the now-familiar cavern room that contained the opening to the tunnel. He heard the sound of retching. Man, if Elbows puked, he'd more than likely choke to death. But it wasn't Elbows; it was Billy tossing his supper.

"I can't go back in there. Don't make me go in there."

The boy had the wild-eyed look of a horse just before he jumps the fence. Tern took hold of his shoulders and shook him. "Go out and find Mr. James. Tell him to send someone else to take your place for a while."

Nearly collapsing, Billy leaned his head against Tern's chest. "I wanted to help him, Joe. I tried. I really did."

Tern patted the boy's back. He felt like he was burping a giant baby. "Billy, you've been great. We never would have made it without you."

Billy swiped his nose on the sleeve of his shirt. "Really?"

"You've got battle fatigue, son. After you find Mr. James, go down to the first-aid station and get some rest."

Billy straightened up to his full five foot five. He squared his nearly nonexistent shoulders. "Battle fatigue—that's what soldiers get."

"Yep, now go on. The sooner you rest up, the sooner you can come back."

Tern could hear Elbows snoring without even sticking his head in the tunnel. He was thankful for a minute's rest. Rummaging through a pile of things sent in by the ladies, he found a tattered quilt and laid it on the floor by the opening. It made a more comfortable seat. He stretched his legs in front of him, clasped his hands behind his head, and leaned against the wall.

He dropped into sleep fast as a fishing sinker plunges beneath the surface of a pond. He dreamed he was a boy again, piled up with his brothers in Grandma's feather bed. The linens were soft as goose down against his cheek and smelled of summer rain.

"Save me, Lord; save me," his brother's voice cried out.

Tern awakened with a start, his heart thumping like a war drum. The house must be on fire. His feet tangled in the quilt. He nearly fell over before he righted himself, taking deep breaths, willing his heart to slow down.

A breakfast plate and a thermos of coffee sat on the ground by the hole in the wall. Billy must have brought it. Tern was ashamed. He had slept while the others worked.

Elbows was calling, his voice barely discernible. Tern strained to make out what he was saying.

"Please, buddy, please—can't you find it in your heart to

help me? I can't die in here. I ain't been saved. If I die, I'll go to hell."

By the time Tern got inside with the breakfast, Elbows's pleas had given way to a whimper.

"I'm sorry," Tern said, edging a collapsible cup, filled to the first rim with coffee, and the straw past Elbows's beaked nose.

Somehow, Elbows managed to clamp Tern's hand between his sharply jutting chin and his scrawny neck.

"Okay. All right," Tern said, gently pulling his hand loose. "I get it. I'll listen."

"I ain't gonna make it, Joe. I cain't take this no more."

Tern wanted to deny and placate as he always had. It made dealing with the man's pain so much easier. Well, easier on himself, anyway.

"Whatever happens, I won't leave you," Tern said, resigned.

Elbows sighed. His breaths came out in little puffs, stirring the air like moth's wings.

Incongruously, a light shone through a small hole in the barrier just beyond where Elbows lay. "Hey, we see the light," Tern yelled at the top of his lungs.

They heard a jubilant shout from beyond the rubble. "Hold on. A couple more hours at best and we'll get you out of there!"

Tern shook Elbows's shoulder gently. "Did you hear? You're the same as free."

Elbows took three distinct breaths through his nose, like he was gathering up strength. "Baptize me," he said.

Tern was flummoxed. Baptize? He couldn't do that. He

had no standing in the church. He didn't even have water, just a bit of sludgy coffee. "Listen, I'll get Turnip. He's a deacon. He'll know what to do."

Elbows fell silent.

Tern slid his fingers across his skinny neck to try to feel a heartbeat. He couldn't find anything but Elbows's Adam's apple and he knew not to press on that. That sharp chin clamped down on his hand again and then released. Elbows's breathing got weird. *Ah* on the inhale, *ha* on the exhale— *ah ha, ah ha, ah ha,* in deep, measured gasps. Was this the death rattle Tern had always heard of? He needed to get someone to help, but how could he leave Elbows alone? If he was truly dying, he might have mere minutes.

Elbows rallied. He took normal breaths. That scared Tern worse than he already had been. Didn't they always rally right before they died?

"I ain't been saved, Joe. I'm scared I'll die unsaved. You got to baptize me."

"I don't have water."

"Use the coffee," Elbows wheezed. "We'll pretend like it's water come from Swampy."

"Do I just pour it on? Do I fling it around?"

"I always thought I'd be dipped—you know, like John the Baptist baptized Jesus. Do you reckon it'll take if I ain't dipped?"

"I reckon God will understand the circumstances," Tern said.

"And sanctify the water," Elbows said.

Picks and sledgehammers grated and banged on the far side of the rock fall. It was like Elbows was being baptized in the presence of a chain gang instead of a church choir.

"I don't know what words to say," Tern said, trying his best to remember what the preacher had said when he was saved.

"Lord, help me!" Elbows cried.

"Lord, help us," Tern prayed. "I'm no John the Baptist."

In the nick of time, Turnip Tippen stuck his head inside their end of the tunnel. "We're about to punch through, Repp. I'll need you to holler out when we do so we don't accidentally disturb the rock that's holding him in place."

"Right—okay, but hold on a minute, Turnip," Tern called over his shoulder. "He wants to be baptized before you go any further."

"That right, Elbows?" Turnip shouted down the tunnel.

"I want to be saved, Turnip. Can you save me?"

"Only the blood of Jesus can save you, Elbows. Do you believe?"

"I always did; I just been kindly slow to respond."

Tern lay as flat as he could, so he wouldn't get in the way of Turnip's important message.

"You've got to confess your sins and repent. You've got to mean it, Elbows, or your baptism won't take."

"I stole a horse and rode it all the way to Jackson."

"Did you bring it back?" Turnip asked.

"No, I got drunk and forgot where I left it." A fit of coughing interrupted his confession. "But I am sorry," he wheezed and coughed again. "I was sorry the minute I put the saddle on."

"Take a minute, Elbows, and talk to God."

While Elbows was mumbling his confession, Tern quietly slid out to speak to Turnip. "You should go in."

"Won't fit." Turnip demonstrated by measuring the width of the opening with his meaty hands. Then he ticked off the four steps on his fingers. "Confess. Believe. Repent. Baptism. He's done the first three. Do the best you can, Repp. There ain't a guarantee this thing won't blow and take us all out any minute."

Back inside, Tern slid the cup with its third refill of coffee to the middle of Elbows's narrow forehead. He tipped the cup. "Leroy, I hereby baptize you in the name of the Father, the Son, and the Holy Ghost. Amen."

Just as the last of the coffee flowed from the cup, the men on the other side of the impediment broke through. "You're in," Tern yelled as carbide lamps bathed Elbows with light. Elbows sighed raggedly. His head lolled to one side, like a baby bird with a broken neck. Tern could have left then, saved himself in case of trouble. But he stayed with the man whom God had used to turn his life around. He supposed that's how it was meant to be.

CHAPTER 30

LILLY STARTED VERY EARLY on her rounds. To save time and energy, she was driving the donkey. Ned had fashioned a bench for her at the front of the cart. In her white high-collared blouse and her navy-blue skirt, she was sure she was the most fashionable doctor in all of Kentucky. If she didn't feel so burdened, she would have laughed at herself. She felt for Aunt Alice's pearls. After she sent Timmy under the clinic to find them, Myrtie had restrung the necklace for her.

Three doors down from the Tippens, she checked on the newborn she'd delivered the night before, glad to see the baby was nursing well and the mother was recovering nicely. She nearly clapped her hands when she arrived at the Tippens' to find Aunt Orie up in a chair.

"Reckon we can go home now," Armina said, sliding plump pillows into fresh cases. "I can't wait to get ever'body in one room again."

Aunt Orie patted Lilly's arm as she leaned over her with the blood pressure cuff. "Child, you saved my life."

"I think we should reserve that honor for Dr. Hamilton," Lilly said. Guilt sharp as the thorn of a faded rose pricked her conscience. She still hadn't spoken to Paul, but when had she had the opportunity? Like everyone else in Skip Rock, she went about her duties hurriedly with one eye on the base of the mountain, where Number 4 beckoned ruthlessly.

Last evening, Mr. James had stopped by the first-aid station. He'd drawn a stick figure on the back of a prescription pad showing Lilly what he figured to be the injured man's position in the mine. He asked Lilly's opinion on the best way to handle Elbows when they freed him and told her to stand by. They'd have need of her sooner rather than later.

While she made rounds, Ned was manning the station. They'd put a note on the clinic door with an arrow pointing up the road, probably unnecessarily. It was no secret where she was.

"How do you feel about going home?" Lilly asked while noting that Orie had surely lost thirty pounds of fluid. Her lungs were clear. Her blood pressure was high, but that was to be expected. The improvement to her health wouldn't last, of course. The illness that caused the ascites was ever present, but they'd borrowed a bit of time.

"I'm ready. I want to sit on the front porch with Bubby

and Sissy in my lap and watch the goats playing and the chickens pecking around."

"Them chickens better not come up on my clean porch," Armina threatened.

"I'm with you, girl," Tillie Tippen said. "The only thing nastier than a chicken is a goose."

Lilly put her stethoscope in her doctor's bag and snapped it shut. She kissed Aunt Orie on her powdery cheek. "You can go home tomorrow. Keep taking your medicine exactly as prescribed."

"I'll do it. Thank you, Doc."

Armina walked Lilly to the door and out into the yard. "I want to tell you something," she said, rewarding Lilly with a rare guileless smile.

"I'm all ears."

"I've found the one."

"I'm guessing it's Ned," Lilly said, nearly dancing with joy.

"I'm guessing you're right. He's got the biggest heart. And that other thing, you hardly notice after a while."

"Are you in favor of him going to Boston to be fitted for a new prosthesis?"

"I ain't looking for a man that needs a woman to tell him what to do. That's a thing for him to decide. I told him I'd be waiting at the depot whenever he gets back."

Lilly took a chance and hugged Armina. Standing stiff as a poker, Armina didn't hug her back, but she didn't step away.

"You couldn't have found a better man. But don't be hasty," Lilly said. "You're young. There's plenty of time ahead."

"Time plays terrible tricks," Armina said in that straight-forward way she had. "Just when you think you've caught it in the hollow of your hand, it disappears. I'm gonna be as forthright as a lightning bug and take a chance on now."

"Am I invited to the wedding?"

Armina's reply was drowned out by the blast of the whistle. The donkey's ears turned toward the sound. A tan-and-black hound ran out from under the porch, howling like he'd just treed a possum. Screen doors slammed up and down the road as folks rushed outside. Tillie's was no exception. All of one mind, they hurried up the road to the mine.

Lilly was at the portal of Number 4 when Elbows was brought out. They'd put him on the stretcher in the position in which he was found, using small canvas sandbags to anchor him as she had requested. He was bent sideways at the waist and one of his legs looked like a rag wrung out and left in the sun to dry. She kept a neutral face as she examined him. She could feel the eyes of his rescuers on her back.

"He's alive, but barely," she said. "Could someone show me exactly where the rock that impeded him struck?"

Bob placed a finger lightly just below the base of the spine. "It was just so."

"What do you need us to do now, Doc?" Mr. James said.

"Send somebody ahead of us to the train station. Have them hold the next train to Lexington." She touched Elbows's wrist at the pulse point. "And someone should collect his mother and father. They'll want to tell him good—" Lilly paused and rephrased. "They'll want to see him before he leaves."

"Let's get him on down to the clinic," Mr. James said. "It'll be easier to load him there, and we don't want his mother to have to come up here."

Lilly scanned the men for a glimpse of Tern. Surely he would have followed the rescuers out. She took a few seconds straightening the sheet folded over the injured man's lower body, to wait for Tern. If only she could look into his eyes and say without words, *I love you, only you.*

Lilly followed the gurney down toward the clinic. She felt like Lot's wife, for no matter how hard she tried not to look back, she did. Carelessly, she caught her toe on a rock and nearly tripped. After Mr. James took her elbow to steady her, she kept her eyes on the path ahead.

Everything fell into place in a timely manner. Within the hour, Billy was back from the depot. A train would be waiting. Ned would accompany Elbows. The injured man couldn't be sent alone.

Grown men holding their caps in their hands wept openly when Elbows's mother bent over her son and gently stroked his cheek. "Leroy, your mommy loves you," she said.

The preacher prayed a long, slow prayer over the slim figure on the gurney. Lilly had to press her lips tightly together to keep from hurrying the reverend along. A woman Lilly had never seen before quoted Scripture as the steamy heat of the August sun bore down on the assembly. The woman began to dance in an odd, hop-skip fashion around the perimeter of the group before she fainted dead away. Lilly broke the neck of an ampoule of smelling salts and waved the bulb under the woman's nose. Her eyes flew open as she gasped and knocked Lilly's hand away.

Elbows's father didn't seem to understand what was happening. "Why are we going to church on a weekday?" he asked his wife. "Is it somebody's funeral?" Lilly could see his eyes were clouded from cataracts.

"Lee," Elbows's mother said. "It's Leroy. Come give him a kiss."

"Leroy, you say?" The old man made a kissing noise in the general direction of his son's face. "He was always a good boy."

The wagon and team of horses were ready and waiting. Mr. James offered his hand to help Lilly aboard. She took her seat beside him. Ned got in the bed of the wagon with their patient.

Myrtie lifted a full basket covered with snow-white linen up to her husband. "This will tide Ned and Elbows over," she said to Lilly.

Lilly tucked the hamper beneath her feet. She looked toward the mountain. Where was he? Where was Tern?

"Is everyone safely out?" she asked, afraid the pain in her voice would give her away. She couldn't ask too many questions without causing suspicion.

Mr. James flicked the reins and the wagon wheels began to roll. "Don't you worry; we won't leave nary a soul behind, neither the known nor the unknown."

His answer gave Lilly pause. Mr. James knew more than he let on. Did his knowing put Tern in even more danger? She didn't think so. Mr. James was the most trustworthy man she knew, but his answer didn't satisfy. "How will you know for sure?"

"We'll count the tally markers. Remember, the men post one on the board in the office and pin the others on their person. If the tally's not right at day's end, we know someone was left behind." He slapped the reins more sharply against the horses' broad rumps. The wagon picked up speed.

Lilly did remember. She put her trust in the system and her faith in God as a silent prayer formed in her mind. *Please, Lord. Please keep my dear one safe.*

CHAPTER 31

TERN HUNG BACK as Elbows was carried to safety. He didn't want any attention focused on himself—good attention or bad. He knocked dirt from the knees of his pants and tucked his shirt in neatly as if that helped the rough way he looked. He'd have to clean up before he went to DC. They'd think he was a bum and throw him out of the depot if he tried to get a train ticket in his condition. But first, he had to get to Lilly. No way was he leaving without telling her where he was going and why.

As much as he hated the thought, his best bet was to stay in the mine until dark; then he could slip into the boarding-house and retrieve his things. Since the men thought he was a drifter, nobody would be surprised if he suddenly disappeared. He'd find a way to talk to Lilly before he got Apache from the livery, then ride a few towns over, secure boarding for the horse, get a room for the night, and hop a train to Washington the next day.

It felt so good to have a plan. He gathered up the raggedy blankets and quilts and made a pallet to lie down on. After turning up the wick, he set one of the left-behind lanterns on a rock beside his makeshift bed. He never wanted to be in total darkness again. Stretching from side to side, he worked the kinks out of his back as he prepared to catch a few winks. He hoped he'd dream of Lilly and not of Elbows.

Tern didn't see the missile hurtling through the air, but he sensed it coming. Before he could duck, the rock struck him square in the base of his skull. One blow and the ground rose up to meet him. He did see the booted foot that kicked him in the ribs and kidneys. Pain exploded through his body like a series of firecrackers as he tried in vain to make sense of what was going on. He was still in the cavern room. Elbows had been rescued. Now someone was beating him senseless.

"You've kilt him," a voice said.

"So? Who cares? If he ain't dead, he soon will be. Dirty scab. Come on—help me hide his carcass."

The voices were vaguely familiar, but in his addled state he couldn't put faces on them. His brain had turned to mush. Tern felt himself being lifted by his wrists and ankles.

"Where we supposed to put him?"

"We'll stick the rat back in the hole he just crawled out of. Serves him right."

"That's the first place they'll look when he comes up missing."

Tern willed himself to keep still—play dead. If they thought he was alive, they'd surely finish him off. He saw stars when his head cracked against the narrow opening as the two men shoved him into the tunnel.

He heard one whisk his hands together. "That's that."

"Not hardly," the man who seemed to be in charge said.

"What have you got up your sleeve now?"

"Company wants us to work Number 4 so bad—well, let's work it real good. Lookee here what I snagged."

"Dynamite? What are we gonna do with dynamite?" Tern could hear fear creeping into the second man's voice.

"Fire in the hole!" the leader said and laughed a mirthless laugh. "Kaboom!"

Tern fought to remain conscious as their voices faded. Alarm fueled a burst of strength. He scrambled like a rat in a maze to the other end of the tunnel, where he crouched down to wait, praying for his life.

When the blast came, it rattled his teeth and shook his bones, but it didn't kill him. The crawlway that had trapped Elbows had protected him—for the moment. But the detonation was so powerful it would surely set other cave-ins in motion, like a long run of dominoes.

Every nerve in his body screamed *run*. But there was no running. There was only stumbling and bumbling and feeling his way over boulders and fallen timbers. There was only gasping for breath behind the scant protection of the mask he'd made of his bandanna. There was only searching in the flat blackness for the feeblest bit of light. There was only hoping that deadly methane gas was not already sealing his fate.

He could feel the walls of the mine vibrating with energy. An evil presence stalked him like a monster loosed from its bonds. Which way should he go? He couldn't find a landmark in the dark. He fought his fear as best he could. It wouldn't help to lose his nerve. Surely the Lord hadn't saved him just to let him die here like a fox with his foot in a trap.

Tern saw a glimmer of light thirty-five feet or more off the ground. Could a lamp or a lantern have been flung up there by the force of the blast? He'd seen stranger things.

At the base of the rock face, he searched for one step up and then another. He wedged his hands into fissures and his feet into cracks and pulled himself toward the light, grimacing with the pain of his injuries. The higher he climbed, the brighter the light became. Obviously the explosion had opened a passageway to the outside. Fresh air poured in through the opening, sharpening his senses and teasing him with the mixed scents of a hot summer day: the sharp green of newly cut grass, tasseled corn mellowing in a field, heavy clusters of purple grapes turning to must. Tern could smell life beckoning.

Dripping with sweat and shaking with the exertion, he inched upward. A mere six feet from the opening, he came up under a shelf rock. He scoured the limestone on either side, hoping to spy an easy way around the ledge. His fingers cramped. If they went numb, he was in serious trouble.

His position was tenuous at best; a rumble from deep inside the mine made it even more so. The mountain seemed like it was trying to shake him off his perch—as if he was of no more value than a bug on a potato vine.

Daringly, he reached one hand at a time and grabbed the lip of the ledge. For a moment he swung like a pendulum, hanging in space by his fingertips, nothing below him but death. By willpower alone, he forced his body to be still as, miraculously, his left foot found a narrow gap in the rock face. Channeling his energy, he chinned himself on the outcropping.

"Aieeee!"

The scream from above was unexpected and nearly made Tern lose his grip.

There was someone else on the narrow ledge! There was no room for him. He gritted his teeth and prayed, "God, get me out of here."

His fingers started slip-sliding off the ledge. He swung his right leg up and planted it on the rock. A hand clamped around his wrist and helped him pull as his knees found valued leverage and he hurtled upward, landing hard on the body of another man. The exit to the outside was just above their heads.

"I'm sorry," the only man standing said. "I'm sorry. I'm sorry. I wasn't in on the plan to kill you."

"Get out while you can!" Tern yelled. "This whole place is going to blow!"

The man climbed up and out. Tern tried to lift the other fellow's limp body over his head, but his arms had lost their strength.

"Leave him," the man outside said, looking down on him. "He tried to kill you, and he would've gladly killed me to save himself."

"Lean in," Tern said, hefting the man as far as he could. "Grab him under the arms and help me."

The man did what Tern asked, and between the two of them, they hauled and shoved the body out. A moment later, Tern was gulping air and spitting coal dust.

The mountain rumbled and vibrated like a volcano on the verge of erupting. Number 4 was meeting its demise. The warning whistle blared and he chanced a look over his shoulder. Rocks shot out from their escape hatch like cannon fodder and rained down around them. He was going to get brained yet. They ran for their lives, dragging the body between them.

When he felt a safe distance away, Tern stopped to catch his breath. He bent over the still form. The man was dead. Dark blood coagulated in the baseball stitches crisscrossing his bald pate.

"We saved him for nothing," the other man said.

Tern balled his fist, swung, and connected. The man went down. Tern cocked his hand like a gun and pointed it at the man's head. "You never saw me," he said.

"Mister," the other man said, rubbing his jaw, "I ain't seen nothing all day."

"Tell Bob's family where to find him," Tern said, stalking away. "They'll want a decent burial."

CHAPTER 32

A WAVE OF DISBELIEF descended on Lilly when Mr. James pulled the wagon up to the front of the clinic. They had heard the whistle screaming from way up the road. Surely there was not another cave-in. Thick, choking dust and a sound like a freight train rumbling down the rail filled the air.

"What now?" Mr. James said, leaping from the wagon seat and reaching up to help Lilly down.

Darrell was waiting on the stoop. "More trouble," he said, unhitching the team. "I'll just get these two to the stable."

Mr. James disappeared into the maelstrom.

"Be careful," Lilly called after him. "Mr. James, be careful."

Covering her head with her hands, she ran inside. Dust

seeped in under the door and around the window frames. The clinic was empty except for the forewarning bird. His cage hung from the coatrack. Thank goodness someone had brought him down from the first-aid station or he'd likely have perished. His tiny lungs could not have withstood another assault.

She opened the cage door, and the biddy stepped onto her finger. Wearily she sank into the chair by the window. The bird hopped from her finger to her shoulder. She could feel his tiny beak pulling strands of her hair loose from its pins.

She wished Ned were there—or Armina. It wasn't a time to be alone. But Armina was safely home with Aunt Orie and the children, and Ned was on his way to Lexington with Elbows. They'd called ahead from the station, and Dr. Coldiron would meet the train. Elbows would have the best of care.

Ned carried Lilly's letter of acceptance in his jacket pocket. He would give it to her mentor. She wondered what the good doctor would think of the special considerations she'd added to the contract.

Lilly had been conflicted over whether to go on the train with Elbows and Ned, but if she had, who would do her job? She studied her motives. She abhorred deceit, even if she was only lying to herself. Her real reason for staying behind was her fear for Tern's safety and her strong desire to see him once again. She was a medical doctor, a scientist. She'd vowed to never let her heart rule her head. Now here she sat, pining away like untold legions of women before her. She sighed.

The truth was she would trade her degree for a piece of tissue paper just to know he was all right.

Rocks pinged on the tin roof like popcorn in a hot pan. A fist-size stone crashed through the window and landed in the middle of the floor. A mighty force was taking down the mountain. She hurried to the surgical suite and crawled under the operating table. The bird squawked in terror, planting his claws into her shoulder. She palmed the tiny body and held him to her heart. When her heartbeat slowed, his did also. His beak went to work on one of the buttons on the front of her blouse.

The outer door opened and closed. Myrtie rushed in, furling her umbrella. Lilly would have laughed if she wasn't so upset. Only Myrtie would use an umbrella against a storm of rock.

"Thank goodness you're all right," she said when she spied Lilly under the table. "I saw the wagon outside. Where's Stanley?"

Lilly crawled out and dusted her skirts. The bird's tiny head poked out of her blouse pocket. "He went up the mountain as soon as we got back from the depot."

"It's just one thing after another," Myrtie said, then tsked. "You and that silly bird."

Others trailed in seeking information and comfort. Soon the office was filled with women and children. Not one to be caught idle, Myrtie busied herself sweeping up the shards of glass. She set little Timmy Blair to work fashioning a cardboard patch for the broken windowpane.

"Turnip said the whole top of the mountain is gone," Tillie Tippen said. "The first-aid station and the canteen are busted. Sorry, Doc."

"I'm worried sick," Mrs. Blair said. "I've not seen Landis since last evening."

Myrtie tapped the dustpan against the rim of the waste-paper basket. "Stanley went right back up there as soon as he and Doc came back from delivering Elbows and Ned to the train. He'll give us an accounting soon enough."

"I won't draw a full breath until I see my husband," Mrs. Blair said, looking faint.

One of the ladies fetched a chair and another got her a glass of water. "Sometimes I hate this place," Mrs. Blair said, sitting down heavily. "What am I going to do if Landis doesn't come home?"

Myrtie studied her. "Honey," she said, "are you . . . ?"

Mrs. Blair rested her hand on the swell of her belly, shaking her head like she wished she could deny the truth. "Yes."

"Just you remember, whatever happens, we'll help you," Myrtie said. "Ever since Doc Corbett came, seems like we womenfolk have pulled together and gotten closer. Don't you all think so?"

Heads nodded in agreement. "Seems like she kindly showed us the way," one woman said.

"Well, she is kin," Tillie said. "That counts for something."

"Mommy!" Timmy yelled from the window where he'd been tacking the cardboard patch into place. "I see Daddy. He's a-walking down the hill with a bunch of other men."

Mrs. Blair's face crumpled. "Praise the Lord."

Timmy flung open the door, and the women rushed out. Lilly forced a calmness she didn't feel. She put the bird back on his perch and fastened the wire door, then stepped outside and joined the throng of people waiting for Mr. James to speak.

The gray dust had settled ankle deep. Way on up the road, she could see the devastation of Number 4. The tall mountain no longer soared proudly into the sky. It stood bowed and humbled, a shadow of its once-majestic self.

Mr. James cleared his throat, and everyone quieted. "I've totted the markers," he said. "There's three men unaccounted for. Jim Harper, Bob Hall—"

A woman screamed. A young man pushed through the crowd. "Bob Hall, you said? Stanley, are you sure it's Dad?"

"Folks, all I can go by is the numbers on the markers. I got number 12, Jim; number 3, Bob; and number 10, Joe Repp. This doesn't mean anything, really. It doesn't mean a thing until we locate them."

"If they're in there, they got a coffin lined with coal," Turnip Tippen said. "Hey, look. There's Jim now."

A man weaved his way toward them. He was short and stout—decidedly not Tern Still, Lilly saw. But he might bring word of the others. If he was safe, mightn't Tern be also—and Bob? She prayed it was so.

A couple of men rushed to bring the straggler to Mr. James.

"Jim, we're missing two others," he said. "Have you any knowledge of the whereabouts of Bob Hall or Joe Repp?"

"I brung Bob out," he said. "I'm sorry to say, he's dead. His body's at the base of the mountain, on the back side."

People gasped. Someone moaned.

"And Joe Repp?"

"I don't know anything about him. It was just Bob and me. We almost made it, but . . . I'm sorry, Mrs. Hall. I tried. I really did."

Fear closed its ice-cold fist around Lilly's heart. She backed up the few steps to the porch and sat down. She tried to imagine Tern eternally absent. It had seemed that he was meant for her; else why had all the puzzle pieces that made up her life finally fitted so perfectly together? He'd saved her in so many ways, first from his own father and then from herself. If not for him, she'd be marrying a man she didn't truly love because she believed it was the sensible thing to do. Was she to live her life bereft? She pinched her lips between her thumb and index finger to keep from crying out. *God, give me strength,* she silently prayed.

She hadn't noticed that Jenny Blair was seated beside her until the girl slipped her arm around Lilly's waist. "He was your beau, wasn't he?"

"Hmm?"

"That Joe fellow? He was your beau. I'm glad I made him dance with you that night. It would have been terrible if he got killed and you'd never even danced together."

Lilly pulled Jenny close. "You're a good girl, Jenny, and a smart one," she said, her voice trembling.

"Mother always says love will find a way. So you shouldn't give up hope."

Jenny was right. In her heart, Lilly felt sure Tern was still alive. Wouldn't she have felt the connection sever if he had been killed? The best thing she could do was go about her business and let Tern come to her.

The small cabin behind the Jameses' had been set to rights. She'd go there tonight. He would know where to find her. For now, she needed to examine the man who'd been caught in the explosion. Adrenaline could be masking any number of injuries.

She opened the clinic door and motioned for the man to come inside. Instead he shoved his hands in his pockets and turned his back. *You can take a horse to water . . .* , Lilly thought. She couldn't force him to accept care. He'd be back if things got bad.

"You need to eat," Myrtie fretted, piling mashed potatoes and cream gravy on Lilly's supper plate. "You're thin as a rail since this dreadful business started."

Mr. James ate methodically, one forkful after another. He hadn't said one word since he came in, but he kept giving Lilly looks. She was certain he knew more about Tern Still than he was letting on.

"Sit down and eat with us, Myrtie," Lilly said.

"I've been nibbling," Myrtie said from the stove. She dropped pieces of floured chicken into a skillet of bubbling lard. "I want to get some things cooked up for the Halls.

Poor Lula—she's a widow now. I'm glad she's got that grown son to help her."

She put a lid on the skillet and brought a colander filled with peas to the table. She began to pop them out of their shells with her thumbnail. "What of that Joe fellow, Stanley? Does he have family hereabout? I could fry another chicken."

Mr. James shoved his plate away and without a word got up. The screen door slammed behind him.

"Forevermore," Myrtie said. "What's that about?"

"I expect he's just tired," Lilly said. "Tired and grieving."

Myrtie popped another pea. "Ain't we all, but people's got to eat."

Lilly folded her napkin and placed it beside her plate. "Should I talk to him?"

"I wish you would," Myrtie said, dabbing her eyes with the corner of her apron. "Maybe he'll open up to you. Him and Bob have been friends since they was boys, you know."

Lilly found Mr. James by the garden fence, sharpening a hoe. Cleve chased a toad in and out of the half-runner beans. Each time the toad jumped, he stuck his nose to its backside again.

"Told you that dog's a hunter," Mr. James said. He tested the edge of the hoe against his thumb, then filed it some more.

"It's almost too dark to work in the garden," Lilly said.

"I know." He looked toward the house. "It was good of Myrtie to hold supper for us. I should be kinder to her."

"You're one of the kindest people I've ever known, Mr. James. Myrtie understands the strain you've been under."

"At least we got Elbows out," he said.

"Yes, there's that to be thankful for." Lilly toyed with her pearls. She couldn't be silent a minute longer. "I know about Joe Repp. I think you do also."

Mr. James laid the head of the hoe over the one spot on the fence that was not covered in abundant morning glory. "I knowed all along that he was not a regular miner—I ain't the only one with suspicions, sad to say. I warned him he was stirring a hornet's nest. He should've listened."

"Maybe he did, Mr. James. Maybe he left as soon as Elbows was safe."

"You might as well hear this straight up, little gal. I think somebody—maybe two somebodys—was laying in wait for him. I don't believe he had a chance."

Lilly swayed. She leaned against the wire fence. "Why do you think so?"

"A while ago, when you motioned Jim Harper to come into the clinic, he stuck his hands in his pockets. I noticed he winced and turned his back before he pulled them out. He had burns all over them. Looked like powder burns to me."

"I don't understand."

"Bob had burns too, only his were worse. His body was burnt on the face and all down the chest. Those fellows set dynamite to blow up Number 4. I'd stake my life on it."

Mr. James lifted the hoe from the fence and whacked the ground sharply, like he had more corn to plant. "Either Joe—his real name's Tern, but I expect you knew that. Either Tern Still caught them in the process, or more likely they killed him first and then set the explosion to hide the evidence. They killed two birds with one stone, so to say."

"Either way, I've lost him."

"It seems to be so," Mr. James said while hanging the hoe on the fence again. He whistled the dog out of the garden and latched the gate.

Lilly tried again, punctuating her words with pleading. "But it doesn't make any sense—why would those two men want to hurt Tern? Why would they destroy the mine?"

"They've had a belly full," he said. "Poke a chained bear long enough and he'll finally rise up against you."

Mr. James's face belied his tough facade. He looked at her with such empathy Lilly thought she'd crumble.

"I ain't saying it's right. Violence solves nothing, but it's bound to happen. Sad thing is, Repp or Still, whoever he truly is, was on their side. He wanted to make things better."

Lilly turned away. She bit her lip hard. A rambling length of morning glory trembled in the warm evening breeze, reaching out to her, searching for safe haven. Its delicate white blossoms glowed in the darkness like little beacons of light. It seemed imperative that she lace the seeking vine in among the other flowers. There, with a final tuck and twist, the vine was secure.

Lilly summoned her resolve. In medical school she'd learned there were times it was best to turn off her emotions and let duty be her guide. "I should go back to the clinic. I don't remember locking up."

"Wouldn't do any good with the window busted. Don't

fret. I'll get Darrell or Billy to stay there tonight." He patted her shoulder awkwardly. "Wait right here. Myrtie will want to walk you home."

※

Tern lay out in a grove of trees until well past dark, studying what he should do next. His heart ached more than his battered body when he decided it was better not to seek Lilly out personally before he left Skip Rock. The less she had to do with him at the moment, the better. He didn't want people thinking she was in cahoots with him. No telling what they might do if they thought that.

But no way around it, he had to leave. He had to report to his superiors in DC so the mayhem that was befalling the miners in this place could be set to rights. He had to try, at least. But he'd be back for her. Just the thought of that sweet reunion lightened his spirits.

Along about midnight, he slipped stealthily up the boardinghouse steps and into his room. He left everything in place except for his written reports, some money, his holstered gun, one change of clothes, and a pair of shoes. Nobody would notice that little bit missing. He bundled everything into a raggedy pillowcase he scrounged from the bottom of a stack in the chiffonier. Other necessities he could buy on the road. He still maintained his apartment in the city, so once he got there, he'd be set.

It was easy enough to slip through the night to the clinic.

The windows were dark. It seemed nobody was around. Good. He'd leave Lilly a clue. He looked around for a flower-pot or something easy to hide an object in. There was noth-ing. Taking a chance, he tried the door. The knob surprised him by turning in his hand. Stealthy as a burglar, he crept in. He could hear snores too loud to be a woman's. Ned was probably sleeping in the back. No matter, he'd be quick.

Two steps in, he saw a desk. That must be Lilly's. He tiptoed over and fished a number 10 tally marker from his pocket. An eerie feeling stole up his spine. He was being watched. Slowly he raised his hands and turned around, sur-rendering to the inevitable.

A tiny rustle of feathers greeted him from a birdcage hanging from a stand by the window. The forewarning bird was bathed in a patch of moonlight. Tern had to cover his mouth to keep from laughing out loud as the bird stared at him inquisitively.

"Buddy," he whispered as he unlatched the cage door, "I don't know who's luckier, me or you." He slipped the tally marker under the first page of newsprint lining the cage floor. "Tell Lilly hello for me," Tern whispered.

The bird tilted his golden head as if he understood perfectly.

At the livery station Tern sneaked around to the back of the paddock. Trees swayed in a sudden hot wind, and heat light-ning surged overhead. It took some work, but he managed to mash a section of the wire enclosure to the ground. Three other horses followed Apache over the trampled fence. Tern wasn't worried about them. They were all fat, contented-looking mares. They'd go back in as soon as they got hungry. Looking at the ladies, Tern suspected Apache had been enjoying his stay.

With regret, he left his saddle and saddlebags behind. It had to look like one of the horses tore down the fence—not him. Riding bareback, he hunched over against the rain that had started to beat down and maneuvered Apache on up the road. Except for the fact that he was leaving his heart behind, he was glad to be shut of Skip Rock, Kentucky.

CHAPTER 33

LILLY PROPPED THE DOOR with the rock that had broken the windowpane three days before. *All things work together for good,* she thought bitterly as she scooted the rock a little to the right with her foot. *Now I have a rock to prop the door.* "Forgive me, Lord," she said. Lately, all her prayers were apologies. She hadn't been able to really pray since the tragedy—she'd taken to calling it that. *"All things work together for good"*—what was the rest of that verse? Something about being called? She'd have to look it up. There had to be some comfort for her somewhere.

Yesterday had been dreadful—just dreadful. Finally gathering her courage, she'd taken a carriage to the depot to use the public telephone. It was in a tall and narrow, boxlike room, and it had a folding door for privacy.

Inside that room she'd shouted down the line all the way to Hamilton Hospital in Boston, Massachusetts. Her hand was rigid on the receiver when finally a nurse got Paul for her.

"Darling girl," he'd said, as cheerful as could be. "Are you on your way here?"

She wished she hadn't heard his voice. She was all right until the moment he spoke. "Paul, I'm not coming. I won't be coming, not ever."

If he replied, she couldn't hear him over the static on the line. She smacked the wooden telephone box sharply with the flat of her hand.

"—missing a golden opportunity," Paul was saying. "You will tire of that backward place soon enough."

Lilly fanned her blouse. The telephone box was stifling. "Please listen. I can't change how I feel. This is where I need to be."

"And what of me, Lilly? Do you not need to be with me?"

She leaned close to the mouthpiece. "Forgive me, Paul. Please say you forgive me."

She heard a woman's voice say, "Dr. Hamilton, you're needed in surgery."

"I only wish you the best, dearest," he said. "Always and only the best."

A loud click signaled the disconnection. She'd stood in the box for the longest time staring at the receiver. What she'd done seemed so callous—so antisocial—yelling across the miles instead of telling him in person. How strange the world had become when you could fetch a person like a dog just by picking up a telephone. Perhaps a letter would have been kinder.

A man tapped on the glass of the box. He smiled and held up his pocket watch. He needed to use the telephone. Lilly dried her tears, hung up the receiver, and pulled open the door.

Paul had taken it well. Of course, he would—he was nothing if not a gentleman. And perhaps he wasn't as upset as she thought he would be.

Relief to have that dreaded task finished flooded her, though her heart still ached. But she didn't cry. She would not let tears predict Tern's fate. She would wait on him forever if she had to.

And now, she still waited. Right outside the clinic door, life went on. A heavy rain had washed the grit and dust away, leaving everything looking fresh and clean. A man tipped his hat when he saw Lilly in the doorway. Two boys raced around him. "Last one in's a rotten egg," one yelled to the other. The man shook his fist at the boy's backs. A lady walked down the alley toward the commissary, an empty basket on her arm. She stopped to speak to a woman who was shaking a rug over the side of her porch. If you didn't look toward the mountains, you could pretend that nothing had changed. But Lilly wasn't good at pretense.

The first night after the tragedy, she'd been too restless to sleep. She kept a lit lamp in the window for company while she paced the floor. Against all logic, she'd nursed a mustard seed of hope that love would win—that Tern would come to her. And love did win, though Tern didn't come. She knew she would always love him—always belong to only him.

The thought of him lying crushed under tons of rubble staggered her. He didn't even have a proper grave. She sat on the edge of her desk and put her face in her hands. Tears leaked through her fingers as her shoulders shook with silent sobs.

"I'm sorry to intrude," Myrtie said, coming in, "but ye didn't have any breakfast. You'll get sick if you don't eat—or go bald."

Lilly raised her eyebrows. "Bald?"

"That's what happened to my sister when my brother-in-law drowned—silly man was noodling for a catfish. But anyways, she lost most of her hair because she wouldn't eat." Myrtie took an apron from a hamper and tied it around her waist. "She's still half-bald."

Lilly's patience was wearing thin. She wished fervently that if Myrtie wouldn't go away, at least she'd stop going on about nothing. But she fell for the bait. "Noodling?"

"You know, fishing up under the banks, using your hands instead of a pole. My daddy lost a finger that way. He caught a turtle instead of a fish."

Lilly regretted that Myrtie had learned about her relationship with Tern. It had been easier when she could keep her feelings of loss to herself. But nothing slipped by Myrtie for long.

Matter-of-factly, Myrtie stacked papers and file folders, clearing a place on the desk for a plate of blueberry muffins and a little pot of raw honey. She poured tea from a thermos into a china cup and stirred a teaspoon of the honey into the cup.

Lilly's temper flared hotter than her grief. In a whirlwind of dark emotion, she pitched the muffin plate out the door and followed it with the honey pot. The cheery yellow-and-black bee on the pot's lid sailed away, as if it had sprouted wings. She missed her mark with the honey jar. The small earthenware pot thudded against the wall. Tiny beads of amber sweetness dotted the doorframe and pooled on the floor in a sticky mess.

She hated this backward place, and she wished she'd never come here. Stupid place—stupid mines—stupid people—stupid her! She should have done what a good doctor would do and obeyed her head, not her heart. Oh, betraying, treacherous heart. Nothing was worth this pain.

From the back room, she heard the squeak of the pump handle on the sink and the splash of water into a bucket. Myrtie came out, trailing soap bubbles, and set to work on the spilled honey.

"I'm sorry," Lilly said those empty, meaningless, despised words again. *Sorry . . . sorry . . . sorry.*

"I've been where you are," Myrtie said, kneeling with her back to Lilly. "Be days and days I thought my heart would burst open with pure longing after my boy died." Her rag went round and round. "It all seemed so unfair and useless. My baby was only three years old." She dipped the rag into the water and wrung it out. "How could a boy be alive one minute and gone the next? I never got a satisfactory answer."

Lilly's rage was gone. Her pain had made her selfish and cruel—there was no excuse. She knelt behind Myrtie and wrapped her arms around her friend. "I'm sorry, Myrtie," she said. Hollow words, she knew, but they were all she had to offer.

They rocked together in the cradle of shared heartache, Lilly drawing strength from her older, wiser friend. Tears flowed and mingled like freshet streams into a river until you couldn't tell one sorrow from the other.

Finally spent, they sat with their backs against the wall, too exhausted to stand. Lilly rubbed the back of Myrtie's work-worn hand with her thumb.

"How did you get through it?" she asked.

"You just do," Myrtie said. "Sorrow's a tall mountain you climb one inch at a time. You ain't supposed to do it quick; else you won't profit from the journey."

Lilly laid her head on Myrtie's soft shoulder. "But I don't want to," she said.

"I know." Myrtie patted Lilly's cheek. "But weren't he worth it?"

Lilly closed her eyes, welcoming the good memories. She felt the press of her cheek against Tern's chest. She could smell the clean linen scent of him. She allowed her heart to leap with joy as it had whenever he came into view. His arms surrounded her once again and swept her off her feet. She sighed, giving in. "Yes, he was. Loving him for this short time was worth every tear, every heartache. It was worth climbing the mountain."

"You'll be surprised what that mountain will learn you," Myrtie said.

Lilly blotted tears from her face with one of her embroidered hankies. "I'd get up if I could."

"Mayhaps someone will come along with a winch," Myrtie said.

They both laughed a little at the thought.

"Somebody threw perfectly good muffins out in the yard," Timmy Blair said, bouncing through the door. Crumbs spilled out the corners of his mouth and down the front of his shirt.

Lilly got the giggles and Myrtie soon joined in. They laughed until cleansing, lighthearted tears flowed.

"Forevermore," Lilly said when she found her voice again. "Timmy, help me up."

Jenny followed her brother. She held the lid to the honey pot. It was missing a piece.

Lilly looked at Myrtie. "I'm—"

"Don't say it," Myrtie dismissed. "I've had my fill of sorrys. Jenny, I wonder would you mind standing on this chair and reaching me down that honeycomb?"

"How'd you get honey way up atop the window, Doc?" Timmy asked, stuffing another piece of muffin in his mouth.

That set Lilly and Myrtie off again. Lilly got a stitch in her side, she laughed so hard. "What are you children doing here?" she finally managed to ask.

"Mother sent us. She thought you might need some help," Jenny said, wiping the window frame with the soapy cloth Myrtie handed her.

"Well, seeing how you're here to work, Timmy, how about scrubbing the stoop with this bucket of water?" Myrtie said, gathering up her things. "You kids stay out of Dr. Corbett's way."

"Yes, ma'am," they said in unison.

Lilly sat at the desk, gathering her thoughts. She had rounds to do, if she could remember who was on her schedule.

"Can I play with the forewarning bird?" Jenny asked.

"He'd like that, Jenny."

Jenny opened the door and the canary flitted from the perch onto her head. "Look."

"Um-huh." Lilly shuffled papers, paying half a mind to the girl.

"I should clean his cage," Jenny said.

"There's clean newsprint in the back room," Lilly said while thinking she'd run up to see Aunt Orie this afternoon, then stop and check on Hiram and Lynn and their brood— see if Cleve had painted himself again. It would be good to get away for a while. Maybe Jenny and Timmy would like to go along.

Jenny transferred the bird back to the wooden rod that made his perch. The canary made chirping clicks of contentment from his roost.

Lilly smiled sadly. Except for food and water, she hadn't paid much attention to the bird lately. She watched Jenny fold the soiled paper and drop it into the waste can from under the desk. The trash made a pinging sound when it hit the bottom.

"Sounds like a coin," Jenny said, folding a clean sheet of newspaper and putting it on the bottom of the cage. "I hope it's a quarter."

Lilly went back to her work. "Whatever it is, you may keep it."

The girl closed the cage and picked up the can. "I'll empty this outside so I don't make a mess."

Lilly reread the telegram delivered last evening from Ned. Elbows was fair. Doctors expected a full recovery. Ned would be home tomorrow—all such welcome news. She uncapped her pen and dipped it in the inkwell. She'd catch up on her notes before she left for the Eldridges'.

"It wasn't a quarter," Jenny said, coming back in with the waste bucket.

"Oh, just a nickel or a penny?" Lilly said.

"Not even that," Jenny sighed, disappointed. "Just this old thing." She dropped a smooth, round object on the desk.

Time stood still. "Where did you get this, Jenny?"

"It was in the bottom of the cage. Didn't you hear it hit the can?"

Lilly covered the disk with her hand. She didn't have to examine it, didn't even have to turn it over to read the number on the front. She knew what it was and the gift of it nearly took her breath. "Jenny, will you send Timmy to find Mr. James?"

Each day Lilly went about the business of being the only doctor in Skip Rock. Each evening she waited for Tern.

A tally marker, suspended from a fine gold chain, nestled in the hollow of her throat. She'd vowed to wear it until she was in Tern's arms again. Her pearls rested unperturbed in their velvet casket—a reminder of another life.

When Ned came home, he had brought Lilly's revised contract from Dr. Coldiron. She'd gotten everything she asked for and then some. When the time was right, she would arrange education classes for women. They could use the schoolhouse after hours. Lilly hoped Myrtie would agree to be the teacher.

Her other petition was easier to instigate. Ned jumped at the chance to be trained as her medical assistant. He only needed to convince Armina that once they were married, she would need to move to town. Lilly would let him do that convincing on his own.

She slept little and ate less. Her dresses hung on her slim frame, aggravating Myrtie no end. When her faith wavered, she held the tally marker in her hand. On the tenth night she prepared for bed in the way that was now her custom— fully dressed, sitting by the open door. Like any other doctor worth a grain of salt, she could rest perfectly well in a straight-backed chair, sleeping in fits and starts.

This night was different from the others. She was weary and restless, startling awake at every screech owl's call, every dog's howl, every bump in the night. Resolved to no slumber, she stepped outside. The stoop was bathed in moonlight. She sat on the edge of the small porch and gazed out into the night. Cleve slid out of the darkness, quiet as a cat, and sat down beside her, bearing witness to her vigil.

She put one arm around the dog, leaning into him for comfort. They sat that way for minutes that stretched into half an hour and then an hour. Lilly grew numb and slightly chilled.

"We should warm a cup of milk," she said.

Cleve turned his long nose toward her as if to say, *"Two cups, please."*

But she didn't move. She'd wait just a little longer. She patted the dog's side gently, then rested her hand below his rib cage. A low growl vibrated against her fingertips. Ears at attention, the dog stood snarling at an unseen presence.

"Stay," she said.

"Ma'am," she heard a teasing voice call from the shadows, "call off your dog."

Every heartache, every fear, fell away at the sound of Tern's voice. Lilly's heart snapped the scene like a camera snaps a picture. All was clarity and lightness of being. She would remember this moment forever.

With her word of release, Cleve bounded off the porch, all bark and no bite.

She waited, gathering her strength.

He didn't come demanding, just took Cleve's place beside her on the porch. His arm circled her waist and pulled her closer. Her quiet tears wet the front of his shirt.

"Please, don't cry," he said, kissing the tears from her cheeks before claiming her mouth with his.

His love broke down all of her barriers. She was safe at last. "Don't ever leave me again," she said.

Tern wiped her tears with his thumb. "I can't promise to never leave, but I promise I will always come back. I'll always come back to you, Lilly."

LILLY COULD HEAR the music from the road. She might be riding in a wagon between her Daddy John and Stanley James instead of in a fancy white carriage, but there was organ music.

Daddy John patted her gloved hand. "Your aunt Alice will have her way," he said.

Lilly straightened the restrung pearls at her throat. "Indeed, she will. Who else would bring an organ and an organist all the way from Lexington?"

"Looks like everybody turned out," Mr. James said.

Lilly could see folks sitting on the low stone wall that outlined the church property. The church windows were all open as well as the door. Boys hung like monkeys from the branches of the big oak in the side yard. Under the trees were the two extra benches they'd taken out of the church to make room for the organ and two wheelchairs. But still there were buggies full of people who had not found seats.

"Hope they saved us a place," Timmy Blair said from the bed of the wagon.

Lilly turned to the boy. "Remember, Timmy, you will be in the procession, so you won't be seated."

"Yeah, I remember," he said, tugging the sleeves of his suit jacket down over his knobby wrist bones. Lilly despaired. The jacket had fit him perfectly less than a month ago when it was ordered from Sears and Roebuck. "But what if they eat up the cake?"

"What did Mother say while we were getting all dressed up?" Jenny asked, pretty as a picture in a frock of blue dotted swiss. The girl touched a finger to her tongue, then rubbed at a spot on her white patent-leather slippers.

"'A wedding ain't about the cake,'" her brother replied in a singsong voice. "But that don't mean it ain't important."

Timmy scooted on his knees until he was just behind Lilly. He put one slightly sticky hand on her shoulder. "We should have brought Bossy, for she is why we know each other."

Lilly laughed. "I think that would have been perfect. She would've enjoyed the show."

"You ain't leaving for good, right?"

"No, Timmy, Mr. Still and I will be gone for only two weeks. I'll be back, I promise."

She and Tern were taking a wedding trip to Troublesome Creek. Right after their engagement, her mother had come to Skip Rock. Lilly knew her intent was to meet Tern Still and take his measure. Her mother was the most generous, forgiving person in the world, but still Lilly had been filled with apprehension. Would her mother understand, as she did, that Tern had nothing to do with his father's actions?

Her worry had been for naught. Mama took to Tern like a cat to cream. He softened after the time with her mother, as if someone had filed his sharp edges away. Mama explained to him what had happened to his own mother. Lilly herself had never heard the full story.

Adie Still had died in childbirth, weakened as she was from scarlet fever. Mama had attended Adie in her travail. His father, disturbed by grief, had kidnapped Lilly in an act of retaliation against Lilly's family. Adie had loved her children, and she had loved Tern's father.

"I don't know why you would want me in your family," Tern had said, "except that I treasure your daughter."

Lilly could still hear her mother's sweet reply.

"Son, your father has long since been forgiven, and you were never held at fault in any way. You brought our daughter home to us. I thank the good Lord for you. I think He meant for you two to be together all along."

So they would go home to Troublesome and finish putting

all the ghosts to rest. Tern wanted to visit his mother's grave. He hoped he could locate his father's, and he wanted to find his brothers. He might travel far and wide for his work, for he was still with the Department of Mines, but he was a drifter no more.

Lilly was proud of her husband-to-be. He was a settler of disputes, a champion of the workingman. The miners here gave him wide berth, but Mr. James said they would come around in time. Their mistrust of the government was hard-earned.

Mr. James pulled the wagon up to the walkway that bisected the stone wall. Myrtie bustled about in her glory, organizing the procession. She hurried Mr. James inside to take his place beside the groom before pulling Timmy aside for a quick dab of Vaseline to tame his cowlick. Lastly, Myrtie tweaked Lilly's veil and straightened her train.

Lilly carried a white Bible and a corsage of white roses and orange blossoms bound with blue ribbon—the ribbon a special request from the groom.

Jenny walked in first, scattering white rose petals. Timmy followed with the ring that was loosely stitched to a satin pillow. Titters of amusement followed him up the aisle.

The maid of honor, Armina Eldridge, wore a dropped-waist gown of blue mull. Her short blue veil was edged in Brussels lace. Lilly's sisters, Mazy and Molly, as bridesmaids, were dressed to match. Her brothers, Jack and Aaron, along with Cousin Ned, were handsome ushers. Soon there would be another wedding—Ned and Armina would marry after he'd been fitted with his prosthesis.

Lilly felt beautiful and cherished in her mother's wedding gown. The cream silk had deepened in color over the years and brought a warm glow to her fair complexion. How thoughtful of Aunt Alice to save it. Myrtie had removed the bustle and added a ruffle of Brussels lace for length. Her floor-length veil was a cascade of tulle held in place by a coronet of orange blossoms. Resting in her right palm, underneath her elbow-length white kid glove, was the number 10 tally marker.

"Don't cry, Daddy," she said as they stood framed in the doorway.

"I won't," he said, wiping a tear from his eye.

Lilly thought she might cry herself from pure joy when she saw her handsome groom waiting for her at the end of the aisle. The strains of Wagner's "Bridal Chorus" filled the air, but Lilly paused. She wanted to take it in: the church decorated with swags of jewel-colored fall leaves, the people crowding the windows looking in, her family by birth and her new family—Ned and Armina, Myrtie and Mr. James, Darrell, Turnip and Tillie. And oh, Hiram and Lynn and the children—she hadn't expected them. On her way up the aisle she stopped to kiss her mother and Aunt Alice, then Aunt Orie in her wheeled chair. Everyone laughed when Elbows lifted himself halfway out of his chair. She kissed him, too.

And then her daddy was putting her hand in Tern's. Her veil was lifted and she could look straight into those mesmerizing blue eyes. Everything else fell away. It was as if they were the only two people in the room.

Lilly's something old was the love her husband-to-be had carried in his heart for her since he was just a boy. Her something new was the renewal of that love. Something blue was every second they would ever be apart. There was nothing borrowed. Everything from here on out was for keeps.

About the Author

A FORMER REGISTERED NURSE, award-winning author Jan Watson lives in Lexington, Kentucky, near her three sons and daughter-in-law. Jan's first novel, *Troublesome Creek*, was the 2004 winner of the Jerry B. Jenkins Christian Writers Guild Operation First Novel contest. *Troublesome Creek* is followed by *Willow Springs*, *Torrent Falls*, *Sweetwater Run*, and *Still House Pond*.

Besides writing historical fiction, Jan keeps busy entertaining her Jack Russell terrier, Maggie.

Please visit Jan's website at www.janwatson.net. You can contact her through e-mail at author@janwatson.net.

Discussion Questions

1. Lilly has a tough time gaining the respect of the people in Skip Rock. What prejudices does she face? Can you think of a time in your life when gaining acceptance was difficult? How did you get through this time?

2. Being in Skip Rock stirs unwelcome memories for Lilly. During a moment of fear, she recites Psalm 23:4— "Though I walk through the valley of the shadow of death, I will fear no evil." What are some Bible verses you rely on when you're afraid?

3. Tern harbors a secret that makes his fellow miners suspicious of him. How does his double life affect his interactions with the people of Skip Rock? Do you think his motives for sneaking around are enough to justify his deception?

4. What do you think of hardworking Armina and her tendency to be prickly with others? Why is she often

resistant to accepting help from those around her? What are some of the good things Lilly did in their relationship? Were there things she could have done better?

5. When Lilly's fiancé, Paul, visits Skip Rock, Lilly begins to have doubts about their relationship. Have you ever felt your past and your present don't mix well? If you faced a crossroads like Lilly's, which would you choose: the future you had imagined or the new path unexpectedly before you?

6. Tern feels a deep connection with Lilly because of their shared childhood experience, but he worries Lilly will fear him when she realizes the truth. Do you think he should have revealed himself to her earlier?

7. Paul believes Lilly is wasting her God-given doctoring talent in a place like Skip Rock. What do you think? Have you ever felt unsure about how best to use your gifts?

8. After contemplating his own demise in a mine accident, Elbows begins to take spiritual matters more seriously. Have you ever had an experience that made you view your faith in a different light? What was different in your life afterward?

9. Near the end of the story, Tern sits with Elbows to keep him company and later refuses to leave a man

behind in an emergency, despite that man's actions
toward Tern. What does this say about Tern's character?
Have you ever been tempted to treat someone poorly
because of the way they treat you? What were the
circumstances?

10. Over time, Lilly gains acceptance among the women
    of Skip Rock and even helps to bring them together.
    What's special about a fellowship like the one she shares
    with Myrtie and the other women? Do you have a
    group in your life you can share with? How can you
    help each other journey through life?

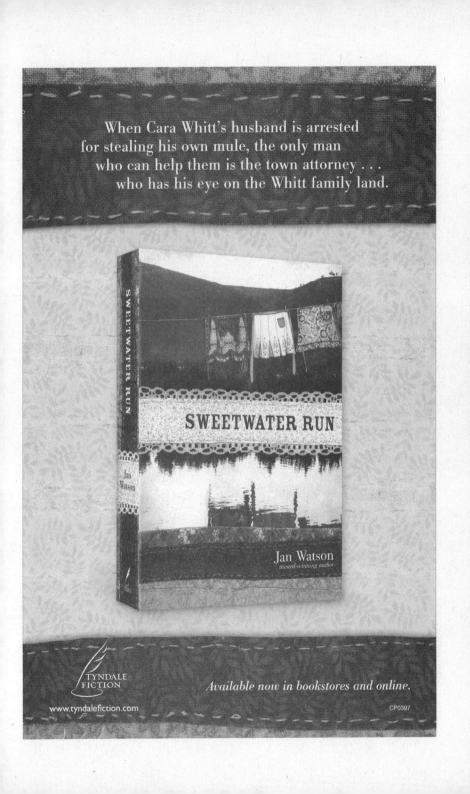